I0562996

A Lilli By Any Other Name

by

Virginia Barlow

Calhan Brides, Book Three

Copyright Notice
This is a work of fiction. Names, characters, places, and incidents are either the product of the author's imagination or are used fictitiously, and any resemblance to actual persons living or dead, business establishments, events, or locales, is entirely coincidental.

A Lilli By Any Other Name

COPYRIGHT © 2024 by Virginia Barlow

All rights reserved. No part of this book may be used or reproduced in any manner whatsoever without written permission of the author or The Wild Rose Press, Inc. except in the case of brief quotations embodied in critical articles or reviews.
Contact Information: info@thewildrosepress.com

Cover Art by *The Wild Rose Press, Inc.*

The Wild Rose Press, Inc.
PO Box 708
Adams Basin, NY 14410-0708
Visit us at www.thewildrosepress.com

Publishing History
First Edition, 2024
Trade Paperback ISBN 978-1-5092-5674-7
Digital ISBN 978-1-5092-5675-4

Calhan Brides, Book Three
Published in the United States of America

Dedication

For Becky. Thank you for all your support and love!

Chapter One

Northwestern Territory, Canada
August 1874

The stranger came late in the afternoon on a Tuesday.

Rebecca Lillian Van Rassner froze when she rode into view of their little two-room cabin and drew her mare to a stop.

Zeus, Papa's alpha dog, growled at her mare's feet, snarling and showing fangs. Part wolf, part husky, the coarse gray hair on his back stood on end as he crouched, ready to spring.

Carlton Genova found them.

"Heel." Her heart rose to her throat and choked her. Fear twisted her gut.

A strange horse stood outside their cabin tied to the hitching post. White as the first snowfall in winter, the stallion wore a handsome saddle with fancy stitching, a bedroll tied to the back, and a long rifle running alongside.

Caution overruled the urge to race to her father's rescue. He taught her better. Bursting into the cabin could get her killed or worse. She shivered in the frigid air.

Scanning the perimeter of the clearing, she clutched the saddle horn and ignored the panic trickling down her spine.

The stranger must have followed her tracks back to the cabin...and Papa. She closed her eyes as guilt crept along her cheekbones.

Her father taught her to sweep her trail away each morning when she left to check the line, and today, she hadn't. Figuring the sun would melt any evidence before it became a problem, she ignored Papa's cardinal rule. And now the consequences of her actions, or lack of them, waited inside the cabin with Papa.

After four years in the Northwest Territory with no evidence of pursuit, she grew less vigilant. And her father would have plenty to say about her carelessness. If he were still alive.

The pit of her stomach fell. She'd never make it back to New York and her old life if her uncle succeeded. She deserved a husband, a house full of servants, three children, and her place in society.

She glanced down at Zeus to see if he detected others lurking nearby.

The dog kept his gaze riveted on the cabin. Stiff and rigid, his ears were tucked flat against his head, and the hair on his neck and back stood on end.

Whoever rode the strange horse came alone.

Shoving her terror aside, she focused on the scene as Papa taught her.

The dark, rich soil around the cabin bore one set of prints, those belonging to the stranger. Large boots dropped to the ground beside the horse and strode to the cabin door.

Frozen in silence, the tranquil area held foreboding undertones. Smoke curled from the chimney into the lofty trees overhead and dissipated beneath the branches.

The air smelled of wood smoke, frost, wet leaves, and birch. A chilly breeze nipped at her nose and cheeks as she angled her head to see beneath the trees opposite her. Leaves rustled across the ground and in the branches overhead. A gray, overcast sky darkened the clearing, creating an eerie atmosphere. The door to the log cabin stood closed, and the calico curtains hung stiffly in place.

Papa wouldn't go down without a fight, and the unnatural silence unnerved her. There should be scuffling, swearing, the crash of broken glass, and the crack of a revolver. The quiet meant one of two things. Either Papa killed the stranger, or the stranger killed him. In which case, the killer would get what he came for. Her.

"What do you think, boy? Is he alive?" she whispered to her dog without taking her gaze from the cabin.

The alpha gave a low growl.

According to Papa, Carlton Genova had spies everywhere and could find a splinter in the middle of the forest. He was correct if his man could find them in the middle of such a vast wilderness. Papa hid their cabin in dense forest and used the surroundings to mask their existence. He covered the exterior of the cabin and barn with leaves and mud for camouflage. Large trees overhead dispersed the smoke from their fire, and thick brush made the trail in and out of the small clearing impossible to find.

Especially if she swept her back trail like she'd been told.

Taking a deep breath, Lilli removed the rifle from the scabbard and slid to the ground.

"Whoa." She tied her mare to the tree and crept

closer, with Zeus at her heels. Flattening against a mountain alder, she peeked through the branches at the cabin. On any normal day, the stranger wouldn't get within a hundred yards of their home without Papa's bullet in his heart. But the damn bear trap changed everything, and she would find the son-of-a-bitch who set it on their property.

Sideling along the perimeter of the forest until level with the living area, she ignored her shaking knees and dashed to the side of the cabin. The window with the best view of the living area sat to her right. She must assess the enemy's position in relation to Papa before she went barging in. The rock in her stomach dropped an inch, and her breath came fast. She squeezed her eyes shut for a moment to get control of her emotions. Whatever scene awaited inside the silent cabin, she would deal with it. Even if there was blood.

Dizziness hit her like a falling tree, and Lilli swallowed. Wishing she hadn't been forced to leave Papa alone did no good. She had one choice now: to keep her wits about her so she didn't make a mistake.

Dropping the rifle to her side, she sucked in a breath and peeked through the window into the cabin.

Papa sat in his favorite chair with his injured leg propped up on pillows, staring toward the back of the house. He said something she couldn't make out and waved a hand at the back door. Boots thumped toward her, and she stepped away from the window, putting her back against the cabin.

She let her breath out slowly. Papa lived, and the stranger hovered near the back door. Waiting for her? Or a coincidence? She couldn't decide and shrugged. His motive made little difference now because either way, she would take him by surprise. Tiptoeing along the side of the cabin, she stepped around the corner and stopped outside the back door.

Six years of hiding, countless lies, and untold sacrifice came to this one moment. Lilli counted to ten to calm her nerves. Her actions in the next few minutes would decide their fate, and she refused to cower before Carlton Genova and his hired killer.

Memories of her beautiful mother and the brutal way she died stiffened Lilli's spine. Her fear gave way to blinding rage as the screams of the past raced through her. She wasn't the same cowering innocent now. Her breath came fast, and her heart sped up. She'd kill the son-of-a-bitch for taking everything from her. And she'd start with his hired help.

Cocking the rifle, she strolled to the door and swung it open. Lifting the butt of the weapon to her shoulder, she stepped into the dimly lit cabin and strode into the living area. Blinking fast to allow her eyes to adjust, she sniffed the air for the scent of gunpowder.

Unprepared for anything but blood and mayhem, she faltered when her rifle came up against a broad red woolen-covered chest.

Lilli blinked.

"Easy there, son. You must be Willie." Smoky blue eyes gazed down at her from beneath dark blond hair. "Take your finger off the trigger and set the gun down. Slow and easy." The stranger caught the barrel of her rifle and pointed it toward the floor as he stared into her face.

Frozen to the spot, she couldn't do a thing but gape.

The man stood six feet if an inch and oozed authority. His hair lay neatly combed to the side of his well-shaped head, except for an errant lock resting on his forehead. Intense blue eyes held her gaze while the scent of the forest, leather, and warm male assaulted her senses. His arm bulged as he gripped her weapon. "I mean no harm. I'm here to help."

She didn't believe in Saint Nikolas or the Easter Bunny, either. "Who the hell are you, and what do you want with my father?" She winced when her voice wobbled.

He smiled. "Officer Max Calhan of the Northwest Mounted Police." His gaze swept over her baggy breeches, buckskin coat, and short black hair before meeting hers.

Of all the things she anticipated, having an officer standing in front of her holding the barrel of her gun never crossed her mind. He had nothing to do with organized crime or the Genova family. Or did he? Carlton Genova had spies everywhere.

"Put the rifle down, Willie. Officer Calhan is no threat. I invited him to stay for supper." Papa leaned around the stranger to speak to her.

Raising her eyebrows in disbelief, she stared at her father, wondering if he fevered in her absence and addled his mind. Her father didn't like strangers. Nor did he invite them to supper.

When Papa cocked an eyebrow at her in return, she growled with frustration. Sighing, she let the hammer down and frowned over the inconsistency of this entire situation. Two minutes ago, she thought her father's life in danger, and she burst through the door determined to defend him or die.

Only to discover her father having a drink with the officer as if they were lifelong friends. Her heart still beat like a runaway horse, and she would require a minute or two for her organ to drop back down to her chest where it belonged. She lowered her chin as she fought for composure.

"And who is this?" Officer Max Calhan of the Northwest Mounted Police dropped to his haunches to scratch Zeus' ears.

She knew the dog followed her into the cabin and gazed down in dismay as their ferocious enemy-eating alpha licked the stranger's face. Now she thought about it, the dog hadn't made a sound once they entered the back door. He picked a fine time to let his husky half come to the surface. Their lead dog tilted his head so Officer Calhan could scratch behind his ears and whined for more.

Not only did she wake up on the wrong side of the bed, but the wrong side of reality as well.

What the hell happened to the two males in her life? "This is Zeus, the traitor. He and my father have a lot in common." She couldn't believe the animal who snarled and showed fangs three minutes ago purred like a kitten at the feet of this stranger.

Rising, the officer met her regard with one of his own. "You're upset because he doesn't consider me a threat?" His smile made her weak in the knees.

"Something like that." They had too many secrets to start having a social life now. Especially with a smart, intelligent officer whose gaze missed nothing.

"I've been told I have a special gift with dogs and women. Most canines are a good judge of character." His deep voice and musky scent filled her senses.

Her eyebrows rose. "And women aren't?" She could have bitten her tongue off when the word slipped out.

Her reaction wasn't that of a fifteen-year-old male, and heat rushed to her face. She had proof of one statement and didn't doubt the other. Zeus didn't like anybody. Yet he responded to the lawman as if they were well acquainted. And since said lawman thought of her as a boy, she wouldn't get the chance to find out about his other statement.

He studied her face. "Not in my experience."

Lilli swallowed. She dressed and acted like the son Papa never had to avoid detection ever since they escaped from New York six years ago. He called her "Willie" because it sounded like her middle name. The name Papa used most.

A hasty retreat seemed the best option to hide her blunder. "I'll take Zeus out to the barn and check on the other dogs." Fleeing out the back door, she hurried to her mare and rode to the barn to put the animal away for the night. After checking on the dogs and having several stern talks with her pounding heart, she closed things up and returned to the cabin.

Officer Calhan and her dad sat at the table going over a map of the Northwest Territory.

Dark blue eyes gazed up when she entered and roamed from her head to her toes. A smile tugged at the corner of his well-shaped mouth. "Would you care for some help with dinner?" The sincerity of his tone and the intensity of his gaze made her falter, and she turned away before the telltale heat in her cheeks gave her away. Men didn't blush, and she shouldn't either. She didn't trust the man, and the sooner he left, the better.

Whisked away from civilization at the tender age of thirteen, she had never come face to face with such a man before. And didn't care to, now. All the men she knew belonged to the *Dene* and kept their distance. Except Mateus. And he didn't count.

Butterflies filled her belly as she risked a glance at the lawman's handsome face. Sincerity and concern shone from his eyes as he leaned over the map and talked to Papa in a quiet voice. Nothing about him screamed cold-hearted killer. In fact, her gut told her the opposite.

He must have sensed her intense regard, for he glanced up and smiled.

Warmth flooded her cold being and spread through her body. For the first time in six years, she wished she wore silk dresses, petticoats, and her hair piled high on her head. But her distrust of men ran deep. One mistake, and they'd be dead. Clearing her throat, she adopted a masculine pose.

"No, thank you." Dropping her voice, she did her best male impersonation as she strode over to her father's side. "You promised to rest." Her scolding fell on deaf ears as her father shrugged.

"Get us some food, will you, boy? We'll eat while we discuss this business about the trap."

Four days ago, Papa stepped on a bear trap concealed along his path to the river. The metal contraption broke his leg and ripped giant holes in his flesh. Lilli had to use a pry bar to open the jaws and several large pieces of toweling to stop the bleeding. She never would have gotten him home if Mateus hadn't come along to help her. Their *Dene* friend stopped by once a week to help Papa with the hides. As old as her father, the man knew more about the bush than anyone she knew.

"I want to find the bastard who set the trap. He had no business on my property, and to conceal it like he did was pure evil. I want to know who and why. Because of him, I'm laid up at the beginning of the season. I'll lose fur and money if I don't get back out there. The boy isn't strong enough to do what needs done all winter, and once the snow starts, things will get a lot harder." Papa took a sip of his drink and glared into the fire.

Glancing through her lashes at the lawman as she searched for a spoon, Lilli resisted the urge to cringe when he assessed her arms.

"Lifting traps will put muscle on him. The boy is skin and bones." Their visitor pointed at the map. "Is there anyone along this stretch of the river? I don't believe someone rode for miles to set a trap for no other reason than to harm you. I'm wondering if whoever is responsible got their directions confused. It's an easy thing to do if you're not used to the bush."

Her uncle would ride to the ends of the earth to annihilate her, and he didn't have to know a direction. Lilli turned away to stir soup in a large pot over the fire, keeping her chin tilted away from the keen eyes of their visitor. He might not pose a threat at this exact moment, but that didn't mean he wouldn't. Their lives depended on keeping her identity and her sex a secret. Wondering why he patrolled this far north, she glanced in his direction.

As if he sensed her question, their visitor traced a line on the map. "I've had several complaints about missing pelts and tampered trap lines in this area during the past few weeks. I don't come this far north as a rule and had no idea you were here until I spotted your prints early this morning." He glanced at Lilli. "I back tracked you to the cabin thinking you might be the thief. Now I know you're here, I'll stop by from time to time to make sure you're doing all right. In the meantime, if the boy runs into trouble while you're laid up, leave a message for me at Fort Simpson, and I'll ride back up this way."

Papa frowned as Lilli set a bowl of steaming hot soup in front of him. "I don't want you to worry about Willie. I'll take care of him. I want you to find the bastard who set the trap." His gaze rested on her face, and she knew he had something to say about her tracks.

Their visitor leaned back in his chair as Lilli set a bowl down in front of him. "Thank you."

She mumbled an appropriate answer and took her seat as far from him as she could. Sitting with her legs spread wide and a scowl on her face, she hoped her concern for Papa didn't give her away. Time to act like the boy she pretended to be. Sniffing, she cleared her throat and spit into her napkin.

Glancing up, she caught the officer's assessing gaze and swallowed the lump of fear in her throat. She may have made a mistake using her napkin, but she couldn't spit on the floor. She knew who'd clean it up.

Officer Calhan might not be the enemy, but he didn't need to know the truth, either. Her baggy breeches and shirt hid her curves, and binding flattened her breasts. Papa's lover at the fort, Marian Adams, kept her hair cut short like a boy's. Only four people knew her real identity—Papa, Lilli, Marion Adams, and her daughter, Charlotte.

Rubbing her nose on her sleeve, Lilli tilted back in her chair and slurped her soup. Belching aloud a few minutes later, she resumed her dinner with as much noise as she could and hid her smile of satisfaction when Officer Calhan shook his head in response.

Their visitor glanced at her several times while he

and her father talked about the day he hurt his leg.

Her gaze fell on the tin can Papa kept close by for his tobacco. When the lawman's gaze met hers again, she belched, cleared her throat, and spit into the can. That should keep him off her scent.

Chapter Two

"How old are you, Willie?" Officer Calhan's deep voice jerked her back to the present with a jump.

"Um." She risked a quick glance at her father. They agreed to keep the deception simple and easy to remember. "Fifteen."

Papa nodded his approval. Marion believed her to be a young man until she learned differently. Fifteen is the age she guessed her to be.

"I have a nephew who is fifteen. You're shorter than him and not as broad across the shoulders. Do you know how to shoot? I know you have a rifle, but can you use it with accuracy? A man can get into big trouble in a hurry out here alone." He studied her face. "You're also a better cook. I don't think Jeremy knows the first thing about making soup."

"I can shoot, throw knives, and hunt. Papa says I could knock most of the soldiers at the fort on their asses. I'll take you on any time you want." Thrusting her chin out in challenge, she rose to her feet, scratched her crotch, and gathered up dishes.

Whenever Papa took her to the fort, she jotted down the soldier's behavior so she could practice at home. Crotch and backside scratching occupied the top of the list, alongside bragging. She did all three for maximum effect whenever she got the opportunity.

"Save your strength for the trap line." The officer's

gaze followed her, so she picked up Papa's whiskey glass and downed the contents in one swallow as she strolled past, hoping her performance passed muster.

She figured if she were a son, she would steal the liquor to impress their guest. Men were quite competitive, as far as she could tell.

Whatever else happened, she must maintain her male persona. Her uncle spent the better part of the last six years searching for a middle-aged man by the name of Finnegan Van Rassner and his daughter Rebecca. No one knew about Frank Rossi and his son Willie, and she planned to keep it that way.

The liquid burned all the way down her throat and hit her queasy stomach like a fireball. Clamping her lips shut, she swallowed so the liquor didn't shoot from her mouth with as much force.

Her eyes watered, and her throat constricted. Coughing, she hurried to the wooden counter where the washing pan resided to unload the dirty dishes she carried. Leaning on both hands, she dropped her chin to her chest and sucked in air. God, whatever made her think she could drink the horrid stuff?

"Are you all right, Willie?" Papa's amused voice told her he understood her distress.

"Yeah." Her voice squeaked. She would be once the stranger left, and her mind functioned again. None of the soldiers at the fort made her as nervous as Officer Calhan. His gaze took in way too much, and she didn't like it.

"Did you take your tonic today?" Anxious to change the subject, she strolled over to the other side of the dish pan and took Calendula salve from the shelf, hoping no one noticed her higher pitch. "We should check your bandages. With all the walking you've done today, we need to make sure your leg didn't start bleeding again." To her consternation, the cough returned.

"You coddle me worse than my own mother. God rest her soul. And my leg is fine." Her father winced when he shifted position, effectively proving his statement false. "We can rebandage my leg after our visitor leaves."

Her eyebrow rose as she took bandages from the shelf and put some water on to boil. He would put up a fuss then, too, and they both knew it.

"Do you mind if I take a gander? I had medical training in New York when I applied to be an officer and again with the Northwest Mounted Police. Sometimes rust and bacteria are introduced into the skin on the teeth of the trap. Another pair of eyes might help." The officer glanced from one to the other.

"Thanks for the offer, but I'll be fine." Papa splashed whisky into a clean glass. "I've got all the medicine I require right here."

Lilli disagreed. And although she wished their guest would leave, another opinion would be appreciated. Last night, when she bandaged her father's leg, the area around the lower puncture wound caught her attention. Bright red and hot to the touch, Papa winced and hurried her through the procedure. She didn't like the amount of pain she read on his face and wanted to take him to the doctor at the fort. Brushing her concern away, he made light of his condition and refused to go anywhere for help. She didn't plan to waste this opportunity. Especially if their visitor had medical training. "We would appreciate your opinion. Wouldn't we, Papa?"

He grunted and took a sip of his whisky.

Pouring the boiling water into a dish, she glanced at her father. If the officer weren't here, she would scorch his ears for not keeping off his leg. Her knowledge of wounds, medicine, and the like came from Papa, her sole source of information from the day they arrived in this place. Before her mother's murder, the family doctor would come to their estate in New York to tend to their illnesses.

Out here, they were on their own.

Dried blood stuck the layers of bandage together and had to be soaked off to unwind the cloth. When the last layer fell away, Lilli removed the sticks running along either side of the leg. The lower three punctures on his wound gaped open. Raw, red, and swollen, she sucked in a breath of dismay.

"These wounds look worse than they did last night. They're all swollen. Are those blisters?" She pointed at several angry bumps along the side of the affected area.

"Yes." Officer Calhan washed his hands and probed the side of the wound with his fingers. "They're bleeding. What kind of salve have you been using?"

"Calendula. Mateus traded me for some tobacco." Papa shifted his leg. "Last night, the lower part of my leg hurt like blue blazes. Today, the pain isn't as bad. I think it's healing."

"Is Mateus another trapper?" Officer Calhan washed the wound with a clean cloth and then applied the salve.

Lilli let Papa answer. She didn't trust the stranger and tensed when he asked questions.

"He's a friend. He stops by from time to time. You won't find a better tracker anywhere." Her father winced as the upper cuts were cleaned.

Wrapping the length of bandage around the wound,

their visitor repositioned the sticks and pinned the edge closed. He stood up. "As soon as you can, you should go to the fort and have the doctor stitch up the lower wounds. They'll be less likely to fester and will heal faster. In the meantime, I'll have a chat with him and see what he thinks about the blisters. My concern is the bacteria and rust I mentioned earlier. I think they may be causing the blistering. You should stay off your leg and keep it elevated like you have. Let Willie do the running for you. If your fever or your leg gets worse, don't let the grass grow beneath you. Get to the fort. I'd hate to see you lose your leg."

Lilli swallowed. Her, too. She needed Papa. How could she get back to her normal life without him? "Thanks for stopping by." Officer Calhan's nearness made her jumpy, and she didn't like it. His six-foot frame filled the cabin, along with his woodsy outdoor scent. The fluttering in her belly increased every time he got within ten feet, which included the entire evening. The sooner the Mountie left, the sooner she could question Papa about his visit and why the hell he let the officer into their cabin.

"My pleasure. Thank you for dinner." Officer Calhan set his black hat on his blond head and shook Papa's hand. "I will stop by on my way back through to check on you and give you an update on my investigation. Have a good night."

Papa grinned. "This glass guarantees me one." Holding up his whisky, he saluted the officer on his way out.

She waited for a full five minutes before turning on her father. "I thought we weren't going to be friendly or allow anyone into our cabin. What the hell happened while I went out checking traps?"

"You tell me. Officer Calhan didn't know we existed before today. And wouldn't now if you'd covered your trail like I taught you."

****

Max rode toward the fort deep in thought.

Whoever had been stealing fur and robbing traps must be stopped. Two other trapper cabins occupied the five-mile trek from his current location to Fort Simpson. Both men swore they kept to their own business and complained about being robbed. Max didn't like the whole setup. What man in his right mind had time to travel for miles to steal pelts? The fool ran the risk of being drawn and quartered if the trappers caught him. None of it made any sense.

He rode to the top of a hill and stared into the distance. God, he loved the wide-open spaces, the clean, crisp air, the scent of pine, and simple choices. He came north to make a difference. To help those in need receive justice and those who committed crimes to pay the price. Simple. Easy. And something New York and the wealthy knew nothing about. With their high-priced lawyers and politics, a decent man had no chance at fairness or impartiality. And wealthy women got away with murder if they associated with the right people and had the coin to pay. The old familiar ache settled in his gut, and he shifted in the saddle.

Shaking the memories away, Max frowned as Willie Rossi crossed his mind. The boy had to be one of the strangest youths he ever met. He never encountered a boy of his age getting offended over a comment about women or spitting into a napkin. This kid jumped when his father spoke and anticipated his needs, like a wife or daughter.

Nudging his horse with his knees, he turned toward Fort Simpson.

His nephew Jeremy didn't do one thing his mother asked unless she threatened him. And Willie did the chores without being told. He passed out soup and cleared the table as if he did it every night and expected to for the rest of his life.

Max remembered being fifteen, and clearing dishes hadn't been high on his list of things to do. The boy should get out more. Get a little sun. A few months on his brother Chase's ranch in Texas would put some muscle on the kid's body and some confidence in his stride. Willie lacked exercise and good old-fashioned camaraderie with men who knew how to work hard. And play just as hard. The boy didn't smile and shied away from human contact. Resentment, fear, and mistrust clung to the kid like perspiration on a sweltering day. Max wondered how long it'd been since Willie laughed or had any fun.

Guiding his mount through the trees, he remembered the fear in the boy's eyes when he burst into the cabin and aimed his rifle at Max's heart. If eyes are mirrors into a man's soul, what he glimpsed in Willie's made him pause. Terror, panic, and extreme grief made the boy clumsy and frantic.

Max clucked to his horse, Spartacus, and urged him to a trot.

Whatever the boy witnessed, and the two hid from must have been soul-consuming, for he recognized the same torment in Frank Rossi's eyes when he opened the cabin door and gazed into the business end of a pistol.

The great Northwest Territory collected many kinds

of people. Among them were trappers, traders, and outlaws. Some men buried their cabins deep in the bush to avoid the law, some to avoid society, and others because they enjoyed the solitude. Frank and Wille came for another reason. One Max would discover and help with as best he could.

As for the bear trap, he wondered if the same person who robbed all the fur lines set the trap. Whether by design or by mistake remained to be seen. But anyone dumb enough to set a trap on someone else's property by mistake wouldn't last the season. If he got lost now, wait until a full white out descended.

Max's mind returned to Willie. Something about the boy bothered him, but he couldn't decide what. His coughing, spitting, swearing, and bragging were all meticulously carried out as if the boy had a schedule to keep. Shaking his head at the absurd idea, Max urged Spartacus into the Big Laird River toward Fort Simpson.

After a good night's rest, he'd travel further north in search of other cabins. Somewhere in a ten-to-fifteen-mile radius, the thief made camp or huddled beside his fireplace to stay warm. Max would find him and obtain justice for the trappers he robbed.

After his experience in New York, he swore off women and rode north into Canada. He fulfilled all the requirements to be a law officer a year later and volunteered to go wherever they needed him. He became one of the first few men to patrol the Northwest Territory and arrived at Fort Simpson later the same year. He believed white should be white. Black should be black. And the wealthy should adhere to the law as much as anyone, with no gray lawyers in between.

Chapter Three

Lilli knew their traps were robbed before she finished the trek to the river. Zeus snarled and lunged down the path. Growling and circling the area before sniffing the nearby markings. Large boot prints around the area made her furious and her dog insane with the desire to chase the thief down. "Balls! The dratted bootlicker!" She kicked a clump of bushes and swore some more. Leaves covered a lone, hefty rock lodged on the side of Papa's trail, and her boots did little to protect her from injury.

Officer Calhan had better hurry up and catch the thief before she set out to hunt the bastard down on her own.

Lilli bit her lip, wishing the officer would drop by again to check on Papa's leg. This morning, when she unwrapped his wound, the blisters were larger and oozed. Heating up a little water, she placed Papa's foot in a basin and washed the affected area while her father mumbled cuss words beneath his breath. His pale face and his grip on the arms of his chair told her he hurt worse than he let on.

She wanted him to go to the fort, but he refused. And she ended up rubbing more Calendula salve into the area and rewrapping the wound.

"Why isn't the salve working? I feel like the puncture wounds on the bottom are getting worse." She cringed when she poked one with her finger, but her father just shrugged.

"I don't feel a thing there. My sole is the only place on my foot I can stand to have you touch. Now, why don't you go check the lines? I'd like to catch the bastard who's robbing us. And we won't until you quit lollygagging and coddling me." Grasping his walking stick, he rose to his feet. Exertion beaded his brow. "If you hurry, you'll be back by dark."

"I'll go if you sit and don't get up until I get home. I want your promise, Papa. And I don't care who knocks on your cabin door. Your bone won't mend if you don't give it a chance." She gave her father her most intimidating frown.

He chuckled. "All right. Be gone with you."

Two hours later, she stood gazing in dismay at the first empty trap. They couldn't afford to lose any more pelts. Papa used to be the Beaver King before he married her mother and moved to New York. The Hudson Bay Company gave him the title when he traded more pelts than any other individual. And the name stuck. Now, twenty years later, they caught half as many as he used to in the old days, and the thief took most of them.

Her toe smarted from kicking the rock, and Lilli hobbled over to a lean against a tree. Worrying about Papa's leg and their future took up so much time and energy, she fell asleep the second she closed her eyes at night. If she could figure out who robbed their traps and get Papa to the fort to see the doctor, her weary mind could get back to worrying about whether her mother's killer found them or not.

Five minutes later, Lilli drew her cap further down over her ears and followed the boot marks. The man took the contents of two traps and left the rest, his prints traveling off to the northwest. Maybe he wandered off to rob whoever lived in the same direction. From what Officer Calhan said the other night, several other trappers experienced the same thing they did and wanted justice. *Get in line.*

Gazing down at Zeus, she commanded him to heel to keep him from running off after this unknown person. Once she had Papa situated, she planned to let Zeus hunt the thief down, but for now, she must get back to her father. Hoping Officer Calhan stopped by with some news, she hurried through the rest of her line and turned towards home. Putting her mare and a sulky alpha dog away for the night, she opened the back door of the cabin and stepped inside.

"I found more prints today, Papa," she called to him as she took off her coat, hat, and mittens.

Her father sat up on the edge of the chair. His face glowed red in the evening light, and she paused as fear clutched her heart.

He didn't look right.

"Papa!" Rushing across the floor, she clasped him by the shoulders and put a hand on his forehead.

He burned with fever!

Cussing under her breath, she gazed down into her father's drooping eyes. "I'm taking you to the doctor. No excuses."

He hadn't eaten a thing since she left this morning. She knew by the cleanliness of the cabin and shook her head. Bustling around, she retrieved biscuits from the bread tin and added butter and cheese. Handing one to Papa, she informed him she would get the wagon ready and disappeared, munching on her own.

Two hours later, they turned in at the fort. Lilli kept her coat collar up, and the flaps on her hat down to conceal her face as she stopped in front of the small building allocated for the army's doctor.

After applying the brake, she slid to the ground and hurried around to the wagon bed where Papa lay. Grasping the back, she lowered the end and sensed the man behind her before a hand dropped out of nowhere onto her shoulder.

She didn't think. She reacted, and her recent fear for her father's health gave her strength. Grabbing the unknown man's arm, she twisted around, turning the appendage as she went. With a swift kick to the groin and a sweep of her leg, she knocked the large man onto his backside at her feet.

"Jesus, Willie. It's me." Officer Calhan's deep voice grunted from ground level and sent tingles through her body.

Rising to his feet, he dusted his breeches off. "You need to calm down, son. I came over to see if you needed help." His gaze ran over her face. A gleam of approval lit his eye. "Who taught you to fight like that? I haven't landed on my ass so hard since Connor grew up and quit practicing on me."

Lilli sucked in a breath as a warm glow spread through her body. "Who's Connor?"

"My older brother. I've got two younger and a sister." He tilted his head as his gaze swept her face. "Did one of the soldiers teach you?"

She ducked her head and thanked the gods the night hid her expression. No one gave her praise or a kind word. Ever. And she didn't know what to do with his approval. "No. Papa did." Uncomfortable with the conversation, she changed the subject. Lowering her voice, she hoped she sounded gruff. "Papa is worse. He's burning with a fever. So I brought him in." The men she studied never wasted time with extra words.

He frowned. "Doctor Talan left to check on a patient about an hour ago. He won't be available until morning." Max leaned over the back of the wagon and touched the side of Papa's neck.

Dread and fear settled in her stomach like a stone. She shifted feet. "Will he…make it until morning?" She didn't like the way the question came out and cleared her throat.

He studied her face and softened his voice. "Your father is a tough man. He'll survive until the doctor gets here. I wouldn't worry." He clapped her on the back and gave her a smile of encouragement.

Max Calhan acted as though he cared.

Uncomfortable with the warmth invading her belly, she coughed. Wondering if she had given her disguise away with her breathless question, she thought of what a man would do in the circumstances. Glancing around for somewhere to spit, she closed her eyes and gave it her best shot. She hoped to convey unconcern and her ability to manage the situation, and failed.

Her companion glanced from her to the spit and back. "Put more force onto it, and it won't land on your boots."

Her face heated when she glanced down and noted the shiny blob staring up at her from the toe of one boot. Mortified, she swallowed. "How?"

"Use your tongue to create pressure and lean into it like this." A perfect arc of clear fluid flew from his mouth and landed a good foot away.

Lilli nodded. Pursing her lips, she spat again. And this time, the blob landed an inch away from her leather sole. Who would have thought the handsome officer would stoop to instruct her on the proper way to spit?

He grinned and ruffled her hair. "You're getting better."

She didn't know how to respond. His touch sent shivers down her spine and made her belly flutter. But Lilli didn't want camaraderie or an older brother. Not from him. She wanted him to see her as a woman and not a fifteen-year-old kid. An impossibility in her current situation. Dropping her head so he couldn't see her expression, she inched away. "I don't like to be touched." She told the lie with a straight face and ignored the guilty knot in her stomach.

"I apologize." He frowned and cleared his throat. A moment of silence followed before he glanced back at her face. "Do you have somewhere to stay? If your father is in the fort, I can bring Doctor Talan to you as soon as he gets back. I know you're worried, but I don't see anything life-threatening about his condition." Compassion glowed in his eyes, but he made no move to touch her. "If you need a friend or someone to talk to, I'm here."

And she wished she could take him up on his offer, but too many things must remain unsaid. Glancing down the row of buildings as the night breeze blew against her heated cheeks, she bit her lip to keep the words inside. The lawman's gentleness affected her more than it should have. She couldn't remember the last time someone offered sympathy or kindness.

Swallowing the lump in her throat, she squared her shoulders. "We can stay with Papa's friend, Marion

Adams." This whole situation with the bear trap would cost them more than Papa's leg if their secrets were exposed. She wished the muscle-bound officer would stop being so likable because she had a tough time not taking him up on his offer and blabbing her life story all over his broad shoulders.

Lilli stepped back into the shadow, putting distance between them. She didn't trust her reaction. Max Calhan stood too damn close and saw too damn much.

"Perfect. I'll help you get your father settled, and then I'll inspect his wound while we wait for the doctor." He strolled to the front of the wagon and climbed onto the seat as he spoke. "Are you coming?"

Tugging her hat forward, she lifted her collar higher before climbing onto the wagon seat. She leaned to the left to avoid contact and kept her face tilted down. Even three feet apart, his closeness made her side tingle. Clucking to the horse, she drove around to Marion's little cabin behind the commissary building.

Together, they lifted Papa out and into the little bedroom of Marion's home. Charlotte, Marion's daughter, held the door open.

The dark-haired widow bustled around, making sympathetic noises as Papa protested, and Officer Calhan asked for clean towels, water, soap, and bandages.

Charlotte stood close to Lilli as Max unwound the bandage. "He doesn't look so good," she whispered.

"I know." The girls had been friends since the moment they met. She hadn't considered their intimate conversation out of character for a man of fifteen until Officer Calhan shot them a second glance.

"You two friends?" He bent over his task as he asked the question.

"Yeah." Lilli glanced at her friend and assessed the situation through different eyes. Most young men would be awkward with petite, dark-haired Charlotte, her ample bosom, and big brown eyes. Until this moment, she hadn't considered how their friendship might appear to others until the officer's eyebrow climbed into his hairline. When they visited Marion, all pretense dropped.

Anxious to maintain her persona, she widened her stance. Shoving her hands into her pockets, she shifted to the side and avoided making eye contact with Charlotte.

Once the wrapping fell away, the odor from the festering wound took them aback.

Max took off his jacket and rolled up his shirt sleeves, revealing tanned muscled forearms.

Lilli gaped. She followed the length of his arm to bulging biceps, straining the sleeve of his shirt, and lingered on the width of his shoulders.

Her interest must have been obvious because Charlotte shoved her shoulder, and Marion coughed.

Tearing her gaze away, she snapped her mouth closed. Flushing with embarrassment, she stared at the opposite wall, hoping Max didn't notice her wayward eyes.

"His infection is getting worse. Let's get this wound washed and dry." The officer washed his hands and took a seat beside her father.

Marion cleared her throat and cast a worried glance in Lilli's direction. "Have you known Officer Calhan long?" She shot her a pointed look.

The woman wanted to know if the officer knew her secret, and Lilli gave a slight shake of her head.

Papa drifted in and out of consciousness while she

explained about the visit to the cabin and the bear trap mystery. Several times, he woke up enough to swear and demand Max leave him alone. Perspiration broke out on his brow and ran down his face as he drifted off again.

Marion nodded when she concluded her explanation.

"I see. Then, you're strangers." Relief crossed her expressive face. "Willie, go with Charlotte and make your papa some Willow Bark tea while I help the officer finish up." She inclined her head toward the back of the house and waved the girls off.

Lille glanced back to see Marion dabbing Papa's brow with a clean linen cloth and making sympathetic noises while Officer Calhan worked.

Grateful for the reprieve, she hurried toward the back of the house.

Out of sight of the others, the girls whispered while they worked, bringing Charlotte up to date on the traps, Papa, and the handsome officer.

"Papa burned my ears for not sweeping my path the morning Officer Calhan stopped by." She spoke in a low tone to avoid being overheard.

"I imagine so. No doubt, the situation reminded him of Montreal. I'm surprised he let you come to the fort at all." Charlotte tilted her head and studied Lilli. "I worry when he leaves you behind."

Her uncle almost caught them in Montreal. He had men watching, and one put a gun in Papa's ribs on his way home from work. Her father's quick thinking and reflexes were the reason they escaped. He left his assailant unconscious in an alley and moved north the same day.

"I know. But I have dogs. Papa never leaves me

home without one of them." Most of the time, she amended. He had taken them to the fort twice, leaving her all alone. And she never got over the anxiety.

But what Charlotte didn't know wouldn't hurt her.

They returned as Max finished cleaning the oozing wound.

Papa lay awake and frowned at her when she entered. "I would have been fine at home."

"Not with this kind of infection. Willie did the right thing to bring you here." Officer Calhan did a final inspection and rose to his feet. "Doctor Talan will take good care of you."

Marion hurried off to collect clean linen. "I imagine the doctor will give you opium for the pain. In the meantime, I have your favorite whisky." A few minutes later, she returned with the promised bottle and a glass.

"I think we should allow his leg to dry in the air while we wait for the doctor." Officer Calhan plucked his red wool jacket from the hook by the front door and gave Lilli a smile. "He should be fine in a few days. Don't worry. I'll let you know as soon as the doctor arrives. Try to get some rest if you can."

Such a thing proved impossible because her ears were filled with Papa's deep voice and Marion's answering one as the two girls retired and locked the door behind them.

Charlotte had a new dress, and after a good deal of nudging, Lilli put it on. As she smoothed the delightful floral calico with her hand, her mind turned to Max. Would he think her pretty in this? Surprised by the idea, she frowned. Why did it matter what Officer Calhan thought? She had no answer and turned away from the mirror. If she were smart, she'd stay as far away from the handsome officer as she could get.

The warmth in his eyes as he patted her shoulder came to mind. Papa wouldn't like his attention, and she shouldn't either. But she couldn't help but wonder what real affection would feel like. The last person to hold her close and whisper, "I love you," died six years ago in New York City at the hands of her uncle. Her entire being yearned for love, acceptance, kindness, and security. And she hadn't experienced any of those things since. A deep sigh escaped before she could stop it.

Charlotte held a delicate lace-edged chemise and a matching pair of pantalets toward her. "Mama ordered these for you when we bought the dress."

Lilli shoved her feelings aside. She didn't know how to answer her friend and ran a finger over the fine fabric. "Your mother is very kind, but I don't think Papa will allow me to wear them."

"What he doesn't know, he cannot argue with. With these on, you can be female under all the men's clothes. Think how much better you will feel with the fine fabric next to your skin. I imagine your red woolen underwear is scratchy."

"Oh, yes." The first few months she wore breeches, a shirt, and woolen underwear, were both torture and bliss. The breeches and shirt were so much more fun than any dress. And she loved the freedom to move. On the other hand, the underwear damn near killed her. Hot, sticky, and scratchy in awkward places, she loathed the things. But Papa only laughed and said she'd get used to it. Four years later, she hadn't changed her opinion.

The delicate underwear caressed her skin, and she smiled with delight. "Tell Marion I love them. And thank you."

Later, after her friend fell asleep, Lilli stared at the blank white walls and sighed. She wondered what Mama would make of the situation if she were here. Dainty, elegant, and refined, her mother possessed the regal bearing of a princess and would approve of the feminine undergarments Marion gifted her. The Northwest Territory would hold no interest for her, nor would their way of life. She tried to imagine Mama using the old wooden outhouse and failed. Used to maids, cooks, cobblestone drives, and indoor plumbing, her mother wouldn't last a week out here. She doubted Mama would care much about the way Papa drank, either. He blamed his wife for leaving him and reverted to the wild side of his nature. The part he set aside the day she agreed to marry him.

Lilli sighed again. She missed Mama, her gentle touch, and her loving nature. Life in New York seemed further away than ever.

Wagons rumbled by, and the sentries strolled past every few minutes. One would suppose the fort fell silent along with the sun, but it did not. On previous occasions, the girls were too busy talking to pay any attention to the noise outside. But not tonight. Anxious to think of more uplifting things than the life she lost, Lilli drifted off to dream of Officer Calhan's supple, tanned skin, gorgeous blue eyes, and bulging muscles. If only…

Chapter Four

Doctor Talan took one look at the wound the next morning and ordered a steaming basin of water to clean the diseased tissue. After giving Papa a healthy dose of opium, he started the process and asked Marion to brew more Willow Bark tea. Two hours later, he finished the last stitch and applied salve over the lower half of Papa's leg. He positioned a leather brace around the break and wrapped the leg with clean bandages.

"The decrease in sensation along the lower right portion of your foot has me wondering if we should consider amputation. I don't detect any odor or obvious gangrene; otherwise, we would be having a different conversation."

"You're not taking my leg." Papa sat upright and glared. "Out here, losing a limb is a death sentence."

"The problem is the broken leg. You've fractured your tibia and must stay off your leg if it's to heal properly. Your other wounds created by the trap's teeth must be cleaned and bound every day. Are you staying at the fort so I can treat you?" Dr. Talan rose to his feet and studied her father's face.

"No." Papa could be stubborn as hell when the mood struck him. "I have animals and traps to tend. I haven't been out this last week, and what has been done, the boy did. I don't have time to lose if I want to make this year's quota."

They had secrets to keep as well, and Lilli knew by the way Papa frowned she would get an earful when they were alone. He didn't allow her to come to the fort for fear of being discovered.

The doctor's gaze swiveled to Lilli. "I see." His gaze wandered over her arms and back to her father.

She shifted her feet as she waited for the usual comment about her lack of biceps and how hard work would toughen her up. But none came.

"This is serious business." The doctor shook his head at her father. "The foul odor of your wound suggests you might be developing gangrene. Now, I'm not saying that is what this is, but it could be. Some of the symptoms are present, and the repercussions of poor treatment are deadly. We're talking amputation and death. Are you willing to risk it if I allow you to go home?"

Papa frowned. "I am. Willie will help me with my foot, and the gods will help me with the rest. We've come this far."

Dr. Talan folded his arms and gave her father a stern look. "These kinds of injuries are difficult to treat. For the bone to heal, the leg must be immobile. A tibia break can take up to five months to heal. Your other wounds require movement to ward off gangrene. I've stabilized the bone with a leather brace and stitched the wound. Leave the brace in place and clean the wound twice a day. Stay off your leg as much as possible. I warn you, the next few weeks won't be pleasant, but if you follow my instructions, there's a good chance your leg will heal fine. I recommend opium twice a day and Willow Bark tea until your fever subsides. I will measure out the proper amount of drug for thirty days. I want to see you when this runs out to determine how the wound is healing. Sooner if your leg gets worse." He turned away and measured out the white powder into a plain paper packet.

When he finished, he named a sum for his services, and Lilli paled. She counted out the coins she tucked into her pocket on the way out of their cabin with a grimace. Every year, Papa drove to the fort at the end of August to buy supplies for the winter. This year, they had half the amount of the previous year, and paying for a doctor didn't help the situation.

When the door closed behind the doctor, Marion sat on the edge of the bed by Papa. "You could stay here with me for a while. Willie, too. I wouldn't mind a bit, and neither would Charlotte. You would be close at hand for the doctor and get the care you need. I don't like the thought of you so far away when you feel poorly." Her cheeks turned pink when he took her hand in his. "You know I care for you, Frank. Stay with me. It's been six years. Genova cannot be searching still."

Papa gazed at her with sorrowful eyes. "I'm sorry, Marion. There's too much danger, and I can't take the risk. He'll strike when we least expect it. We have stepped beyond what's acceptable as it is by coming here now. What if someone recognizes me? If they do, Genova will come for my daughter." He shook his head. "Even after all this time, my answer is no. We should get back to the cabin and stay out of sight. It's the only way."

Lilli stepped outside the back door while the two said their goodbyes. Papa deserved happiness after what he'd been through, and although she didn't mind Marion, she had the feeling the woman cared more for Papa than vice versa.

Oh, her father liked the woman, judging by the smile of satisfaction on his face when he left her room on their trips to the fort, but she suspected his interest lay more in companionship than being in love. The one thing Lilli knew for sure, her mother, Molly Genova Van Rassner, occupied the coveted position as love of his life, even in death.

Hitching the mare to their wagon, Lilli said good-bye to Charlotte and waited on the seat for Papa.

She often wondered about the odd phenomenon of love when she rode out to check the traps. How did one know if they loved another, and what characteristics must one have to attract a good man? In retrospect, for a man to hold her interest, he must track, shoot, hunt, and fight better than she did and stand a good head taller. No man could be taken seriously if he were too short. After the first good fight, she would stuff him on the tallest shelf where he couldn't get down and leave him there until he apologized. Such a situation would not create a happy household, and a smile curved her lips. The man she married would have to be valiant, strong, and brave to deal with her and her temper.

As a woman, society expected her to control her feelings and temper her voice. Now that she pretended to be Willie, she yelled, cursed, smashed her fist into the wall, and kicked things when she got riled. And her sore toe bore witness to the fact. But if the truth were known, she would be the model of grace and virtue for the chance to be her true self once more.

When the moment arrived, she would don her silk dress, pile her hair high on her head, slide her silk stockinged feet into satin slippers, and walk like a princess. Somewhere, beyond fear and danger, a good man waited for her. She'd have the house, the children, and the life she envisioned. There would be family, friends, happy times, and so much love everyone around her would be sucked inside.

A deep sigh escaped as she gazed with unseeing eyes into the distance. But first, the danger must be gone so she could live without fear of attack. Lilli read fairytales as a child, and she thought them wonderful. But common sense said she'd have to go find the prince and rescue him because no male of royal blood stepped foot this far north for any reason. Happy ever after would have to wait. In the meantime, the silky new underwear did feel better than the red woolen ones.

Her gaze caught on an odd little man hurrying past Marion's little cabin on his way to the commissary. He stayed in sight the whole way. His thin shoulders drooped under the heavy bundle of furs he carried. Black and white peppered hair, wizened skin, and thin features, his gray eyes glanced at her and away as if he didn't want to attract her attention. The man had several minks in his bundle. Papa's traps were robbed before she got the chance to empty them, and she knew they contained several of the little animals by the sign they left. Dropping her gaze to his feet, she gaped at the brilliant beadwork on his leather shoes. Someone spent a considerable amount of time stringing beads and sewing them to the thick hide. Her gaze returned to the pile of fur across his shoulders. How did he manage to get so many? On their best weeks, they did a quarter as much.

"How's your father?" Max Calhan stood beside her.

Jumping in alarm at his sudden appearance, she told him the doctor's opinion. Wrestling with the fact he snuck up on her, she frowned. Under normal conditions, she would be aware of his presence long before his gorgeous body came into view. Her gaze returned to the odd little man with all the pelts, and she concluded the man distracted her, so she hadn't been aware of Officer Calhan's approach. Papa would be disappointed in her if he were in his right mind.

"Which window is Charlotte's?" Max's question snapped her back to the present with a start.

"The one facing the road. Why?" Her gaze searched his face while an odd sensation fluttered in her belly. Something happened last night. She could feel it.

"Let her know to close her curtains tighter. I discovered a man outside her window after dark and sent him off with a warning. This is a busy fort, and any number of men could get a glimpse inside her room. She should be careful." He turned to gaze down at her. "Our job as men is to protect the women in our lives. You should keep a better eye on your friend when you're at the fort."

Her mind refused to function as a chill ran through her. *Someone peeked in the curtain last night while they tried on clothes.* Swallowing the lump of fear in her throat, she nodded to let the officer know she understood and agreed. Had her uncle found them again?

"Let's go, Willie." Her father appeared at Marion's door, and she jumped.

"Okay." For once, the secluded cabin appealed to her, and she couldn't wait to get back.

Papa insisted on riding on the seat instead of laying in the back. After several failed attempts to mount, Officer Calhan gave him a hand up, and they were off with her father's leg propped up on the front of the wagon. His tall, lean frame filled the seat beside her as he shifted for comfort. Sunlight glinted on his black peppered hair and oil-slicked breeches. He rolled the sleeves of his woolen shirt up and leaned back with a sigh.

Silence followed for long minutes as they drove through the gates and out onto the main road.

"Taking me to the fort put our lives in danger. What if Genova had a scout there searching for us? All the years of hiding and sneaking around would be erased in seconds if he did. When I make the trip, I'm careful, and I go after dark so we're not seen. Strolling around the place in the middle of the day is plum crazy. What were you thinking? You know how things are. I don't care how bad off I am. Don't take that kind of chance again. And pull your cap down over your ears so no one gets a good look at your face." Papa's deep voice rumbled beside her.

If she told him about the man peeking in the window now, he wouldn't let her out of the cabin for the next hundred years.

If ever.

"I brought you to the doctor for help because I can't do without you, Papa. If something happened to you, where would I go? What would I do? You're all the family I have left, and we both know I can't go home." Her voice quivered despite her command to remain steady and strong.

A deep sigh escaped him. "I know." A lengthy silence followed. "But there is another you can trust."

Her gaze swung to his. "Who? Where?" The grisly scene of her family's murder replayed in her mind until she dropped her chin and willed the memory away.

"I'll tell you when the time is right, but for now,

know you are not alone. I have a contact in New York who keeps me up to date on events there. As soon as the threat is gone, I will take you home." Papa's voice trailed off as he stared into the trees. "Molly would be horrified *and* proud of you if she could see you now. I don't doubt she'd scorch my ears for teaching you to shoot and fight. At the same time, she'd be so happy to see what a beautiful young woman you've grown to be. And capable. Molly would love that about you."

Lilli choked on her words. "I hope so." Papa never offered compliments, and she didn't know how to react. In her younger years, any words of encouragement came from Mama, not Papa. And more than anything, she wished for her mother's smile of approval. If she were more capable, they'd have a bigger pile of pelts and more coins inside the sock in Papa's drawer. "A man came into the fort with mink. He wore the most peculiar shoes I've ever seen with beads and fancy stitching."

Her father stiffened and cast his gaze in her direction. "Moccasins?"

Lilli nodded. "Yes, but not like any I've seen before. They had soles like boots. Do you know him?"

Papa growled low in his throat. "No, but the one who set the trap on my property wore moccasins like you describe. His sign trialed off to the east. I had plenty of time to study the marks as I lay there waiting for you to find me."

She swallowed. "Do you think he's the one?"

"Trapper, mink, leather soles, beadwork, fringe, and a slight build. Yes, I do. I found a bead in the mud beside the trap." Papa sounded sure of his conviction.

"I didn't say he had a slight build, but he did. And he didn't like the attention I gave him, either." The man's face flashed before her mind, and she shuddered. "I can send a note to Officer Calhan as soon as Mateus comes."

"There's no need to bother the officer. We can deal with the bastard on our own. First thing tomorrow, I'll go check the lines and search for more signs. I'll find the scoundrel, and when I do, I don't want the officer anywhere close."

"Agreed." The small man deserved to be caught and punished for his crimes. Because of him, Papa's might lose a foot. Up here, an eye for an eye reigned supreme. "But what about your leg? You're supposed to stay off it." She knew he wouldn't the second the words left the doctor's mouth, and his response came as no surprise. She kept her mind occupied so it didn't dwell on ugly words like gangrene, amputation, and death.

"I have my walking stick, and I'll be careful. We both know I'm not going to sit around." He cleared his throat and shot her a sideways glance. "Speaking of the law, you should put some distance between you and Officer Calhan. He's not the sort of man you should get close to or confide in. We took some awful chances the last few days, and I won't take more. Did you tell him who you are? He kept his gaze on you more than I cared for." Her father's discerning eye inspected her face.

"No." She choked on Papa's assumption she would do something so foolhardy. The fact Papa asked made her mad as hell, and she told him so.

He shrugged. "There will be no more trips to the fort for you. I'll go alone in a week or two to get supplies."

She shot him a disapproving glare and opened her mouth to argue.

He held a hand up to stop her. "Okay. I'll have Mateus do it." He sighed. "But either way, I can't afford to take any more chances with your welfare." The finality of his tone told her he wouldn't be swayed, so she leaned forward to rest her forearms on her knees.

The opium must be working. She figured he would be more verbal in his displeasure about her bringing him to the fort once the pain pounding in his lower extremity no longer demanded all his attention.

"I'll be fine." Thank God she didn't grow a conscience earlier and tell him about the window peeker.

"You will be if you do as I say and stay away from the man." Papa's tone brooked no argument. "The last thing we need is for him to find out you're female and old enough to court."

"Yes, Papa." He needn't worry. Officer Calhan wouldn't glance twice at a girl like her. And nothing on earth could induce her to get too close to the over-observant muscle-bound lawman to find out. He was smart, kind, handsome as the devil, and patient, but she knew better than to trust a stranger.

Unless he surprised her.

Which he did.

And not in a good way.

The next morning, her father took the rifle and the dogs out to check the trap line despite her arguments. The first snow covered the ground, so he took the sled. Climbing on after Lilli harnessed the dogs, he gripped the sled and gave her a stubborn stare. "I'm not going to lay around when there's work to be done." The Willow Bark worked wonders for his fever, and the opium made him feel like the old Finn Van Rassner from yesteryear. Or so he said.

He must be doing better because he walked easier and didn't grunt with pain. She worried and argued about him going out alone. "You're supposed to stay off your leg."

"And exercising is the only way to prevent gangrene. I'll be fine, Lilli. I have my crutch to lean on and all the stockings you could find covering my injured foot. I've been running traps and traipsing across this country since I wore knee breeches. I could do this in my sleep if I had to. The opium took the edge off. Now, stand aside."

Lilli held Zeus's harness as she stared up at her father. "Let me go. I will get there and back, and then we can check the cages down by the river together. You know where to step. I won't. If the man who set the bear trap sets another one, I'll step on it like you did." She hadn't told her father the other traps were being robbed on a regular basis, and their pelt count suffered. She knew if she did, he would ride the line until he got answers, and his leg would suffer the consequences. She planned to keep him close to the cabin until his wound mended.

He narrowed his gaze as if he could read her mind. "Take a branch and test the area before you take a step." He swayed on the seat and caught the side of the sled with his left hand for balance.

"You're not well enough to be out on your own, Papa. You've been on the cot for a week and burned with fever yesterday." His dizziness concerned her a great deal. "Give me a minute to get my other jacket, and I'll come with you."

"I feel fine. Now, don't coddle me." He shifted his leg and sighed when she turned away. "If I'm not back in four hours, come find me. I need exercise, girl. And freedom. I haven't laid in bed so long in my life, and I look forward to the ride."

She didn't get a chance to answer because he whistled to the dogs and drove away, leaving her staring after him.

The day lasted forever.

She took her mare to the river and used a limb to test the path as Papa said. Tracks along the way made her hesitate. She knew how to use the pistol in her belt and knew how to fight, so she shouldn't be nervous. But for some reason, she was. Unsure if Papa's injury shook her from the safety of her little world and carried the memory of her mother's death. Or if her encounter with the strange little man made her plain jumpy, she didn't know.

Standing still in the middle of the winding path to the river, the hair on the back of her neck stood on end, and she held her breath. She sensed the presence behind her before she had any indication of company. Flexing her shoulders, she glanced side to side to assess the direction of the danger.

Stepping behind a tree, she slipped the pistol from her belt and focused her attention on the area around her. The slight rustle of leaves floated on the crisp breeze, bringing the scent of dark earth, pine trees, and arctic cold.

And then she caught a glimpse of a figure out of the corner of her right eye. Rounding the tree, she lifted her pistol, but the dark figure caught her arm and propelled her back behind the tree. She grunted when she hit solid bark and shook her head to clear her vision. Boxing the man's ears, she jerked her knee up hard into his pelvis and smiled when he grunted with pain.

"Stop." The hoarse command made her grin.

Satisfaction disappeared like frost in the sun when her assailant refused to succumb to her blows. Throwing both his arms around her and knocking her to the ground, he rolled with her held tight against him into a clump of bushes.

Dizzy and disconcerted, her defensive attack made no impact. She lifted her head, but he pulled her back down as the report of a pistol cracked through the frigid air. Shocked, she sucked in a breath and stared up at the blurry figure who saved her life.

"What the hell?" She yearned to see her mother again sometime. But not this way and not this soon.

Chapter Five

Making a quick check for obvious injury, she sighed when all her body parts responded wound-free.

"Get off me!" Bringing her knee up, she missed her target and hissed with fury. Bucking her hips and slugging the bulky figure with all her strength, she ignored the stinging in her hands and gave him more.

The man grunted and clapped a large hand over her mouth. "Be still. He may be close. If you promise to keep your skinny ass on the ground out of sight, I'll find the bastard."

She recognized Officer Calhan's voice and sucked in a breath. His long, lean frame pressed her to the ground, and his face hovered above her own. Why the hell didn't he have on his red wool jacket? She mistook him for a stranger dressed in a dark-colored jacket and breeches. Blinking up into his amazing blue eyes, she shook her head, surprised she hadn't guessed his identity sooner. His musky male scent clung to his jacket and blew across her face when he spoke. Warmth flooded her belly, and she sucked in a breath. His mouth hovered inches above hers, and the weight of his body enveloped her in his heat. She tingled in response. Papa's words of caution flew from her mind as she melted beneath the weight of his body. She wanted this intimate moment to last forever and shifted beneath him to accommodate his heavy frame. Her belly jumped when he leaned closer, studying her face. With a dry mouth, she gazed into his beautiful blue eyes and wondered if he planned to kiss her. Envisioning his hard mouth moving against hers, she closed her eyes and lifted her face. The air thickened around them, and Lilli forgot to breathe.

"What the hell's wrong with you, kid?" Max rolled to his feet with a grimace and brushed debris from his jacket. Glaring, he took a step away from her. "Don't ever do that again." Running a hand through his hair, he stared down at her. "Stay here. And for God's sake, stay down. I'll be back."

He disappeared as suddenly as he appeared, and she bowed her head with mortification. He recognized the interest in her eyes but thought her a boy of fifteen. God, could this day get worse? Heat rose to her cheeks as she recalled how he fit against her body, pressing into her softness. No man had gotten within twenty feet of her since the day Papa packed her into the Northwest Territory for safety. Trembling beneath the lean, hard heat of Max's frame made her flutter with awareness, and he must have guessed her thoughts by his hasty withdrawal.

Self-incrimination made her wince. She knew better than to let anyone get close.

Deepening shadows filled the area around her as she rose to her feet. Ignoring the heaviness in her chest, she glanced around. A bullet hole, eye level on the other side of the tree, caught her attention. Max knocked her to the ground to save her life. She'd been so consumed with getting free and then equally so of his closeness that she forgot about the shot. What if he hadn't come?

Terror shivered over her. First, the bear trap and Papa, and now this. The man peeking in Charlotte's window danced across her mind. She wanted to believe the villain was a drunk soldier stumbling back to his room. But instinct said otherwise. Had her uncle found them?

Retracing her steps to the edge of the path where she tied her mare, she frowned at the possibility. Taking Papa to the fort had been foolish, and she may well have destroyed everything. Her life, Papa's, her future, and any chance she had of returning to the life she knew. Allowing Max Calhan into their lives and confidence had to stop.

The object of her thoughts fell into step with her a few minutes later, maintaining several feet of space between them. "I asked you to stay put for your own safety." The sharpness of his tone made her wince.

"I don't care." The silence stretched between them as she kept walking.

"I do. If I hadn't spotted him through the trees, you'd be dead. And that's one message I wouldn't like to deliver." A deep sigh escaped her companion. "Whoever he is, he's gone. His tracks crossed the trap thief's and then veered this way. They may be working together. I followed the shooter when he ventured this way to make sure you were safe. I caught up to him as he pulled out his rifle. I got one glimpse through the trees and followed the angle of his site to you. Did you see him?"

"No. Just a blur." If she had, *he'd* be dead. "I can fight and shoot as well as any man, and I don't need your protection." She bit her lip as a new worry occurred to her. "Did the new tracks go anywhere else?" Did the shooter work for Carlton Genova?

He glanced side-ways at her. "Yes. He stopped at

two other cabins. You shouldn't be out alone. Where's your dog?"

Her shoulders sagged with relief. Her uncle's man would stick around for the kill, and he wouldn't visit the neighbors unless he thought they were connected to her. Lilli cleared her throat and used her gruff voice. "With Papa." Embarrassment burned her cheeks. A dog would have warned her of danger. She knew what he thought about her going off alone, although he didn't say a word.

He maintained six feet of distance between them, and she sighed, thinking hard about how to explain her reaction without giving her secret away. Swaggering, she spit on the ground as they walked. She practiced for hours the other night and could make an arc as wide as his. "I didn't recognize you without your uniform." A man wouldn't blurt out the truth or give a lengthy speech.

"Which is why I'm not wearing it. The thief would spot my red jacket long before I found him." He stopped and searched the area before continuing. "I assume your father went north to check the rest of your line?" When she nodded, he shook his head. "I didn't think he'd stay in bed." His stallion stood twenty feet from her mare tied to a different tree.

"He has the sled. And the dogs." She swung into her saddle and picked up the reins. "Thanks for…." How did a man say, "Thanks for saving my life," without sounding weak?

"Yeah." He mounted his horse and turned south. "Keep a dog with you from now on, kid. They'll keep you out of trouble." He rode away into the forest without glancing back.

Any normal day, she would have Zeus and knew his worth. The bush had been her home for the past four years, and she knew how to survive here. The fact Max Calhan thought her a fool made her mad and embarrassed. Papa taught her better, and she didn't need the officer to check up on her. Speaking of her father, she should go back to the cabin to see if he returned.

When she flung open the stable door an hour later, the sled and the dogs were there waiting for her to put them away. With a sigh of relief, she hurried through the task and back to the cabin.

Her father sat in his favorite chair with a glass of whisky in his hand. The paper containing opium powder lay open on the table beside him. His leg resided on a chair in front of him piled high with pillows and blankets. His white face and shaking hands spoke volumes.

"Were you able to check the entire run?" She picked up the packet and frowned. "How much of this did you take? Doctor Talan gave us enough for a month, and at the rate you're going, this won't last more than another week or so."

Her father shrugged. "I'll get some more. What did you find on the small line today?"

Lilli swallowed as she told him about her encounter with Officer Calhan, minus how they landed on the ground.

Papa's hands gripped the side of his chair. "This shooter visited other cabins?"

When she nodded, he sighed. "He's not one of them, then. Mateus should be here tomorrow. We'll go to the fort for supplies and medicine. When I get back, I'll check the line. I don't want you out anymore where you're an easy target. I swore Genova wouldn't get his hands on you, and he won't."

"I'll be fine. I took Zeus everywhere before, and since he went with you today, the matter slipped my mind. It won't happen again. You should stay off your leg. I'll go with Mateus. Problem solved."

Her father gave her a long look. "No. I admit I need your help until my leg is healed, but I cannot risk you. Stay inside until I return."

She understood his reason, but rebellion took over. "I'll go crazy. At least let me come when you check the small run. That's where the danger has been. If we go together, neither one will be taken by surprise."

"Seven traps on the long run were broken into when I checked on them today. Did this happen last week, as well?" Taking a sip of his whisky, he gritted his teeth as he shifted his injured leg. "God damned drugs should start doing their job."

She glanced from him to the packet in her hand. "Yes, to the traps, and you can't have any more opium, Papa. I'm concerned about what you've taken so far. More won't help."

He grunted. "I'll decide how much is enough. Until I'm better, I'll allow you to come along to check the small line, but no more. I'll send for enough powder tomorrow to last for a while, so you won't have to go out to do my job."

"Our job." She folded the edge of the packet over and placed the paper on the shelf beside the Calendula salve. "Once I get dinner, I'll wash and bandage your leg."

****

Max tracked the would-be shooter to the riverbank two miles downstream from the location where he saved Willie's life.

He frowned over his earlier encounter with the strange young man. He recognized desire in the youth's eyes when he pinned him to the ground and shook his head. Accustomed to lust on a woman's face, he hadn't been expecting it on the boy's. Growing from a boy to a man affected people different. It could be Willie's natural inclinations came into play at the close physical contact. Understandable from the boy's point of view but intolerable from his. He remembered being surprised by his body's response to different things at the same age. As well as his inability to control it. But as a grown man, he sure the hell could. Beginning with the thin, awkward youth. He had no stomach for men who crossed the line with underage individuals, and he damned sure wasn't one of them.

His frown deepened. For being such a scrawny individual, the boy possessed a surprisingly soft body. The memory crossed his mind as he rode south.

He knew a young man well acquainted with the Calhan family who possessed a frail constitution as if he were born with feminine genes. Willie could be the same, which would make sense of his unusual appearance and attitude. But desire?

Distaste filled him, and he shook his head. He had plenty to worry about beside the boy and his journey to manhood. Whatever the reason Willie behaved as he did, Max vowed to keep a good distance from him in the future and focus on apprehending the man responsible for attempted murder, thievery, and unlawful trapping on private property.

Frank Rossi deserved justice for the wound on his leg and the pain he endured. As for Willie, the extra work hadn't harmed him a bit. Good hard physical labor would put some meat on his bones and keep his mind occupied. And his body.

Most trappers out here with a half-grown son shared the work, even putting the larger share on younger shoulders, but not Frank Rossi. He favored Willie and kept him inside, out of sight. Odd behavior for a trapper.

Max asked around at the fort and discovered the pair had settled in four years prior. He accepted his position at Fort Simpson six months ago, and although he patrolled the area, he had no idea they existed until he stumbled onto their cabin that day. The soldiers reported they came to the fort at night and avoided people.

Frank hadn't been very talkative the day they met, but he did mention his reputation with the Hudson Bay Company from his younger days, and Max wondered what made him leave Canada after creating such a name. And even more important, what made him come back? Twenty years hung between the two events with no explanation. Twenty years and Willie. The soldiers spoke of Frank as a wild man, a risk taker, and prone to walk outside the line of acceptable behavior. Did he get into trouble and come north to hide? Or did his return have something to do with Willie?

The incident at the fort popped into his mind a moment later. At first, he thought the man peeking in Marion Adams' window might be a drunk soldier on his way home, but as he approached and asked for a name, he discovered the stranger stone-cold sober and a civilian. A few inches shorter than his six-foot-three frame and a good deal thinner, Max met the man's glittering, soulless eyes as they turned toward him. The stranger's hand flexed above the butt of a pistol slung low around the man's hips.

"You'll be dead before you clear leather. I don't think a quick peek into a lady's bedroom is worth dying over. Do you?" Max squared off with the tall, wiry man and unhooked the leather loop on his holster to draw if necessary.

The stranger stared at him for a long moment and then shrugged. "No. I've seen girls before."

Two soldiers stopped on their way to the bar. "Is this man giving you problems, Calhan?"

The stranger shook his head and stepped back. "No trouble. I apologize and bid you good night." Hurrying away toward the fort's gate, he disappeared.

Max frowned as he thought the situation over.

Willie paled when he spoke about the incident the next morning. At the time, he thought the boy cared about Marion's daughter, Charlotte. Now, he wondered if he had misread the entire situation. There could be an altogether different reason beginning with why someone would want to kill the kid.

Something put the look of terror in the boy's eyes the first time they met and again this evening. If trouble came for the Rossis, Max wanted to know who, where, and from what direction so he could be prepared. Too many people came north and disappeared into the vast territory, never to be seen again. No one knew if their past caught up with them. They suffered an illness, an accident, or all three.

He lost his father in a senseless ambush at fifteen years of age and remembered the feeling of hopeless rage he endured. He and his two younger brothers swore to keep others from suffering as they did and joined different law enforcement offices, hoping to make a difference. Reese became a U. S. Marshal and patrolled the mid-west. Chase signed on with the Texas Rangers and patrolled the south while he trained as an officer in New York.

But after his gut-wrenching experience with Elsie and her parents, he couldn't face the injustice of the wealthy or those they influenced and rode north. He took the first assignment the Northwest Mounted Police offered. With every family he preserved, every father or mother he saved, the savage injustice of his own father's death diminished. And whatever he had to do to help Frank Rossi and his awkward son, he'd do. No boy should lose his father at such an early age.

Shaking his head, he followed the tracks until they crossed the river and up the other bank to the fort. Losing his lead in the busy confines, Max rode for the bar, hoping he got lucky and recognized the man in the trees among the patrons. If he could figure out who shot at the kid, he could find out why and stop the murder.

Dismounting, he took a minute to stretch his sore muscles while he relived the moment Willie knocked him to the ground beside the wagon. One thing was for sure—the kid could fight despite his lack of height, weight, and strength.

Inside, he ordered a beer and settled into the corner, where he surveyed the crowd with growing frustration. No one resembled the man he spotted with the rifle aimed at Willie. Several trappers complained about their lines being tampered with, and another man found a bear trap disguised along his trail like Frank Rossi had.

Max took notes on a sheet of paper with a pencil he kept in his pocket. The more he studied the culprit, the more determined he became to capture the son of a bitch. The thief's escapades covered fifteen miles of prime trapping along the Mackenzie River and half a dozen trappers on both banks. If he didn't catch the thief soon, one of the furious men shouting threats would, and they would exact their own revenge.

He ordered another drink and leaned back. Sooner or later, he would find the bastard, and he preferred sooner. He might not be around next time to save Willie's life and didn't like the way his chest clutched at the thought.

****

The next two weeks passed with no sign of Officer Calhan. Lilli couldn't make up her mind if she were upset or relieved because his gorgeous blue eyes popped up in her mind every day. And at night, she dreamed of the way he felt when he knocked her to the ground. All masculine and hard she lay beneath him, surrounded by his heat and scent. Licking her lips, she wondered what kissing him would be like. Would his mouth be hard or soft? Would he slide his lips along hers or press them against her? She closed her eyes, imagining how he would feel, and jumped when Papa yelled to attract her attention. Hurrying over to pour him some whisky, she returned to her dish pan with a sigh of regret.

Papa drove to the fort with Mateus to pick up supplies the following day. He spent the rest of their coins on canned goods and enough opium to last another month, according to Doctor Talan. He returned with half the supplies they needed to see them through the long winter, and Lilli swallowed to hide her concern.

She'd have to make up the difference somehow, and the responsibility weighed heavy on her mind.

The swelling in Papa's leg went down with all the exercise, although the sensation along the right side of his foot did not improve. She discovered the lack by accident when she dropped an empty bottle and followed a trial of blood to a fragment sticking out of her father's foot. He had no idea he'd been cut and acted as surprised by it as she did.

Oozing from the wound grew less and less as the days went by, and although Papa swore he recovered, Lilli had her doubts judging from the amount of opium he ingested with his morning coffee. She worried about the break, too, wondering how his bone could heal when he refused to stay off it. Figuring the pain came from his broken leg, she offered to go in his stead every day so he could rest.

And every day, he refused. Papa wouldn't discuss anything but his determination to gather pelts and replenish their stack of coins.

He allowed her to accompany him on his daily trek to the small line but no further. Together, they checked the path for traps and covered each other's backs as they did their work. The strange little man in the beaded footwear did not appear, and as the days got shorter, the air grew more frigid.

After the second snow, Lilli hoped for a break in the weather before winter settled in for good. But nature refused to cooperate, and she spent Saturday afternoon waxing the runners on the sled and tightening the leather lashings.

Her father came home complaining of a headache and made a straight line to the shelf for the white powder he loved so much.

"You had twice the dose the doctor recommended this morning, Papa. I don't think you need any more." She plucked the paper packet from his hands and slipped it inside her pocket, out of reach. "The medicine makes you sick. You breathe harder than you ever have, and you've been getting dizzy."

He caught the back of a chair or the wall for balance a lot more in the last week than he had when he first got hurt.

"Give me the medicine, girl. Don't make me fight you for it." His dark eyes stared into hers, and she faced him, noting the pallor of his skin.

Sweat clung to his forehead and upper lip, and she frowned. "Are you fevering again?' Placing her hand against his skin, she discovered him cold and clammy. "Let's get you to your chair, and I'll make you some tea. You're cold."

"Give me the paper, Rebecca." The anger in Papa's voice sliced through her.

He never raised his voice, and she glanced at him in surprise, taking a step backward. "You didn't say how the trap line fared today." Hoping to distract him, she poured him a glass of whisky. "Why don't you sit down and rest."

"Give it to me now, Rebecca Lillian. Don't make me take it from you." His tone dropped as he stared at her.

Papa never called her by her full name, and apprehension tingled down her spine. He planned to take the drug from her by force if she did not concede. He taught her every fight move she knew, and the chances of her winning this round were zero. His punches hurt like hell. And in his current state of mind, he wouldn't be gentle. Plucking the packet from her pocket, she held the object out. "Here."

With a grunt, he poured a good amount into his tea and limped to his chair. "Next time, don't get in my way.

I'll decide what's best for me. Not you, and certainly not some doctor." After a long swallow, he glanced at her. "I'll go to the fort tomorrow for more. You will stay here and check the trap line."

As she lay in her bed later, she tugged the covers over her shoulders and fought with her emotions. Papa had never scolded her or spoken to her in such a way before. When they trained, he showed no mercy, but never in a cruel way. Unlike the look he gave her earlier. She shivered under her heavy quilt.

As for the drug, the packet should have lasted a month but survived two weeks. She knew they had enough pelts for one more packet and no more. With any luck, he would be recovered by the time the new packet expired, and they could get back to collecting fur for the coming year.

The next morning, she discovered her father, the dogs, and the sled gone long before the first rays of the sun flickered through the trees.

Papa never touched the pelts after they bought supplies for the winter until they went to the fort the following spring. The drug's hold on him overpowered his good sense, and she wished she knew enough about the dangerous white powder to help him. The Papa she knew and loved disappeared while an unfamiliar one took his place.

She didn't like the new man and had no idea how to deal with him.

Chapter Six

Carlton Genova set his crystal cut glass down on the desk in front of him and steepled his fingers. "Did Fingers find the girl or not?" He stared at his secretary and thought of several ways to kill the fool. Then he changed his mind. Most of his ideas were messy, and he didn't care to buy a new Persian rug today.

"He, uh, is not sure, sir. Fingers said he found a man close in age and build to Finnegan but didn't get to see his face because the people with him covered him with a blanket. The man has a son, not a daughter, and when Fingers took a gander through the window for a closer look, a Northwest Mounted Police Officer chased him off." The man paled and glanced back at the half-open door behind him as if gauging the distance. "Fingers tracked them across the river and took a shot at the boy, but the same mounted police officer popped up out of nowhere and shot Fingers in the shoulder."

"This is the third time I've come close to catching the bastard and failed. I want answers, not excuses. And good work, Smithers, on digging up Finnegan's past. Without your help, we wouldn't know where to search next. Who would have guessed Finnegan Van Rassner and the Beaver King were the same man?" Carlton's gaze wandered over the gleaming oak desk in front of him and drifted to the cream-silk walls of his office. "I plan to be a very wealthy man in the next few months, and Molly's daughter must be found and disposed of. Do you understand me, Smithers?"

The older gray-haired man swallowed and ran a finger inside the neck of his stiff high-collared shirt. "Yes, sir."

Six years and two missteps weighed on Carlton Genova's conscience. He hated killing Molly. Of the three sisters, she treated him better than the rest. The blame for her murder lay with the old fool who fathered them. Since he changed his will, lethal methods were required to gain access to his inheritance. And he wouldn't be cheated. Not by Molly, her sisters, or her offspring.

Carlton swung his gaze back to his trembling secretary. "Add Fingers to the list and send the new man north. Let him know I expect a quick return on my investment."

The old man paled. "Yes, sir."

Retrieving the parchment from his desk drawer, he dipped his quill into the inkpot. "I almost forgot to scratch dear sister Louise's name off the list until you reminded me just now."

He found the bitch cowering in France at her husband's aunt's chateau. A chuckle escaped him. As if he wouldn't find her despite her efforts to hide. His man slit her throat when she left the estate to go shopping, and none of her four outriders lived to tell the tale. Telegrams with such tidings brightened his day, and he drank to the occasion.

Three names remained on the kill list—Finnegan Van Rassner, Rebecca Lillian Van Rassner, and Eloise Saint Claire, the other twin sister. He smiled as he envisioned crossing them off, too.

Soon.

"I will not tolerate another situation like Montreal or Winnipeg again. Make sure the recruit understands his instructions. One whiff of something amiss and Finnegan Van Rassner will disappear like a ghost in the night. He's a smart man and not to be underestimated." Carlton placed the precious parchment back inside the drawer and glanced at Smithers. "Make sure you bring me good news from now on. I'd hate to place an advertisement in the paper for a new secretary."

The old man's knees buckled as he shuffled backward to the door. "Yes, sir."

His secretary all but ran from the room, and Carlton frowned. The wealth belonged to him as the son the old man's wife never gave him. What did it matter if his mother came from humble blood to serve at the grand estate and spread her legs for her master? Or that she bore him a son out of wedlock? He carried the old man's blood in his veins the same as the holy trio he called half-sisters. Sure, they turned up their noses, called him a bastard, and ignored him in his younger days, but all that changed the day his father died. And Carlton planned to make them all pay for the indignities he suffered. He ate and slept in the servants' quarters with the rest of the help. He had no special tutors, lavish birthdays, or fine ponies to ride. He wore coarse linen, polished silver, and shoveled dung under the stable master's eagle eye. Even the old man's wife went out of her way to make his life miserable after his mother died by requiring more and more duties heaped upon his shoulders.

He remembered standing in the stable door holding a pitchfork as the family left for Europe on vacation and wondered what such grandeur would be like. With bated breath, he willed the old man to turn around and invite him along. But alas, his father stepped into the carriage without a glance in his direction and closed the door. With a tap of his cane on the roof, the carriage wheeled away, and Carlton vowed he would have his revenge if he had to kill to get it.

Bitterness welled up in his chest, and he spit into the spittoon on the floor beside him. No sanctimonious legitimate issue would keep him from what rightfully belonged to him, whether they were pure bred or not. God, how he hated the word *legitimate.* Almost as much as he disliked *bastard.* Although the latter contained more character and a good deal more potential. A potential he had every intention of exploring once he got his hands on his daddy's money.

****

Papa returned after dark, yelling through the back door for her to help him put the dogs and sleigh away.

Lilli passed him outside the back door as he brushed past. "How did your trip go?"

"Fine. How many pelts did you gather today? I'll need to make another run to the fort in a couple weeks for more opium. The doctor gave me what he had and cleaned my leg."

"Is your leg getting any better? What did he say about the break?" Her gaze searched his face, hoping he had good news. If the wound healed, they wouldn't need to revisit the fort until spring.

"He told me to keep taking opium for the pain. Is there dinner? I'm starving." As he strode away, she noted his limp and swallowed.

She trusted the doctor to say something if he worsened, and the fact he didn't meant good news.

Didn't it? Or did Papa not answer to keep her from worrying.

Once her father healed, with a few good weeks of trapping, they would be back on course, and everything would be all right.

She hurried through her chores in the stable and stopped short on her way back inside. Her father sat in his chair, sound asleep with his whisky glass by his elbow. Up before dawn and in bed long after normal people retired, she couldn't remember ever seeing him doze off before. The pallor of his skin and the sweat dripping from his brow made her frown. His breath came fast and shallow as he murmured incoherent words in his slumber. Hurrying over, she touched his brow and discovered his skin cold and wet.

What caused the excess moisture beading along his upper lip and on his forehead when he didn't have a fever? Unsure of what to do for him, she did the dishes and swept the floor, keeping her eye on him as she worked.

An hour later, Papa jerked awake, shouting for her to get down. His hands scrambled to find a non-existent pistol from his belt as he gazed around the room with wild eyes. "You can't have her. I'll kill you if you take another step!"

Lilli risked a glance behind her and found the room empty except for the two of them. "There's no one here, Papa. You were dreaming."

She allowed Zeus in the house since the day someone shot at her, and the dog lay asleep in front of the hearth, giving no indication of danger.

Her father sat upright, gazing at her in confusion. "Where are we?" Glancing behind her again, he gaped and paled. "Molly? Is it you? Tell me you're real. Tell me you're here. My God, let me look at you. You're so sweet, so perfect, and so beautiful it breaks my heart."

"Papa. There's no one here." Lilli repeated her sentence, but he continued as if she didn't say a word.

"I tried to get to you in time, but Carlton beat me home. I arrived too late and found you—" He choked and rose to his feet, stumbling forward. "I would give anything to have you back."

Silence filled the little cabin as her father's words transported her back in time to the awful day when she lost her mother. Curled in the corner of the closet where her mother stuffed her, she heard more than any child ever should.

How her mother knew they were in danger, she wondered about for years. One minute, they were on their way out the massive front doors, and the next, Mama gave a cry and shoved her into the coat closet. "Stay here, darling. Don't come out unless I or Papa open the door. No matter what you hear. Promise me."

Armed men swarmed into their beautiful home less than a minute after her mother closed the door. They shot everyone in sight and scoured the rooms, killing servants and family alike. Alone with nothing but her imagination, she listened to their boots thumping upstairs and across polished wooden floors while she held both hands over her mouth to contain her horror. More boots thump down corridors and into the kitchens, while her heart hammered against her ribs. Doors slammed, feet ran, and she cried silent tears, afraid the door to her nightmare world would open and they would find her. Screams of terror were followed by gunshots and then silence. More shooting followed, and then angry voices shouted before the boots thumped away.

Thank the gods they never opened the closet door, or they would have found a frightened thirteen-year-old girl huddled in the corner with both hands over her mouth. Tears streamed down her cheeks as she fought with her grief and shock.

Lilli had no idea how long she cowered in the corner, too frightened to peek out at the bodies littering her once-happy home. She didn't want to put a picture with the sounds traumatizing her mind and heart.

Then, Papa swung the closet doors open and gathered her into his arms. He cradled her head against his side to block her view as he helped her to the stable and his waiting carriage. She took one peek and spotted a bloody ribbon tied to the gleaming banister. The memory burned into her mind, and she never touched a red ribbon again.

Ever.

Transporting her to the other side of Manhattan, her father left her with her best friend, Emily Astor, and her family while he met with the police.

She would never forget Mr. Astor's kindness during the longest two days of her life. She couldn't eat, couldn't sleep, and cried until Papa ushered her to the family cemetery for a quiet, private burial.

Her father and Mr. Astor spoke in hushed tones after the burial, and Lilli discovered the reason behind the senseless slaughter. Following her grandfather's death, the family learned he left his entire estate to her mother, Molly. At her death, the wealth would become her daughter, Rebecca Lillian's, followed by Molly's twin sisters, Louise and Eloise. Carlton Genova, Molly's bastard brother from a willing housemaid, became enraged after the reading of the will and threatened to annihilate every member of the Genova line as punishment. Beginning with Molly and her daughter, Rebecca Lillian.

Lilli had no idea about any of this until her mother burst into her room, stuffed a few articles of clothing into a valise, and swept her downstairs. There, she stopped and, after a moment's hesitation, stuffed her daughter into the closet before closing the door. Later, she discovered Carlton Genova tied a red ribbon around the banister at the bottom of the stairs, warning her mother of her impending death.

Molly's quick thinking saved Lilli's life, and she would be forever grateful for Mama's maternal intuition. From there, Papa whisked her to Montreal, where they lived for a year in a small apartment until one of Genova's men attacked her father on his way home from work. They moved to Winnipeg the next day and spent another year on a farm until, once again, Genova sent an assassin.

Papa's paranoia kept them alive, and after the second attempt on his life, he moved to the Northwest Territory, north of Fort Simpson. They made their home in the tiny cabin, kept out of sight, and hid Lilli's identity from everyone. For four years, they lived in peace. And now this.

Lilli had no idea who her father communicated with but every few months a letter came to the fort and Marion collected it for Papa. Through this unknown person, he kept track of Carlton Genova and his pursuit of Lilli.

"I never got a chance to tell you how wonderful you were for saving our daughter." Papa's gruff voice transported her back to the present with a start.

"Mama's gone, Papa. You're here with me, and everything is all right." Stepping forward, she took her father's shaking arm with both hands and helped him back to his chair. "Let me make you some tea and bandage your leg. You'll feel better after you've had a cup."

For once, he didn't argue. When she handed him the hot beverage and finished with his leg, he gave her a thin smile. "I'm sorry, Lilli. Sometimes my head aches, and I can't remember where I am. Thank you for helping me. I'll say good night." He drained the mug and hobbled off to his room, closing the door behind him.

When she wiped the table down and removed his empty cup, she picked up the packet of opium and gasped. At the rate he gulped down the stuff, they wouldn't last the week.

She glanced at his door. If he refused to use good sense with the medicine, she would have to be his conscience. The way the powder affected him tonight frightened her more than she cared to admit. Taking a sheet of paper from the cabinet, she folded the corners until she created a packet like the one the doctor gave them. Dumping most of the powder into her hand-made one, she hurried to her room and placed the packet under her undergarments in her top drawer.

Returning to the main room, she set the remaining drug back on the shelf beside the bandages and salve. Pulling in the latches on both doors, she banked the fire and wandered off to bed, wondering how to help the man in the other room become the father she loved once more.

They battled over the amount of powder he ingested until Lilli wanted to wring her hands with frustration. Papa's wound grew better, while his sweating, confusion, and delusions grew worse. Astonished, her father could require so much pain medicine when his leg no longer required so much cleaning. She wondered if the break grew more painful for some reason. She made a mental note to discuss the matter with the doctor the next time she traveled to the fort.

After the first three days, Papa changed his mind about going out to check the lines and sent her.

He sent her to the fort, too. Which shocked her a great deal. Especially after the way he reprimanded her the night she took him in. Confused by Papa's sudden change of heart, she went about her duties, mulling the conundrum over in her head. The powder made him difficult to understand. But either way, she'd be careful, and he required rest if his broken leg were to heal. And she wouldn't complain because going to the fort meant running into the handsome officer.

Less than a minute after Lilli swept her tracks away in the clearing the next morning, a laugh bubbled up in her throat. She liked the freedom the sled provided and rejoiced in the quiet of the forest. Trees didn't argue with her like her father did, and although running the line took all her strength, she enjoyed the moments away from the little cabin.

Following the line to the first trap, she stopped and frowned over the tracks in the snow. Animal and man traipsed across the area since this morning's snowfall. Someone robbed them....again. The cad who swooped down and stole fur with no conscience must be stopped.

"God! What a bastard! We need those pelts you thieving twat!" Yelling into the still whiteness of the freshly fallen snow did little to relieve the anxiety racing through her.

How could she get Papa more medicine if they had nothing to trade? He took everything they had last time, and they didn't have enough pelts for another packet of opium.

Taking hold of the trap, she reset the mechanism in the freezing mud and secured the tether. After rubbing castoreum on a nearby stick from the bottle she kept on her side, Lilli placed the piece of wood near the trap and stepped back to view the area.

One out of every three traps contained a beaver. The other traps were robbed before she got there. They should have had several bundles of forty hides by now, but they didn't even have one.

At home, ten hides hung on round frames made of thin willows to dry. With the few mink, muskrat, and raccoon pelts they collected over the last few weeks, Lilli wondered if they even had enough for another doctor visit.

A sound in the forest made her spin around, and she lost her balance. Down she went with a loud splash into the freezing river, gasping as the icy water closed over her.

Damn! Her feet hit the riverbed, and she gave a strong kick to rise to the surface. Floundering to the bank with her teeth chattering, she stared down in dismay at her wet clothes. If she didn't get warm and dry in the next few minutes, hypothermia would set in. Dashing to her sled, she gathered a bundle of sticks kept on the back for situations of this kind and cleared a spot on the ground. Within minutes, she had a roaring fire and held her frozen hands out for warmth. Stripping her clothes off down to her undergarments with numb fingers, she shook with cold. Stumbling back to her sled, she plucked the fur from the seat and returned to the fire. Huddling beneath the warm, heavy sled rug, she stripped off her undergarments. Placing them on rocks around the fire, she squatted near the flames, careful to keep the fur close to her body and away from the flames.

Chills raced through her system as her teeth and knees knocked together.

Dropping her chin, she clutched the fur to her chest and focused on the warmth of the fire. When the feeling returned to her fingers, Lilli turned the clothes on the rocks and smiled. In another minute or so, her new chemise and pantalets would be dry enough to put back on. Thank God, she wore them today and not the heavy woolen underwear Papa gave her. The woolen variety would require another hour or two to dry. Her father loved her and wanted the best, she knew, but sometimes he didn't understand what she needed. Practical situations he could manage. Like now. He kept essentials on his sled in case he ran into trouble while he checked his line, and she did the same.

The emotional situations were a different matter altogether, like her underwear for example. He didn't understand her need to feel female despite wearing men's clothes, and she hadn't told him about Charlotte's gift for the same reason.

"Hey there," a deep, familiar voice called out, sending shock waves through her system.

Here she sat, naked except for the heavy fur with her undergarments and binding spread out for all to see. "Give me a minute, and I'll come up there." She hoped he would wait on the trail for her, but no such luck.

A minute later, his bulky figure appeared beside her sled. She had thirty seconds to collect her under garments before he got a good look at them, and she took advantage of the time, sweeping everything under her fur out of sight. Except she missed the two most important items, her chemise and the strip of binding.

Strolling around the sled, Officer Calhan stopped short. His gaze dropped to her feet and jumped back to her face. Understanding flashed across his face, and his expression spoke volumes. "Hello... Willie."

Her heart thudded loudly in her head, and she pretended not to notice Officer Calhan's hesitation when he said her name. Embarrassment warmed her cheeks. "Hello. I, uh, fell in the water, and I'm getting warm." God, she sounded like a child explaining the extra cookie in her hand. She dropped her gaze and tightened her grip on the fur.

"I spotted the smoke from your fire through the trees." His gaze dropped to her feet again, and he bent over. Picking up an article of clothing, he held the item at eye level while he turned it around in his hands.

Glancing up, Lilli wished lightning from heaven would incinerate the fine linen undergarment into a pile of unrecognizable ash at his feet.

His gaze dropped to her face. "I imagine you'll want this first." Her new, lace-edged chemise hung from his long fingers.

Scratch the lightning. If God were merciful, he'd send a blanket of darkness to cover her shame. Or fire. Fire would distract the observant lawman so she could dress unobserved and pretend this whole situation never happened.

But it did, and she flushed to the bottom of her very bare feet.

She could feel him thinking. "Yes, Thank you."

Clutching the fur closed with one hand, she jerked her undergarments from his fingers with the other and lost her pantalets in the process.

Another assessing look passed over his face before he bent again. This time, more slowly. "Or do you begin with this?" He held the strip of binding up and tilted his head as he stared at her. "So many things make sense now. You're not a *Willie*. Thank the gods." His gaze swept over her trembling body before returning to her face. "Why do you pretend to be a man when you're not?"

Lilli swallowed. Papa would skin her alive when he found out Officer Calhan knew of her deception. Ever since he stopped by their cabin, things changed one after another and she didn't know if she liked it. "My name is Lilli." She skipped the *Rebecca* part out of habit. The less he knew, the better.

Max dragged a log over to the fire and sat down with his back to her. "I see. And the man who shot at you? Is he involved in this…" He waved a hand up and down her trembling body. "charade. I can't wait to hear this explanation. Talk while you dress. I don't think anyone else is around, but you can't be too sure. I'll keep my head turned, so you don't have to worry. I'll see…anything important. Why don't you start at the beginning and tell me who has you so frightened you dress like a man and answer to Willie?"

Anxious to cover her nakedness, she wound her binding tight and slipped her chemise over her head. Her pantalets and woolen breeches came next, followed by her wool shirt. All the while, she kept her gaze on the back of his head in case she had to dive for cover. "There are some men looking for Papa. Bad men. They know he has a daughter, so I dress like a boy to avoid attention. We plan to keep it that way." Brief, devoid of details, and to the point. Papa would approve. Plus, she didn't know if she trusted the officer yet.

"I see." His voice suggested he didn't and sifted through scenarios in his mind. "Do these bad men have a name?"

"No." And she wouldn't tell him otherwise. Not until she trusted him with her life.

When she slipped the last button through the hole and tucked her shirt into her breeches, she bent to see if her jacket had time to dry. It hadn't. Bending, she placed the fur around her shoulders once more. When she stood, Max faced her with a curious expression while his blue eyes traveled over her from head to toe.

"I'll ask your father about the men."

He shook his head as he studied her. "So much makes sense. I can't believe I didn't see the truth. You're too dainty to be a man." His gaze bored into hers. "The answer is there for all to see. The delicate wrist bones and tiny frame, your dainty features, your big eyes." His gaze dropped to her lips and then back to hers.

Her gut tightened in response. *He wanted to kiss her!*

"How old are you? The truth this time." A husky note entered his voice, and her belly fluttered.

She grew hot all over. Lilli swallowed. "Nineteen." She licked her lips and wrapped the fur closer. "Marion knows, and so does Charlotte. They figured me to be a boy of fifteen when we first met. Papa and I tell everyone that's who and what I am."

"I see." Max took a step toward her, and the air crackled with sudden tension. "I shook my head over the two of you whispering together like girls. First, I wondered if someone should show you how to be a man, but now I'm thinking you need to be reminded you're female." His gaze heated as he took another step toward her. He touched her hair and ran a finger down her cheek. "You didn't like me ruffling your hair the other night. Why is that? Does my touch bother you?"

She shivered from top to bottom, fascinated by the glimmer of desire in his eyes. Her dreams didn't do justice to the real thing. She should put space between them, but Lord, did she want to touch him. Her belly tingled with awareness, and her knees clacked together as he caught her chin and tilted her face up to his. "No one touches me. I didn't know how to react." Her breath ended in a sigh as she stared into his deep blue eyes.

"The other night, when I hit the ground with you in my arms, I wanted to kiss you. You lifted your face to mine and offered your lips. Something about you called to me, and my body responded." He gave her a rueful smile. "But you were a child of fifteen in my mind, and I couldn't follow through. I'm not the kind of man who enjoys that sort of thing. Children should be allowed their innocence, and any adult who robs them of that should be shot." He took a deep breath and shook his head. "For a time, I wondered if I should see a priest and confess the sin my imagination committed with you. You have no idea how much self-talk I've done about this entire situation. I have to say, I'm relieved to discover you're female and over the age of accountability." He stepped into her personal space and stared down at her for a long moment. And then something changed. His lids dropped over his eyes, and he took a step back. "We should get you home before Frank wonders where you are."

Disappointment zipped through her like a thunderstorm, forgetting to rain, and the devil took hold of her tongue. "Will you kiss me now? I mean, now you know I'm old enough and…things?"

He hesitated as if a war raged inside him. "Why?"

Lilli flushed. "Because." She licked her dry lips. "I've never kissed anyone before, and I have to start with someone." Besides, she'd die if someone else kissed her first. She dreamed of the handsome officer for so many nights she couldn't leave and not find out what kissing him would be like.

"I'm sure one of the soldiers would oblige if you asked." His gaze roamed her face. "You're pretty and shouldn't have a hard time finding a willing partner."

"Why don't you want to?" She blurted the question and took a step forward. Her nose stopped half an inch from his chest.

"I don't like women." His answer hung suspended between them.

She wanted to stamp her foot with frustration. "One kiss." She lifted her chin and folded her arms over her chest. "You're my only option. I can't ask the soldiers. They don't know who I am and aren't supposed to ever find out. You either for that matter, but you do. And I'm asking you."

He stared at her for a long minute before he slid an arm around her waist, drawing her close. The chill in the air turned blazing hot, and the heat of his body made her shiver with anticipation.

She let her hands rest on his chest. They itched to explore the broad expanse, and she maintained eye contact so he could see her desire. "I don't know what you have against women, but I'm different. Try me and see." She threw the challenge out, hoping it had the usual result. Men were competitive by nature, according to her observations.

His mouth twisted in a wry smile. His gaze turned predatorial. "Okay. But don't say I didn't warn you." Catching her chin in his hand, he ran the pad of his thumb along her quivering lower lip. When he glanced back to her eyes, her breath caught in her throat. Hot desire glowed in the sapphire depths. "I'm going to taste you."

She couldn't speak. Tingling with excitement and curiosity, she ran her eager hands over his broad chest and down his arms to his biceps.

He felt like bunched steel, hard and warm to the touch.

Shivering with pleasure, she licked her lips and forgot to breathe. Her imagination hadn't done him justice.

"So soft. So perfect," he murmured as he bent his head. His mouth descended, and she grew faint with anticipation.

She had waited for this moment for ages. Standing on tiptoes, she lifted her chin higher, inviting his caress.

His firm mouth settled over hers, and he drew her to him, fur and all. "Open your mouth." His warm lips slid against hers, sending shivers of delight through her.

She opened her lips and gasped when his tongue invaded her mouth to mate with hers. The most delicious heat seeped into her veins and raced through her body, weakening her knees.

He smelled like leather, forest, and temptation. His easy strength sent thrills through her body as she leaned into him.

Cupping the back of her neck, he tilted her head sideways to deepen his kiss. Butterflies took flight in her belly and threatened to escape through her throat. She whimpered and let go of her fur to wrap her arms around his neck.

Kissing a man in real life didn't compare to what she imagined. Desire tightened her belly as she moved against the hard planes of his body. Pleasure zinged through her, and for the first time in a long while, she enjoyed being female.

"God, you taste good." His lips coaxed hers to open further, and he drank from her mouth with a moan, clutching her tight against him.

She forgot to breathe and leaned in for more. Liquid heat poured into her bloodstream. He tasted like coffee, the outdoors, and forbidden fruit. She couldn't get enough.

His hands roamed her back, waist, and hips, molding her willing flesh into the hard planes of his, and her knees buckled. She caught his shoulders and held on for fear she'd fall in a puddle at his feet.

The bulge in his breeches pressed against her belly, making her mouth go dry. Hard and hot, he caught her hips and held her against him.

Answering, wetness pooled between her legs, and she gasped with delight. Her knees grew weaker with each passing moment, and she mimicked his kiss in return.

The dogs mated and had puppies, so she knew the basic mechanics of being with a man, but nothing prepared her for the reality of being held this tight against his arousal.

Lilli pressed closer, anxious to experience every

nuance of being a female, and moaned when he kissed the side of her neck and moved down to the furious flutter racing at the base of her throat.

"Your heart's beating like a runaway sled." He unbuttoned the top button of her shirt and slid his mouth along her collar bone and down to the swell of her breasts flattened by her binding. She grew faint and panted for air.

Being a boy could be fun, but she'd rather be a woman in Max Calhan's arms. The thought danced in her mind as she arched back, wanting more. Marveling at the wonder his lips created, she shivered.

Max lifted his head and stroked her cheek. His lids dropped back over his eyes, and the moment evaporated in the frigid air. "You're shivering. We should get you home now. Some warm liquid inside you will take the chill out."

Lilli dropped her head so he didn't see her disappointment. "I'm not cold." If truth were told, she burned with anticipation and amazement. Gazing at his lips so close to her own, she sucked in a shaky breath. "Please don't tell my father you know I'm not a man. He's having enough…difficulty. He doesn't need to know someone else discovered my secret. It will only add to his worry." She glanced at the trap and then the sky. They needed more pelts. "I have three more traps to check, and then I can go home."

"I'll help you." Bending to assess her jacket laying on the rock at their feet, he frowned. "Here. Take my coat. Yours won't be dry for some time."

Her stomach fluttered anew. "What about you?" She took the proffered article and slipped her arms in the pre-heated sleeves. His scent clung to the wool and made her mouth go dry. The warmth of the jacket, combined with the scent of his skin, made her knees buckle. Her breath hitched when he leaned forward.

He glanced at her. "I have another jacket in my saddle bags. I can wear it. Let's get this done and get you home."

She smiled when his gaze lingered on her mouth. Despite his brusque manner, their kiss affected him, too. Going home didn't seem like a bad idea if Max came with her. She could use some help with her father, and the lawman might know what ailed him. And with any luck, she would convince him to kiss her again.

They hurried through the last three traps, collecting two pelts and finding the other trap tampered with.

Max frowned as he assessed the tracks. "I've been following this man all day. His feet are small for a man his size, and he makes tracks like your father's. This man is light and runs with a short stride. From the direction he's going. I'd say he's headed back to the fort." Glancing at her, he gave her a rueful smile. "I'll see you home." He glanced south toward Fort Simpson.

She knew from the intense way he studied the tracks he wanted to follow them. "I'm all right. I can find my way home. And thank you." She unbuttoned the jacket, but he put a hand on hers.

"Keep it. It'll give me a reason to visit."

The heated glance he sent her kept her warm all the way home.

Chapter Seven

After another trip to the fort with the last of their bundles, Lilli divided the white powder she purchased into several paper packets to ration the drug.

The first week, she convinced Papa to take less opium, and his agitation, sweating, and body aches increased. She made him drink more water and tea, convinced the drug must be flushed from his system for him to return to normal. Neither one got much sleep, and by the end of the second week, Papa's smile returned. He walked with a limp and returned to running the long trapline despite her arguing to the contrary. The more she wanted him to sit and rest his leg, the more stubborn he became.

Concerned for his welfare and knowing the futility of arguing further, she threw her energy into baking, cooking, and tending the small line.

Things went well until the robber struck their trap lines again. And not just the big one. He harvested both lines clean.

Papa cleaned and oiled his rifle the next evening after dinner. "I'm going to the fort tomorrow to see what the others know. They might know where this thief comes from and where he hides. He must be a local, or he would be dead. Or in irons by now."

Lilli stopped stirring the stew. "What about the lines? Do you want me to go?"

Papa shrugged. "I don't know if you'll find anything. We haven't harvested a pelt for two days. The damn robber gets there first. Right now, the important thing to do is find the thief and stop him. We can't live on what he leaves us unless we do." He shot her a glance. "I know you've been worried, and I've spent the last week thinking up a plan to help us survive until spring."

She smiled as she handed him a bowl of hot, thick soup. "It's nice to have you back, Papa. You had me worried there for a bit."

He grunted. "I have too much to do to die yet. Once Carlton Genova is six feet deep, you've married a good man, and given me a grandbaby or three, I'll consider going quietly. Until then, I'm here to stay."

"Maybe he's already dead." She couldn't wait to go home and see Emily Astor, her best friend. With her uncle out of the way, she could return to her life.

While Officer Calhan remained in the Northwest Territory.

His kiss filled her dreams with excitement, anticipation, and longing. She frowned and shoved the idea out of her mind. There were handsome men like him in New York, too. There had to be.

"No. My source will let me know when it's safe. We stay here for now." Papa set his rifle on the hooks above the mantel. "And keep you out of sight." He stared at her downcast face. "Now my leg is healing. We go back to doing things the way we were. Good night."

Years of solitude ate at her soul, and she frowned. She didn't like tending the line, but she loved the freedom of the forest.

Ignoring the tight band around her chest, she jumped up to gather their empty dishes and clean up. She didn't want to stay close to the cabin. She wanted to walk through the fort with her head high and her face in full view of everyone. She wanted friends, family, and a life without fear. Running into Officer Calhan would be nice, too.

Closing her eyes, she relived his kiss and sighed. He'd make an excellent husband and partner. Frowning, she wondered where the thought came from and sang hymns at the top of her voice to quiet the notion.

The next morning, she woke to a blizzard. Papa and his stallion were gone. He left all the dogs but Achilles, one of Zeus' older offspring.

She paced for the first hour. If she could see two feet in front of her face, she'd go after him. But doing so wouldn't help him and would put her own life in danger.

At noon, she made a sandwich and carried in more wood. Opening the back door, she clutched the rope tied between the house and the barn for guidance. Papa put it up every year at the beginning of the season and took it down after the last frost. A person could lose their sense of direction in a matter of minutes in a whiteout and wander off into the forest to die. The rope kept them on course.

She didn't worry about her father until well past time for dinner. Achilles knew the way and would guide Papa through the storm, but he should have been back by now.

Rising from her place by the fire, she rubbed the window so she could see out. Nothing but whiteness filled her view on every side. Sighing, she returned to her reading, ignoring the loud ticks of the clock. Papa grew up in the Northwest Territory and knew what to do in emergencies. And blizzards.

She repeated the words over and over until a sound made her jump.

Achilles!

Throwing on her woolen jacket and stuffing her hands into her woolen mittens, she opened the back door and stared out. "Papa?"

His voice whipped past her ear along with Achilles' excited bark.

Grabbing a lantern, she clutched the rope and hurried toward the barn. And Zeus. He would guide her through the darkness to Papa.

And he did.

She found her father in the tree line, leaning against an oak for support. His jacket hung in tatters as did his breeches. He gasped for air.

An excited Achilles snarled and growled at the forest behind them.

She sank down beside Papa to catch her breath and assess his situation.

Zeus sat by her side, bristling as he stared at the forest. He showed teeth at the whiteness behind her and growled.

"Quick. Get me inside." Blood dripped from a wound on Papa's right thigh, tied with a strip off his shirt. "Wolves."

He needn't say more. They must have smelled the wound on his leg and come looking for blood.

"Home." She commanded the dogs to lead. Slipping her arm beneath his shoulder, they followed Zeus and Achilles to the back door. Lilli let the dogs follow them inside as she latched the door and helped Papa to his chair.

He sank down with a moan. "Get me a glass of

whisky, will you?"

He required more than whisky. A lot more. "I'll get the bandages and some water." She made a quick inspection of his leg for damage. The wolf clamped around his upper thigh, tearing part of the flesh away. A wound of this size would require a great deal of time to clean and bandage. His make-shift bandage stemmed the flow of blood, for now. "I'll put the dogs in the barn and be right back."

He didn't answer.

Glancing up, she noted his blue lips and trembling. Throwing a quilt over him, she told Achilles to stay and took Zeus back to the barn. The dog would let them know if the wolves ventured too close following Papa's trail.

Half an hour later, she sank beside her father with hot water, bandages, Calendula salve, her needle, and a spool of silk thread.

The dog hadn't budged since she commanded him to stay, and she gave him a pat.

"Thank you for bringing Papa back." When her hand came away covered in blood, she discovered the animal sported several large wounds on his back and chest. The blood came from them both. "I hope you killed them."

"He tried. I shot three of them before the others caught up to us. I killed two more with my knife. Achilles got the last one, but not before he did some damage. Do what you can, girl. We're both pretty torn up."

She could see. Four hours later, she tied the last bandage around Achille's chest and sat back on her heels. Every now and again, howls lifted the hair on Achille's neck, and he growled. They didn't get the whole pack. From the sound of the cry, Lilli concluded one wolf remained.

She rose to refill her father's glass and recheck the door.

"Will you get me the opium?" Papa's request made her glance up at him. "I know how bad I got last time, but I won't sleep unless I take some."

His statement hung suspended in the air, and she didn't know how to answer.

One week. He'd been better for one week. Frustration and anger pumped through her. Lilli wanted to charge into the woods and kill the last wolf on principle.

Papa's white face and knuckles changed her mind. He clutched the comforter to his chest like a lifeline and moaned. He never made a sound the whole time his leg healed before.

"I'll make some for you." Rising to her feet, she glanced down at the black and brown dog who saved Papa's life. "And you can have some, too."

Papa's wounds festered and oozed. He moaned with pain and begged for the white powder every few hours until she wanted to scream in frustration. Wondering what they did to anger the universe, she complied with his requests.

Anxious about their future, fearful over the state of his wounds, and exhausted from lack of sleep, she rose before the sun each morning. After bathing and dressing both Papa's and Achille's wounds, she made Papa food, took care of the animals, and left to check the traps.

The first couple of days, she discovered the thief had beaten her to them. But then, her luck changed. Every day, she collected the usual pre-thief numbers and hauled back big, thick pelts. By the time she returned every night, put the dogs away, and prepared food for Papa, she dropped with exhaustion beside him to bathe and bandage his wounds.

"We must take you to the doctor. Your bite should be better by now." Probing the largest one, she shook her head. Angry, hot to the touch, and bright red, she worried her father would lose his leg this time.

"Get me some opium, and I'll be fine," Papa swore when she poured alcohol on the wound. "Give me the bottle." He took a generous swallow and closed his eyes.

"There's enough powder for one more dose, and then it's gone." His headaches, delirium, and excessive sweating returned. As did his shortness of breath and dizziness. She hoped he wouldn't ask for more and cringed when he did.

With Mateus' help, they had two bundles ready and another five pelts drying. They couldn't afford to barter the fur for more opium, and she said as much to Papa. "We're out of flour and salt pork. We need more supplies."

"Shoot a rabbit while you're out checking the traps. Once I'm better, we'll start a new line and make up for all we've lost. For now, I need the powder." He gazed down at her. "Go to the fort for opium tomorrow."

"I thought you wanted me to stay out of sight." She hadn't meant to anger him, but she did.

"These are extenuating circumstances. I need the powder." A muscle ticked along his jaw as he stared at her. "You know how it is if I don't get any."

Yes, she did. Anxiety tightened around her chest. "If you'd let me check the lines, the pack wouldn't have smelled your leg and come after you. What if your new wounds get gangrene? We cannot afford to lose your leg,

Papa."

"This situation is temporary. Once I'm back to feeling like my old self, things will be different. Get me the powder. I'll be better in two weeks." Stubborn and angry, he stared at her.

She knew better than to argue when he got that gleam in his eye. "Okay. Two weeks." With a sigh of resignation, she picked up dirty dishes and put a kettle of water on to boil.

Chapter Eight

All the way to the fort she went over their situation in her mind. If he'd rested like the doctor wanted, they wouldn't be in this situation.

But then the wolves would have gotten her. Lilli bit her lip and shoved the thought aside. She didn't have a limp and would have gotten away.

Papa's new wounds would take time to heal, and with his need for opium, the future loomed ahead like a black thunder cloud.

After collecting coins for the last of their pelts, Lilli paid a visit to the doctor and explained about his wolf attack.

After asking various questions to determine the extent of the damage, Dr. Talon gave her instructions on cleaning the wounds and measured out the powder. Glancing at her over the rim of his glasses, he held her gaze. "Make sure he takes the amount I prescribe and no more. This drug can be addictive."

Talk about the understatement of the century. "Yes, I know."

Walking out of the doctor's office, she met Officer Calhan. One glance into his clear blue eyes and her heart jumped into her throat.

"Hello." His deep voice made her shiver with awareness. His gaze roamed her face and dropped to her lips.

"Hi." She stared back at him and then at his mouth. Hers grew dry while heat flooded her cheeks. He looked better than she remembered. His red woolen jacket stretched for miles across his broad shoulders. She swallowed. The last time they met, he held her against that chest and kissed her with those hard, warm lips.

"I didn't think Frank allowed you to come to the fort alone or in the day." His voice dropped to a whisper. He smiled down at her, and she grew faint in response.

"I…uh…this is an emergency." She held up the packet of powder and explained about her father's new wound. "I'm glad I ran into you." Her voice grew breathless, and she gave him a smile. "Will you stop by the cabin soon?" Taking a step closer, she wished he'd kiss her.

His lids dropped over his eyes, and his voice dropped to a whisper. "We can't talk here." Max glanced around and ran a hand through his hair. His voice grew brisk, and he took a step back. "I'll come out and check on Frank in the next day or so. I'd come now, but I'm following a lead on the robber."

He changed from a warm, would-be lover to a cold, indifferent stranger in less than a minute.

A soldier walked by and waved.

Swallowing, she took a step back. One insignificant kiss, and she damn near gave her identity away. And after *she* made *him* promise not to tell. Embarrassed by her lack of control, Lilli snapped her mouth shut and straightened her shoulders. If he could be cold and formal, so could she. They *were* in the fort with several hundred pairs of eyes. "I hope you catch him. Don't bother coming out to see Papa. He's my problem. Goodbye." She tilted her chin up and turned away. She took two steps before he caught her arm.

"Come with me." He marched her around the doctor's office and between the commissary and the stable. They crossed an open area and walked up two stairs to the boardwalk, running in front of a row of buildings. He opened the door in front of them. "In here. This is my room."

Closing the door behind them, he turned and caught her by the shoulders.

She had a quick impression of wooden slat walls and floor. A large bed covered with a blue and yellow patchwork quilt stood against the wall opposite the door. A blue stuffed chair stood beside the fireplace off to her right. A rag rug covered the floor in front of the chair and disappeared beneath the facing side of the wide bed.

His blue eyes seared her with their heat. "What the hell are you doing? You can't look at me the way you did just now, or I'll forget everyone thinks you're Willie and take you in my arms. I didn't mean to be cold, but if I'm too friendly, anyone watching will get suspicious. And I don't want to be the cause of anyone finding Frank." He shook his head. "I came north to solve problems, not start them. I swore I'd never let another woman get close to me, and then I gave in and kissed you." His mouth twisted. "I haven't been able to get you off my mind." The heat of his hands burned through her coat and shirt, turning her insides to mush.

Her hands grew moist, and she rubbed them down the side of her breeches. "Me, too."

The last of her words were swallowed in his kiss as he slid his lips against hers. She opened her mouth, and he slid his tongue inside to mate with hers. Heat filled her belly and seeped into her limbs. Lips clung to lips as

Max's hands roamed her body.

A moan filled her throat when he tipped her head to the side so he could drink deeply.

Lilli wrapped her arms around his neck and kissed him back with all the frustration she had built up over the last two weeks. Hell, the last six years. God, it felt good to be held and wanted. Desire and longing raced through her, and she gave her body up to the pleasure of his touch.

After a few minutes, he lifted his head and smiled. "I taste desperation in your kiss." Holding her against him, he stroked her back until their breathing returned to normal. "Are you all right?"

The tender way he held her and the caring in his voice created a lump in her chest. "I'm worried about Papa. He isn't acting right. One minute, he wants me to stay out of sight. The next, he sends me to the fort for opium." She indicated the packet of powder in her pocket. "I worry he'll get addicted again. Last time, he got mean, and I didn't know how to deal with him. He's all I have." Trembling, she dropped her chin and swallowed the lump. She could stay here forever, held tight in Max's arms and breathing in his clean masculine scent.

"If you need help, send a note to the fort with Mateus, and I'll come. You don't have to do this all alone. We'll figure it out." His deep voice rumbled beneath her cheek, and his heat surrounded her.

Lilli gave in to the urge to lean on him and sighed. If she died in this moment, she'd be so happy. Having a broad shoulder to lean against for a few moments was pure heaven.

"Okay. Thank you." Glancing up, she met

compassion in his gaze and allowed the golden bubble of his strength to flow over her. She hadn't been this safe in a long, long time.

Such a kind, handsome man would make a wonderful husband.

Lilli frowned. Why did the idea keep popping up in her head?

The first verse of a hymn filled her mind in robust chords, followed by the chorus.

A chuckle escaped him. "Are you humming *Amazing Grace*?"

She flushed and took a step back as she scrambled for a reasonable explanation. Without telling the truth. "Um, yes. The song calms me and helps me cope with Papa."

"Then, by all means, sing." He dropped a quick kiss on her lips. "I have to go, but I'll come by as soon as I have time."

As soon as they emerged from the alley between the commissary and the stables, a soldier stepped up and handed him a note from the commander.

Max gave her a brief nod, and together, the two walked away discussing the robberies.

On the way home, her mind drifted to the thief. He must be desperate. She'd known thieves before, but none of them shot at her. Anxiety over their financial circumstances weighed heavy in her chest.

Papa must have the addictive powder, or he got angry and couldn't sleep. He wouldn't eat, wouldn't sit, and paced covered in perspiration. The thief didn't know what kind of hardship he put them in and didn't care. Without his interference in their harvesting, there would be plenty of coins in the drawer to care for Papa. So much for Papa thinking of a plan. She must beat the thief to the traps, or they'd die.

Rising before the sun the next morning, Lilli strolled in to find Papa gone, along with the sled and dogs.

Achilles lay before the fire and wagged his tail at her approach.

If Papa left so early to tend the big line, she would check the small one. After swallowing a piece of toast and downing a cup of coffee, she saddled her mare.

Whistling to Achilles, she turned east toward the small trap line.

An hour later, she approached Papa's first trap and got a glimpse of black wool through the trees. The bastard beat her to her father's line. He must have circled around after discovering Papa out checking the big line. She could have taken these pelts first if she hadn't stopped to eat.

Plucking the rifle from her saddle, Lilli approached with care. "Whoever you are, this is your warning. Leave our line alone, or I'll shoot." As she topped the bank, a flash of black wool disappeared into the trees. Lifting the gun to her shoulder, she pelted the area behind him so he'd know she meant business. "If I see you again. I'll shoot to kill."

She strolled down to the river. Every trap on Papa's line had beaver, and Lilli could have cried with relief. A few weeks of them harvesting both lines together, and they'd be back on track.

Securing her haul to her saddle, she offered a prayer of gratitude to the gods. She couldn't survive without Papa, and he couldn't survive without his magic white powder. One way or another, they'd survive. After all, they escaped Carlton Genova and his cutthroats for six years. Opium would have to get in line.

The rest of the week followed suit. Twice she caught a glimpse of a man through the trees and fired warning shots to frighten the man away.

All too soon, Papa's powder disappeared, and another visit to the fort loomed on the horizon. When she approached Papa about the situation, he surprised her by asking her to go.

"I have things to do. Don't dawdle at the fort. You'll have the lines to check when you get home." Stirring the rest of the powder into his tea, he turned his back to her and swallowed the drink whole.

She blinked back her surprise. "Both of them? Why can't you do one? I'll be gone for five hours tomorrow."

Papa swiveled to face her and set his cup on the table with a thud. "And I have all the rest to do. Unless you've overcome your aversion to blood and want to help."

When she shook her head and swallowed to hide her gagging, he gave her a thin smile. "I didn't think so. What I do is none of your concern. Do as you're told." Stomping toward his room, he slammed the door.

She stared after him. Papa changed his mind more often than his red woolen underwear. And bringing up her inability to help with the process was a low blow. Ever since her mother's murder, the sight of blood sent her into a panic.

Lilli glanced at the empty paper packet. She couldn't blame Papa's changing attitude on the drug because he measured his dose before her eyes with meticulous accuracy. Although his mood swings, slurred speech, and increased temper made her wonder if he had a secret stash somewhere.

When she loaded the sled, she counted four bundles

of pelts instead of the two she thought waited in the barn. Frowning, she tied them to the sled and shook her head. She must be more absentminded than she supposed. Between worrying about their future, Papa's condition, and dreaming of Max's kisses, she miscalculated somehow.

Shrugging, she whistled to the dogs, and soon they raced through the forest.

Three hours later, she stepped back to her sled after another of the doctor's lectures on the danger of overdose. With a fresh packet of opium tucked inside her pocket, Lilli stopped to check Zeus' harness.

A group of men stood beside the commissary, talking in angry voices.

"He robbed all my traps two weeks ago. I harvested one pelt all week and planned to go thief hunting until Officer Calhan stopped by. He said it won't be too much longer, and he'll have the guy. He thinks he knows where the man holes up.

More angry voices chimed in, voicing threats and violence.

"What about you, kid? How's your dad's trap line?" One of the men turned and addressed her while she settled the fur rug over her lap.

Lilli froze and then tugged her cap lower. "He got our traps, too." She hadn't used her gruff voice in a while and worried they would notice.

"You brought in several good bundles. That's more fur than I have at home right now. Sweeney said you and another man bring in on a regular routine." His deep voice caught everyone's attention, and six pairs of male eyes pinned her in place.

"What's your secret, or isn't the robber hitting your

trap line as hard as he is ours?" The man took a step toward her. Bushy red hair and bright blue eyes gleamed from a black knit cap as he waited for her answer.

"I just said he did. Our traps have been robbed, the same as everyone else's. My dad's been sick, so we've been using up everything we've stored to get more medicine." Tugging her collar higher, she avoided eye contact so no one got a good look at her face.

The man dropped his head and stepped back.:" I'm sorry to hear that, son. Let your dad know he can count on us for help if he needs it."

Several other men murmured the same, and Lilli nodded before whistling to Zeus. She hoped Max would catch the thief soon.

Without the threat of her uncle, she had a vast fortune at her disposal. If she could access her money, she'd make sure the men here survived the winter. They were good men and didn't deserve the hand dealt them.

Chapter Nine

Lilli arrived home well after dark, tired to the bone, cold, and hungry. She never made it to the small line and had two pelts from the big one. But the robber didn't get all the bounty. The other cages were attacked by a wolverine. The ferocious animal killed whatever the robber left. Disheartened and discouraged, she drove into the barn and discovered Max's stallion in the stable.

She froze in her seat. Did he come to see her…or?

She frowned. Did Papa's important errand have something to do with the officer? Considering the notion for a moment, she chewed on her bottom lip. Maybe Papa found information about the thief and asked Max to come so he could share his knowledge in private. What else could it be?

The suspicions weighing her down lifted, and her anger at being sent to the fort and then to check the lines disappeared, leaving her aching, sore, and hungry.

Memories of Max's kisses chased across her mind as she rubbed the sled down and gave the animals their feed. The dogs required her attention, and as she worked, she relived the last time they met. His touch made her forget everything but him and the excitement of his kisses. Heat filled her cheeks over the way she offered her lips in full view of the entire fort. She didn't know when she asked for the first one that she would become addicted. She couldn't get him off her mind or his taste out of her mouth. The more kisses they shared, the more she craved. And to her shame, Max stayed in character while she did not. A mistake she couldn't afford to repeat. If her uncle found them now, with her defenses down, he would win.

Lilli stepped into the frigid night air and stared at the cabin. Her body wanted to experience the pleasure Max could give while her mind warned her to stay away. The two emotions swirled in her belly until the cold demanded she seek the heat of the fire. Determined to keep her wits about her and her libido in check, she straightened her spine and strolled through the back door.

Inside, a mouthwatering aroma filled the tiny cabin. Her stomach grumbled in response as she walked into the living area.

Papa sat in his usual chair with his leg propped up on pillows. He held a dish in his hand, and a glass of whisky sat on the table by his elbow.

Max stood beside the fire, stirring something in the big pot.

They both glanced at her when she stepped through the door.

"Ahh. There you are, Willie. Officer Calhan learned about the wolf attack from the doctor and stopped by to check on me. When I told him where you were out checking the lines, he offered to make us something to eat. Come on in and get a bowl. Haven't tasted food this good since your mother died."

Max didn't come to talk about the thief. She studied the two men as she set her boots in front of the fire and hung up her jacket to dry. Lilli couldn't decide if she was offended Papa thought Max cooked better than her or not. Standing a foot away from the man, she glanced at him and swallowed when he moved his gaze over her from head to toe.

A hot glint entered his eye. "Good evening…Willie."

Damn. Not an effective way to start her celibacy. He remembered the kisses in his room with as much clarity as she did. He called her by her other name, so Papa didn't know he knew the truth. She gave him a grunt and walked to the shelf for two bowls. Setting them on the table within Max's reach, she straightened.

When she turned, she caught him staring at her backside. Frowning, she glared at him, but he just smiled.

"Your father said you've been getting a better harvest from your trap line. Every other trapper says things are worse. Several of them report bundles of pelts missing from their barns." He held a bowl of thick stew toward her, and she stared down, worried her shaking hands would give her away.

His nearness made her nervous, and she swallowed to ease her dry throat. "I'm sorry to hear that." She sat on the opposite side of the table and picked up her spoon. Soup spilled from her spoon to the table. "He hasn't taken any of our bundles. I fired at him the other morning and told him I'd kill him if he came again." Forcing her body to obey, she took a bite and sat the spoon down. Tucking her hands beneath her thighs until they could behave, she glanced up.

"When did this happen?" Max's gaze bored into hers. "I don't like the idea of you alone in the forest. Especially after someone took a shot at you. Did you have a dog with you?"

How could she harden her heart toward him if he kept being so damn kind and caring? "Yes. I warned him off after I went to the fort last time." *When you kissed me in your room.*

His gaze darkened. "I see. And you haven't seen him or any sign of him since?" His gaze dropped to her lips, and she resisted the urge to squirm.

Heat filled her cheeks, and she ducked her head. "No. Not for a week or two."

"Did you get a good look at him?" Max's gaze sharpened on her face."

"No. He was too far away. I glimpsed him through the trees and took my shot." She didn't like the way the officer frowned.

Papa's gaze swung to Max. "Do you know who he is? Or why he set a bear trap on my property?"

"No. I don't." He continued stirring with a frown.

Papa thought the men targeted their line because of his reputation for bringing in more pelts and said as much. "What direction did he come from?"

Lilli peeked at the officer beneath her lashes.

"Both men's tracks were all over. Then the shooter went south, and I haven't tracked him since. Until a few days ago." He glanced at her father. "He hasn't been near your land since he fired at Willie. I think the boy surprised him."

Silence filled the cabin until Papa cleared his throat. "What kind of a gun does he have?"

"Sharp's single shot." Max finished his soup.

Papa nodded. "Typical." He finished his glass of whisky and sat it on the table, changing the subject. "Then there's the wolf. Willie tells me the last of the pack comes sniffing around every few days. It's a long way to the fort, Calhan. And late. Why don't you stay here tonight and get an early start tomorrow." Oblivious to the undercurrent between her and Max, Papa glanced up from his bowl of stew.

The lawman's gaze met hers and held. "I'd be delighted to. Thank you."

He would be here all night, in the same cabin, breathing the same air, close to her....

She swallowed. If he were here, she wouldn't sleep. Not with him so close. And she had to check the small line before the sun rose. A second of disappointment tugged at her chest before she remembered her decision to keep her distance.

She glanced at Max and froze.

Desire flared in the glorious blue depths of his eyes.

"I want to bed my stallion down for the night if I'm going to stay. Care to give me a hand, Willie?" He rose to his feet and shrugged into his wool jacket.

"Not really." Rising to her feet, she collected dirty dishes and set them in the dishpan. Being alone would be catastrophic.

"Willie!" Papa glared. "Go help. You can clean up after you show Officer Calhan where we keep the hay."

Dragging her body toward the door as if offended by the extra work, she tagged three feet behind Max all the way to the barn. Her mind raced with excuses to high tail it back to the safety of the cabin and came up short when he closed the door.

She stood nose to chest with him and sucked in a breath for strength. His scent came with it, and her nose twitched with excitement.

"What's wrong with you? First, you ask for my kisses and then act like the condemned to be alone with me." He put his hands on his hips and studied her face. "Did something happen between now and the day I kissed you in my room?"

She took a step away from the heat of his body so she could think. "I shouldn't have to explain."

"Yes. You do. What happened?" He wrapped gentle hands around her arms and tugged her up against his broad chest. "Talk to me. What frightened you? I can't help if I don't know what's wrong."

Her determination to put distance between them wavered as his masculine scent surrounded her. "You frightened me." She dropped her head and focused on her breathing. God, he smelled good.

"I did?" Surprise flashed across his face. He lifted her chin to gaze into her eyes. "Tell me how."

"I don't like your kisses. Or being touched." The lie stuck in her throat and threatened to choke her.

He tilted his head and gazed deep into her eyes. "Then your death grip around my neck makes perfect sense."

She stared at her arms in confusion. How the hell did they wrap around him so tight without her knowledge? They touched breast to chest, hip to hip, and knee to knee. Lilli swallowed and wondered where all her self-control went.

Max dropped a slow, soft kiss on her upturned mouth while he rubbed lazy circles over her back, sending shivers of delight through her. "Are you sure you're scared of me?" His deep voice rolled over her like warm water on a chilly night, and she moaned against his lips. His caresses melted her icy determination into a puddle beneath her curled-up toes.

"No. I'm scared of me. And of giving my secret

away when I'm close to you. That day in the fort, I wanted you to kiss me again, and I didn't care who might be watching." She opened her eyes and allowed him to see her fear. "The men who are chasing Papa are evil. A mistake like the one I made at the fort could cost him his life."

Max nodded. "I won't let them get close enough." One hand rose to the back of her neck and massaged her tired muscles. "I think about you all the time, Lilli. Your kisses keep me awake at night."

She moaned again and closed her eyes as his hand worked the knots out of her upper shoulders. "God, you feel good."

His lips closed over hers. "I haven't been able to get you out of my mind for weeks."

"Me, either." The heat of his body made her weak in the knees as she opened her mouth for his kiss. Tongue mated with tongue, and Lilli pressed closer, anxious to feel as much of him as she could.

Glorious delight spread through her body at his touch, and she moaned into his mouth. "Max." She wanted more.

Tipping her head to the side, Max dived into the recesses of her mouth and drank. She squirmed against him, locked her arms tighter around his neck, and whimpered with pleasure.

His hands gripped her buttocks and pulled her tight against his hips. His hard shaft pressed into her quivering belly, making her knees buckle. She would have fallen if he didn't have her clamped against him.

"God, you feel so good, taste so good. I close my eyes to sleep, and there you are. You follow me everywhere I go." His warm breath blew against her cheek, and she snuggled closer, moaning with pleasure.

Her breasts pressed against the hard plane of his chest, and his arms held her tight. The musky scent of heated male, combined with the woodsy scent of the forest clinging to his clothes, brought a tingle of danger to her nose.

Thinking of the way his arms bulged and rippled in the firelight, the night she took Papa to the fort made her breath come fast. She released his neck and ran her hands over his arms, shoulders, and chest, marveling at the ridges and steel planes of his body.

Excitement gripped her, and the fluttering in her belly grew as she traced her way over his body.

The heat of his kiss sent her spiraling in a world of physical delight, and moisture gathered between her legs.

"Lilli." Max lifted his head and kissed the side of her neck while his hands rose to her breasts. Her breath caught in her throat.

Bound tight, she couldn't feel a thing but the tips of his fingers above the binding and pressure from his palms. "I can't feel..."

"I know." Tucking her head into the crook of his shoulder, he held her tight. "I want to take your shirt off. I've wondered for weeks now what you look like without it on." He stroked her cheeks. "I want to see you, touch you, and taste you. All of you." One hand undid the buttons on her shirt.

"Come with me." She tugged him toward the farthest stall and closed the gate behind them. "We keep the hay in here."

Turning, she froze when he stepped close and drew her shirt from her shoulders.

His lips stroked and caressed her naked breasts above her binding while he propelled her backward into a pile of hay. "I can't stop thinking about you, and I want to lay you down and make love to you until you cry my name."

Her mouth dried, and her palms sweat. "Then why don't you? Papa doesn't leave the cabin after dark. No one will know."

He followed her down, nudging her thighs apart and settling into the cradle of her pelvis. His lips trailed a path along the naked expanse of bosom and up the length of her neck before settling on hers.

He tugged on the knot, holding her binding in place while his tongue mated with hers. Delirious with pleasure, she arced against him, willing him to follow through with his suggestion. One never knew when such an opportunity would arise again. And with Max, the experience would be phenomenal.

"Sit up so I can take this off." He unwound the strip of linen, flattening her breasts.

She rolled to the side and spotted a bundle of fur stuffed beneath the hay. Frowning, she ran her hand to the side and discovered another bundle.

"Are you two coming back inside?" Papa's voice split the sensual haze in her mind, and she sat upright, clutching her shirt to her chest.

"Yes, Papa. We're almost done." Heat rose in her cheeks as she risked a glance at Max.

The back door slammed closed, and Lilli sighed with relief.

He grinned. "Are you saved or disappointed?" His dark gaze roamed her face and upper torso. "I'm disappointed."

She laughed. "Both."

"I came this close to seeing what no man has." He held two fingers close together. "Come on. Let's go back inside before Frank gets suspicious." He caught her lips for one final kiss. "I'll race you back."

He beat her by two strides. They burst into the door laughing and stopped when Papa's snore drifted toward them.

"He doesn't sleep unless he takes opium. The pain keeps him awake, and he wants more. Despite all my cleaning and bandaging, the wounds get worse. I don't know what to do."

Max frowned. "Have you tried carbolic acid? Dr. Talon ordered some. I could check for you tomorrow if you'd like."

She would and thanked him for the offer.

Lilli did the dishes while Max woke Papa and helped him into his room.

"Leave my door open." Her father's voice drifted toward her, and she grimaced.

No kissing in the dark now, or Papa would know. For once, his opium-induced sleep didn't seem like a terrible thing. Wondering what kind of a daughter she turned out to be, Lilli swept the floor while Max banked the fire.

They met in the living area, and she bid Max an awkward *good night* after helping him spread a pile of fur in front of the hearth.

He responded with a smile, and she wandered off to bed, wishing things were different.

She dreamed of her old life since the moment she left. Her future involved marriage to a man equal in social status and bearing his children. Visions of her vast home and many servants filled her mind when sleep eluded her. She'd have the newest coaches drawn by the finest horses money could buy. Her children would attend the finest schools available, and her husband would be well respected and popular. She would sweep into soirees in the latest fashion and take her place among the elite hostesses of New York.

If Carlton Genova succeeded, she would never leave the Northwest Territory and return home. She would never marry, never have children, and never know the pleasure of laying with a man.

Her mind turned to Max and the pleasure he gave her in the barn. Her lips still tingled from his kisses, and her body hummed with tension.

They could finish what Papa interrupted.

A more mouthwatering male never walked the earth, and he slept a few feet away on the other side of the wall. If her uncle outlived her, she could kiss her dreams of the future good-bye.

Lilli sat up.

She could experience passion, love, and desire right here in this tiny cabin in the wilderness, in Max's arms. And damn her uncle to hell. He wouldn't win. He couldn't.

She rose to her feet and tossed her dressing gown over her night rail. On silent feet, she left her room and tiptoed into the living area.

Max's eyes flew open the second she stepped foot outside her door.

Their gazes met and held.

Lilli couldn't breathe. He'd been thinking of her, too.

Desire flashed across his face as he inspected her

from head to toe.

Swallowing hard, she crept to her father's door and closed it with a soft click. Crossing the wooden floor, she dropped her dressing gown and slid beneath the fur beside him before she changed her mind.

"What are you doing?" Leaning up on an elbow, he gazed down at her with hooded eyes. The heat of his body warmed her through.

"I couldn't sleep." Snuggling against him, she traced her finger over his chest and down his arms. Her eyes widened when she discovered he slept without a night shirt. Warm and supple as caramel, his skin tantalized her in the flickering light of the fire. She kissed his skin and licked his salty flavor from her lips. He tasted as good as he looked, and she wanted more. Caressing the bulges in his arms, she shivered with temptation. Her mouth dried as she glanced up to meet his gaze.

"And you thought climbing in bed with me would help?" He tucked a strand of hair behind her ear and stared at her.

"I…don't know. I wondered if you would kiss me and…touch me like you did earlier." She glanced through her lashes to see his reaction. Wondering if he wore anything on his lower half, she resisted the urge to run her hands down his body to see.

"If I do, neither one of us will sleep for some time." His comment suggested the idea might not be worth pursuing, and she frowned.

"I don't want to sleep. I want you to…show me what happens between a man and a woman in bed. I liked what you did earlier." Her boldness surprised even her. Quivering against his hardening body, she wrapped an arm around his neck. "I want to finish what we started before Papa interrupted us."

Silence thickened the air around them as he studied her face. "Lilli, we are in your father's house, in the middle of his living area, where he could walk in on us."

She shook her head. "He won't. Once he takes the opium, he sleeps like the dead until morning. I could scream for hours, and he wouldn't wake." Her heart beat loudly in her ears as she held her breath. Getting the nerve to come in here and ask took a lot. He had to give in. She knew he wanted her as much as she wanted him.

His gaze dropped to her lips. Leaning forward, he traced the outline. "We're still in his house." He stroked her face and neck as he whispered his response.

She swallowed and inched closer. He had a point, but then, so did she. "And mine. I'm an adult and capable of making my own choices. I might not ever get the chance to be with you again, and I want to experience everything. Please say yes."

"Then let's go to your room." He rose in one quick movement, lifting her high in his arms. In three long strides, he reached her door and stepped inside. Closing the door with his shoulder, he pulled the latch closed.

Lilli grew hot as he carried her to her bed and set her in the middle of the mattress. Her knees clacked together, and her breath came fast as she gazed up at him.

Following her down, he took her mouth in a deep, carnal kiss, stroking her tongue with his. The fluttering in her belly took flight as he molded her trembling body against his. Anticipation filled her veins with tingling excitement.

"Is this what you want?" Stripping her night rail from her body, he settled over her, nudging her thighs apart with his knee. As he lowered his hard body into hers, she gasped. "Yes."

His heat surrounded her and pressed her down into her straw ticking. The hair on his chest tickled her nipples, and the scent of his skin made her mouth dry. Aroused male, woodsmoke, and whisky settled over her. Her breath caught when his arousal settled onto her lower abdomen, and liquid heat filled her belly. She couldn't speak and stared up at him with wonder and anticipation.

"And this?" He cupped a naked breast in his hand as he kissed her again.

She gasped when his lips came down on hers and opened her mouth for his assault. No one told her she could be this excited and anxious at the same time. Shifting against his arousal, her eyes flew open when he ran his fingers over the hardening buds of her nipples. Clad in nothing but her pantalets, she gasped when he bent to trail kisses from the furious pulse at the base of her neck to her right breast. "Yes." Her whisper came out on a low moan as he caught her nipple in his mouth and sucked.

Pinpricks of pleasure danced through her, and she clamped her lips shut to contain her gasp. She doubted Papa would wake, but if he did, all this would be over.

"And this." He licked around her areola and then flicked her nipple with his tongue. His other hand cupped her other breast and rolled her nipple back and forth.

She clapped a hand over her mouth and arced back.

He followed, sucking her other nipple into his hot mouth. "You're beautiful. Lilli. It's a shame you bind these up out of sight. But then, no one knows they're here but me." The huskiness of his voice made her belly jump as he lavished her nipple with his tongue. Her blood turned to fire and settled between her legs. She panted and leaned up to kiss his neck. Her thighs widened on their own, and his rod shifted against her, sending tremors of delight through her body.

Kissing lower, she tasted his chest and ran her hands down his back. Corded muscles sent shivers of delight through her. He could do anything he wanted, and she wouldn't be able to stop him. Not that she wanted to, for the pleasure his lips gave her surpassed any she'd known in her nineteen years. She stopped when she discovered the waistband of his breeches and swallowed her disappointment.

"I sleep naked in my own bed. Not here." He rolled to his side and untied the string. With a quick motion, his breeches dropped to the floor beside the bed, and he rolled onto her again. Hard, hot, and swollen, his shaft pressed into her, and she gasped aloud. Wetness pooled between her legs, dampening her pantalets.

He suckled as he ran a hand the length of her body before returning to caress her other breast. "You taste so good; you make me ache."

She could imagine his rock-hard girth inside her throbbing core and trembled with need. She shifted against him. "Me, too."

"Yeah?" He slid a hand between them and followed the flat plane of her trembling belly to the juncture between her thighs.

Her breath caught in her throat. Did he plan to touch her…there? Ablaze with curiosity, pleasure, and passion, she opened her thighs wider.

He slid his hand into the slit in her underdrawers and touched her swollen mound. She cried out with surprise and delight. God, he felt good.

Swooping down to cover her gasp, he kissed her hard. "You'll like this." Sliding his fingers between her folds, he flicked her sensitive nub and caught her moans of pleasure in his mouth.

"What are you—" She writhed and clutched the bedclothes tight as he guided her with expert fingers along the river of desire and gratification.

She moaned into his mouth and lifted her hips for more.

Then he dipped his finger into her tight, wet sheath and stroked her. She cried out into his mouth and shuddered against him.

"God, you're so wet for me." Slow and deliberate, he penetrated her with his finger, stroking in and out with exaggerated movements. With their mouths fused together to contain her cries, he created a rhythm that had her writhing beneath him. The sweep of his tongue and the rhythm of his hand numbed her to everything but him and what he did to her. When her head thrashed side-to-side, he quickened the tempo and added another finger. Her cry of delight didn't make it past the seal of his lips. She never imagined such exquisite pleasure could be found from a man's hand and rocked against him. If his fingers could create this magical world, what would his manhood be like? Her shuddering increased, and the most intense delight she had ever experienced swept over her, increasing in urgency with the movement of his hand. She didn't want him to stop. Ever. Pumping his hand faster, she clawed at his back and curled her toes as the most delicious paroxysm of pleasure washed over her and sent her spiraling into a vortex of satisfaction. Gratification burst inside her body with such brilliance she wondered for a moment if she had died.

He caught her moans of pleasure with his mouth as she rode the funnel to the last spasm and lay spent in his arms.

He gave her one final kiss and lifted his head. Slumberous blue eyes gazed into hers. "So. How was it?" His wicked grin told her he knew without her saying a word.

"Adequate." She could barely say a word and swallowed her moan when he stroked inside her one more time.

He chuckled. "If I didn't have my mouth over yours, you would have woken our ancestors with your enthusiasm to my *adequate* efforts."

She flushed. "I never knew such a thing was possible. I thought a male must inject his, er..." She floundered as heat filled her cheeks.

His swollen member still pressed into her belly.

"Shaft?"

"Er, yes. Into a female to mate. I didn't know a man's hand could produce such an experience." She trembled at the memory.

"There's a lot you don't know about men, pleasure, and what we can do to each other. This will have to be enough for tonight, my Lilli. Another time and another place, when your father isn't sleeping on the other side of the wall, I'll teach you more." He kissed the side of her neck and rocked his pelvis against her.

She sucked in a breath and rubbed her hips against his. "When?" She wanted to know more. With him.

"When you can scream and moan out loud. And I can pleasure you the way I'd like to." He bent to kiss each nipple and cup her breasts in his hands. "And we aren't in your father's house."

"It's *my* house, too," she insisted and then frowned. "But you didn't—" She dropped her hand and ran her fingers down the side of his stiff member. "What do we do for you?"

"I'll take care of me. For now." He kissed her hard and drew back with a thoughtful expression on his face. "Earlier, you mentioned evil men searching for your father. Who are they? What do they want? I promised to keep you safe, but I need names."

Lilli flinched and stiffened.

How could he ask her to betray her father's confidence after what they just shared? She felt betrayed, and her pervious euphoria dropped like a stone off a tall cliff. "I don't have a name to give you." Her tight-lipped answer made him glance at her.

He studied her expression, and his lids dropped over his eyes." Okay, but I'm working blind here. If I don't know who is coming, I can't stop them."

She shrugged and turned away, staring at the wall. "When I have a name, I'll let you know."

The bed creaked when he rolled to his feet, followed by the slide of his britches on the wooden floor. "Good night." He kissed her on the cheek and left without a sound.

Lilli lay silent for some time, blinking back her tears. She should have listened to her head and kept Max at arm's length. She had the most incredible experience of her life tonight until he took advantage of her vulnerability by asking questions she couldn't answer. If she did, she'd put his life in danger, too. And that was something she couldn't live with.

Chapter Ten

When Lilli woke, the bed in front of the fire no longer existed. The furs Max slept on were rolled up and stacked beside Papa's chair.

Her father sat beside the hearth, drinking a cup of coffee and frowning. "Are you sick, Willie? You should have left hours ago. Officer Calhan made me a cup of coffee before he left when you didn't wake to either of our knocks."

She never slept in. Memories of last night made her flush, and she turned away to slice some bread for toast. "I'm not sick. I don't know why I didn't hear you knock." She did, but her explanation and the accompanying storm would affect relatives unborn to the seventh generation. She agonized over her life and the choices she made until the first fingers of dawn lit the sky. And she still didn't know what path to take with Max. He was like a fire. Irresistible on a cold northern night but deadly if you got too close.

"Don't bother with food. I can make some toast. You'd better get out there and check the line. Laying around in bed won't keep the thief from harvesting our traps." Papa clutched his cane and rose to his feet with a grimace. "We can't afford to lose any more pelts."

"I know." She, more than anyone, knew their financial situation and winced. "Okay. See you in a few hours." Guilt made her stop on her way to the door. "I'm sorry, Papa."

He grunted as she closed the door and hurried to hitch the dogs to the sled.

Thinking back over her night as she checked the line, she concluded staying away from Max Calhan was in her best interest. Hers and Papa's. She couldn't afford to miss the traps, and if allowing him in meant answering questions, she would pass. As it were, the thief beat her to the line. She harvested fur from five traps. Their bundles waiting in storage should be in the double digits. But they weren't.

Pleasure or pelts? And the pleasure came with questions. A girl shouldn't have to make such a choice, especially if Officer Calhan were involved. Thinking about pelts reminded her of the bundles she discovered beneath the hay in the barn. A stone settled in her gut. She'd ask Papa about them tonight.

Sighing, she turned for home and crossed the lone wolf's tracks, running down the path made by her sled. The predator followed her for most of the day. She shivered with terror. Was he stalking her? She untied the loop, securing her rifle to the sled for an easy draw.

Lilli whistled to the dogs and kept her gaze on their surroundings as evening shadows settled over them. The dogs didn't like the scent of wolf and growled as she urged them forward. One lone wolf would be no match for her team of dogs. Although the idea comforted her, she frowned. Why would the animal follow her? As a rule, they avoided humans. Halfway home, the wolf turned around and headed southeast, and the direction of their cabin.

Her heart leaped in response. She left Papa alone, and although he hadn't gone outside since the attack, the uncanny behavior of the predator made her nervous. She followed the wolf's prints to their barn, where they turned and disappeared into the tree line.

Lilli stared at the print, guessing it to be five inches wide and at least six inches long. Wolves can run up to thirty-five miles an hour and jump twelve feet. She withdrew her rifle and unhitched the dogs. Zeus showed his fangs and burst into the barn with the team right behind him. But nothing happened. They growled, sniffed, and whined at the tracks leading away from the clearing. They wouldn't chase unless Lilli was in danger or she commanded them to.

"Everything's okay. Heel." She didn't believe the lie either and made sure she locked the animals up tight before going to the cabin. Maybe the wolf smelled the pelts and came sniffing around for an easy meal. With winter in full force, the predators took what they could find. But why follow in her sled's tracks and then beat her home? The unnatural behavior frightened her, and she entered the house determined to ask Papa.

What she found scared her more than the wolf, and she forgot everything but the scene before her.

Papa lay on the floor by the hearth, burning up with fever. His leg oozed through the bandage and onto the floor. A broken whisky glass lay beside him along with the empty white paper containing the last of their opium.

"What have you done, Papa?" She rushed inside and rolled her father onto his back. He was limp, with cold blue skin. She worried he had died in her absence. Unable to contemplate the horror of his demise, she shoved the worry to the back of her mind. Swallowing her sob, she placed her ear against his chest. A faint thump sounded, and she leaned back, shaking with relief.

He lived.

Glancing around, she discovered a puddle of vomit beside the glass and shuddered. She should take him to the fort, but with the wolf lurking nearby, she didn't want to take the chance. Besides, her father made her swear she wouldn't take him again without his permission. The return of the shooter made him nervous, and when he learned the details, he forbade her from going anywhere but to check the trap lines.

Unless he required opium.

Clutching him to her, she fought to get him to his feet and, after several attempts, gave up. Cleaning up the vomit and broken glass, she rolled out the furs Max slept on the previous night and rolled Papa onto them. Covering his upper half, she boiled water and retrieved clean bandages for his leg.

The task took her longer than usual, and she gagged when the smell of the wound hit her nostrils. Max said Dr. Talon ordered carbolic acid. She didn't have the money for medicine and more opium. One, but not both. Biting her lip, she leaned back on her heels. Papa would demand more opium once he woke, and he wouldn't be pleasant without it. But what could she do?

Her father moaned. "Rebecca?"

She frowned. He never called her by her real name. "I'm here, Papa."

"I believe I fell." He blinked and stared up at her, slurring his words.

"I believe you're right. But it's okay. Stay where you are. I couldn't lift you, so I made a bed in front of the fire. Are you hungry?" She wiped his moist face with a clean towel and tucked his arm under the fur.

She received a loud snore in response. Glancing at

the untidy cabin and back to her father, she shrugged. She could use a good night's sleep. Hurrying through her nightly chores, she stopped when the lone howl of a wolf called from right outside the cabin. She locked the doors and kept her rifle ready. The beast couldn't get inside, but something about the mournful cry sent shivers down her back.

"You must get better, Papa. Do you hear me?" She glanced down at him on her way to bed. He couldn't die and leave her alone. He just couldn't.

Papa woke the next morning, angry as a hungry bear fresh out of hibernation. She cajoled him as best she could and hurried along the lines so she could make it back before the sun set. Nothing on earth could convince her to stay out after dark anymore, for the wolf prowled the perimeter of the clearing during the midnight hours after she locked the dogs up. She carried her rifle to do her chores ever since the predator stepped foot onto their property, and her intuition saved her life.

For two nights later, she met the animal on the path between the house and the barn. Icy fear trailed down her spine as she gazed into his yellow eyes. She knew he would be big by the size of his prints, but staring at the giant beast terrified her to her core. She never considered how prey might feel until that moment.

Fangs appeared. The beast snarled and crouched. Lifting the barrel of her rifle, she glanced through the sight and fired. The wolf leaped as she shouldered the weapon and fell to a heap at her feet. For several moments, she shuddered with equal parts relief and terror before hurrying to the house. One less threat to worry about. If only Carlton Genova could be disposed of as easily.

She fell into a deep sleep the second she closed her eyes.

The next morning, when she went to fetch a shovel and bury the beast, no trace could be found but a sizeable red stain in the snow. On closer inspection, she discovered the predator rose to his feet and left in the night. She tracked the beast north for several miles before turning around and heading back to the cabin. Red snow said she didn't miss, so how could the animal walk away? She had no answers and shrugged. If the animal stayed away from Papa and their cabin, she would allow him to live. More important things occupied her mind, like medicine and their financial situation.

Her mind returned to the pelts in the barn, and on impulse, she walked to the stall in the back and scooped the hay away. Eight bundles of pelts stared up at her, and suspicion danced in her gut. Several times, she returned from checking the lines to discover Papa's boot drying in front of the hearth. He never talked about where he went or what he did while she was gone. And now, she had a sinking feeling she knew.

Strolling back to the cabin, she stopped in front of her father's chair and searched for the right words to ask what she knew to be true.

He glanced up at her and took a bite of egg. "Why aren't you gone yet?"

She folded her arms over her chest and tilted her head to study his face. "Where did the eight bundles of fur in the barn come from?"

Papa shrugged and kept eating his breakfast.

"Did you steal them? I know they aren't ours." The lump of dread in her chest grew.

He glanced up, and the fury in his gaze made her

falter. "What I do in my spare time is none of your business. Your job is to tend the lines and keep your nose out of my affairs."

Lilli swallowed and took a step back.

Daggers shot from his eyes as he glared, and his voice dropped silky soft, scaring the life out of her. "Do you understand?"

She nodded and tensed for a quick retreat. He never raised a hand to her in all the time they were together, but the look in his eye concerned her.

"Take the bundles with you and bring me back my powder. Tell the doctor I'm worse so he'll give me more. And get me some whisky."

Rebellion raged inside her. She wanted to tell him what she thought about the situation, but the violent gleam in his eye kept her silent. "Okay." She ran all the way to the barn.

Hitching the team, Lilli made her trip to the fort in good time. She had enough to pay for a good supply of opium and more carbolic acid. With the coins left, she bought salt pork, flour, and kerosene. Her stomach swirled with guilt. Whose fur did Papa steal? Why should another trapper go without to buy Papa his drugs? Remorse, disbelief, and anger kept her mind occupied during the long drive. Her father's behavior eliminated every good lesson her parents taught her.

And it all started with opium.

The old Papa would never take something of someone else's. Nor would he speak to her like he did today. For a moment, she wondered if he'd strike her. She shuddered and sucked in a deep breath.

The whole situation stank. Stealing was a sin, plain and simple. No matter the religion, they all agreed. And she couldn't allow Papa to continue doing it. All the good he did over the years would be erased by the wrongs he committed today. Where heaven would be a guarantee, hell now loomed before him. But how could she stop him? A frown wrinkled her brow. She couldn't, not physically. But she might be able to make it right behind his back. If she made a note of each new bundle, she could repay Papa's victims once she inherited Mama's money. If she could get him to confess who he took them from, she could sneak back in and leave an IOU for the damage.

Stealing was such a judgmental word. And if an IOU replaced the goods, *borrowing* would be a better description of his activities. And her conscience would allow her to sleep.

Drawing her sled to a stop in front of Marion's, she tugged her hat low and her collar high as she knocked on the wooden door and waited for an answer.

"How's your father?" Marion tugged her through the door and into her arms. "I've been so worried about the two of you. Especially after Officer Calhan gave us the news about the wolves. How's his leg?" She bustled around making tea and clucking her tongue over Papa's health. "He needs to get married and settle down. If he had a wife to come home to, he wouldn't be off stomping all over the woods like he did in his twenties."

Lilli glanced at her. "Nothing would make me happier than to see him settle down." She didn't like Papa stomping all over the forest either. But Marion had a surprise coming once she knew the kind of life Papa lived before coming back to the bush. Lilli doubted her father planned to settle down in a little cabin in the Northwest Territory or at the fort. If he lived through his opium addiction, he would relocate to a chateau in France or a villa in Italy.

And she doubted he would ever marry again.

"Did you come for more medicine?" Marion paled when she asked the question, and Lilli lied once again to put the dear lady's mind at rest.

"A little. He's getting better." She frowned when she considered all the lies she told of late. Did heaven accept promissory notes for that sin, too? Once she could go home to New York, everything would work out for the best. She would never have to tell an untruth again, and she could pay everyone back for all the things Papa borrowed from them.

Giving Marion a smile, she announced she planned to visit the doctor.

Dr. Talon listened to her description of the wound and agreed with Max. Carbolic Acid should help heal the infection. While he measured out the medicine, she formulated in her head. She took inventory of where he kept the opium and carbolic acid. As he handed her the packet and she paid, a man burst in, requesting the doctor's assistance. She made sure the doctor noted her departure by shaking his hand and giving him her gratitude for his help.

She ate dinner with Marion and made her excuse to get back to the cabin, but instead of leaving, she circled around behind the doctor's office and peeked in the window. Dark, empty, and quiet, she smiled and inspected the lock. This one she could unlock in her sleep. A skill she grew quite proficient at over the last few years when Papa locked the barn and left to check the line with the key in his pocket.

With her mind busy on prospective conversations

with her father about his recent activities, she climbed onto the sled and gave a cry of surprise when Max stepped up beside her.

"I didn't mean to scare you. I spotted your sled and came to see how you are. Did your father come, too?" He glanced around them and back at her face.

She drank in the sight of him. "No. He didn't get back from checking the lines until late, so he sent me without him." Lying came easier and easier, she noted with dissatisfaction. If Max believed Papa tended the lines, he wouldn't add him to his suspect list.

"I'm glad he's doing better. From what I witnessed the other night, I had my doubts." He shook his head.

"I'm working with him." She clutched the sled handle, remembering the last time they were together. Max used her attraction to him to get information. Anger and hurt resurfaced. Tucking her fur around her in preparation to leave, she avoided eye contact.

His voice dropped to a whisper. "I don't know what I did to upset you that night in your room." He frowned. "But I'd like to discuss it with you. In private. Soon." He stared at her but kept his distance. "We have unfinished business."

Her hand trembled where she gripped the sled. If he could use her attraction to him, she could use his. "Okay." He would know who had been robbed if Papa didn't cooperate. Raising her voice to normal, she smiled. "What about the other trappers on our side of the river? We had some bundles of fur taken from our barn while we were both out checking lines."

Max frowned. "Both cabins on either side of you have reported the same. Bundles would be easier for the thief to take and a lot less work." He put his hand on his hips and stared at the front gate and then at her face. "The shooter is back. I also came across your father's tracks today, and I don't want him getting involved."

Lilli nodded. *Papa, what else have you done?* "I'll let him know."

His gaze sharpened when they made eye contact. "I'll have the thief in custody by the end of the week. I discovered a pattern in his behavior. Once I arrest him, I'll pay a visit."

Her heart plummeted to her sled runner. She had little time to convince her father to give up his thieving before he became the only suspect. "Papa will be glad to know. Is this the same man who set the bear trap on our property or the other one?

"The other one. But I'll get them both. Tell Frank I'll make sure he gets the justice he deserves. No one has the right to take another person's property for any reason. Putting thieves behind bars is one of the highlights of my job."

She swallowed the lump in her throat and tried not to think about the goods she purchased today with contraband. They sat in front of her on the sled with all the subtlety of a pimple on her nose. "Well, I better get going if I want to be home before dark." The satisfaction dripping from his voice when he mentioned putting the thief behind bars made her uncomfortable. And the whole situation got awkward as hell.

Max frowned. "Is your gun loaded? You shouldn't be out alone. Especially with the shooter around again."

"I'll be fine. Bye." She drove away without a backward glance. Guilt and shame plagued her until she shouted for them to leave her alone. "I'll stop lying and contemplating sin to help Papa as soon as he is well. Now go away!"

And they did.

Until she climbed into bed and closed her eyes, and then they returned in a nightmare. Waking in a cold sweat, she spent the next few hours handwriting dozens of IOUs.

Chapter Eleven

Max stared after Lilli's sled with a frown. She shouldn't be out alone. He remembered the feeling of her in his arms and wanted to run after her. But doing so wouldn't do either of them any good. He damn near lost control last time and didn't know if he could stop a second time. He protected women. He didn't ruin them.

He figured she felt the same until two minutes after the last ripple of pleasure left her body, and she turned cold as snow. He analyzed the situation time and again and drew a blank. Did he say the wrong thing? Did he do the wrong thing? Although he never had a woman complain about his performance before. Then what? Did she regret inviting him to her bed, and her virginal instinct got the best of her? Memories of her flushed face, arching back, and moans of satisfaction made him shake his head. Lilli's wanton, uninhibited response negated the idea.

Women were a mystery, for sure. Take his ex-fiancée Elsie, for example. Her elfin face flashed before his eyes, and he ignored how his stomach tightened in response. Innocent blue eyes, a cheerful smile, and a sunny disposition covered a heart as black as midnight. He should have trusted his gut when the first signs of her inconsistencies spilled out. If he had, Edward T. Baker would be alive today.

Elsie Roth came from old money and lived a life of

luxury. Although she had everything a woman could ask for, she harbored a dark, competitive nature beneath her sugar-sweet exterior, which Max knew nothing about. Until it was too late.

He met her in New York, where he trained to join the marshal service. His brother Connor introduced them at a party, and Max fell hard for the dainty brunette.

Her father warned Max to stay away. Elsie should marry someone of her own status and social position, but he didn't listen. In love and full of visions for the future, he escorted her to every function he could attend. Although he enjoyed the lavish estates, expensive dinners, and connections with New York's elite, he disliked the snobbery and condescension people of her class used to convey their importance to those less fortunate.

One day, as they walked arm in arm down Fifth Avenue, Elsie showed him a sapphire ring in a jeweler's window.

"I want that ring. Think how jealous Mary Vander will be when she sees it on my finger." Turning, she kissed his cheek and smiled. "Will you buy it for me? I would know you loved me forever if you did."

Max glanced from her to the window and back. She wore his diamond on her third finger, and he didn't have the funds to buy jewels like the one displayed.

"Do you want the ring as a token of my love or to make Mary jealous?" The two shouldn't be in the same sentence, and unease settled in his gut.

"Well, to make her jealous, of course." She glanced at him and then back at the ring. "But I will accept it as a token of your love." She squeezed his arm, and they continued their walk.

When he remained silent, she tapped her fan on his arm. "Oh, don't brood. Everyone knows the price of a ring determines the value a man places on his beloved. Of course, they're jealous of me because I have you, and I'm happy with my choice." She twisted his gold band and solitary diamond around her finger while she spoke.

Her voice didn't sound as though she were happy, and Max had plenty to think about.

"I will have that ring." Determination rang in her voice, and he should have paid attention.

A week later, another man purchased the very same ring and proposed to Mary Vander. Unable to console Elsie, he promised to escort her to the Vander family mansion. Rumors said they purchased a famous marble statue which they planned to display on the evening of Mary's engagement party.

"Papa says I must go. If I must suffer through an evening of Mary Vander gloating, so do you. I can't believe she got the ring. And now she has a statue, too." Her voice ended in a fresh round of tears, and Max struggled with his feelings. Elsie had never acted like this before she agreed to marry him.

He dismissed the flash in her eyes and the way she turned away from his caress.

The night before the big party at the Vander Mansion, someone attempted to steal the statue.

Max arrived with his patrol to help with the investigation. There, they discovered the statue covered in cloth and tied with ropes as if the thief were interrupted.

Searching the grounds, they found one of the night guard's bodies below the library window. The other night guard, Mr. Edward T Baker, went to jail for the murder. An eyewitness, Elsie Roth, testified he shot the other guard right in front of her.

She came to visit Mary Vander and happened to be there when the attempted robbery occurred. During the investigation, Max discovered Elsie paid the dead guard to steal the statue, creating a diversion for her to take the sapphire ring from Mary's room.

Edward T Baker caught her in the act and confronted her. In retaliation, she accused him of the murder she committed. The night guard died from a forty-four to the chest, and Edward T Baker didn't own or carry a gun.

But Elsie did.

Max inspected the weapon and discovered she fired two bullets that night. They dug the other bullet from the garden window casing, where she shot the guard to keep him from revealing her part in the crime.

Later, Max discovered the sapphire in Elsie's handbag, and she laughed when he asked her about it. "I told you I would have the ring."

He arrested her on the spot and sent her to jail. But Mr. Roth opened his wallet and hired the most successful lawyer in New York to take the case.

The jury ordered Edward T Baker to be hanged for murder, and Max's charges were dismissed as the result of jealousy.

Elsie Roth arrived in court beside her new fiancée, Charles Goodwin, with a winning smile and a flashy new ten-karat engagement ring. She portrayed the essence of innocence and virtue.

And made Max sick to his stomach.

Although he fought hard to bring the truth to light, Roth's attorney had an answering lie for every accusation. Ridden with remorse for an innocent man's death and shocked, Elsie and her father could disregard life, decency, and truth to such an extent he swore off women and rode north.

A year later, he bought a newspaper in Quebec and read about Elsie's wedding to Charles, her equal and the man her father wanted her to marry all along.

Max burned the paper and smiled as the flames licked Elsie's face to ashes. Determined to learn from his mistakes, he vowed to remain single and avoid serious relationships as if they were the plague. When the position at Fort Simpson came up six months ago, he took the job without hesitation.

A group of laughing soldiers walked past, bringing him back to the present.

He considered Lilli and his brows knitted. Frank dropped his overprotective attitude on such short notice he wondered about his reasons. If Max had any senses, he would have put some distance between them before things got serious. He already learned that lesson.

Strolling toward the saloon, he stepped inside and walked up to the bar. Ordering a beer, he took a seat at the table and sat with his back to the wall. Ignoring the urge to saddle up and follow Lilli home, he analyzed the men sitting around the dim interior of the saloon.

A handful of soldiers and trappers sat on wooden chairs, playing cards and sipping alcohol. A few men sat at the long bar nursing their beer while one of the fort's whores played the piano. The woody caramel scent of whisky mingled with the yeasty, earthy scent of beer. Cigar smoke hung in the air, and the murmur of voices washed over him. Glasses and coins clinked as a woman laughed at a nearby table.

Tracing the woodgrain on the table beside his beer,

he took a sip of his drink and studied the room. A stranger sat at the end of the bar with spurs on. His woolen jacket and polished boots proclaimed him a city dweller. Glancing toward the door every time someone entered or exited made Max wonder if he had a nervous condition or if he planned to meet someone.

Leaning back in his chair, he narrowed his gaze. The man kept his collar up and his hat low so Max couldn't get a good look at his face. Something about the angle of his head seemed familiar, but he couldn't remember a name or a location. A pair of pistols hung on the man's side, tied to his thigh with a thin strip of leather. *The man he caught peeking in Charlotte Adam's window!*

Max frowned. Fort Simpson didn't attract many gunfighters. Killers, yes, but not the kind of man who wanted to meet in the street and fire at ten paces.

Mr. Lawson, the stable master, strolled in the door and took a seat beside the stranger. The two pretended they didn't know each other while swapping notes on the gleaming counter. Lawson pocketed his and ordered a beer. When the bar keeper set the mug down in front of him, the stable master threw a coin on the bar, and moved to the next seat down, as if leaving a stool between him and the gunfighter made them less acquainted.

Max took a sip of his beer, his gaze glued to the pair at the bar.

The stranger sipped his ale and unfolded his note. His head swiveled toward the door as his hand dropped to the butt of his right gun and hovered.

Interesting.

A soldier strolled in and hustled over to Max's table. Mr. City dweller stiffened.

"Sir, Commander Jorgensen asked me to fetch you.

There's a trapper in his office saying someone robbed his barn." The soldier twisted his cap in his hands and shifted his feet.

Max glanced up. "Get someone to take his statement, and I'll look into it."

The man at the bar shifted in his seat, plunked coins on the wooden counter, and slid to his feet.

"I did, sir. But the commander wants you." The young man shifted again. "He said it's urgent."

Max placed a coin on the table beside his glass and rose to his feet.

As the gunslinger passed, Max glanced at his face. He wore the expression of a man on a mission.

The stranger disappeared through the door ten seconds before he did.

When he stepped out into the frosty evening, the man strolled around the corner of the livery and disappeared. His gut told him to follow.

The soldier hurried in the opposite direction. "Are you coming, sir?"

He gazed at the soldier and back toward the livery. "Yeah."

He couldn't arrest a man for a gut feeling and shrugged. Another day, and another time. Something said he and the stranger would meet again.

The trapper reported more of the same, and Max went to bed thinking the situation over. One thief wore leather soles with fringe. The shooter wore boots with the same tread as Frank Rossi but with shallow imprints and a longer stride. And then there were Frank's.

The next morning, he went to the commander's office to listen to another complaint.

He arced a brow when the man handed him a piece

of parchment.

IOU the sum of twenty-five dollars for items received. RVR

There were two different thieves, without a doubt. "Most thieves don't leave notes with their initials." Max ran his hand over the paper. "This is superior quality parchment. I'd start with every man bearing these initials. If that doesn't work out, find out where the paper came from. Someone went to the trouble of leaving clues. Whether he wants to be found or whether he has a conscience about what he did remains to be seen. Something prompted the note, and either way, we'll find him."

"Do what Officer Calhan commands and report back to me when you have answers." The sergeant in charge gave his order and walked away.

The soldier nodded and tucked the note into his pocket. "This paper didn't come from the fort."

Max raised an eyebrow. "How do you know?"

The young man turned red. "I write my girl in Quebec every week, and I buy parchment a lot."

He nodded. "I'll be in my quarters if you find out anything about the notes. I plan to leave at first light, but I'll be back in a few days. Keep me posted."

All the way back to his rooms, he pondered over the stranger and the new thief. Thievery must be as contagious as smallpox. First, the trap thief, then the shooter in the forest the night he tackled Lilli to the ground—

Max stopped in his tracks. The stranger at the saloon tonight and the man shooting at Lilli where *one and the same*!

Turning on his heel, he retraced his steps and circled

135

the livery, searching for clues. City dweller, wealthy, stranger, killer, tied down pistols, Lilli, and a note. And Charlotte Adams' window. His gut twisted in a knot. Did the stranger plan to shoot Lilli, or did he take a shot to warn her away? Who was his target? Lilli? Frank? Or someone else? And what about Charlotte Adams?

With so many different tracks going in so many directions, it took him a few minutes to find the stranger's. Then he did. Tracks like Frank's, shallow imprint, and a longer stride trailed northwest. Did he go to Lawson's or circle around to Rossi's? His heart rose to his throat.

Frank and Lilli.

Saddling up, he added more ammunition to his saddlebags.

The trap thief would hit Olaf's cabin at first light if he followed his usual pattern, and Max planned to be there early to catch him in the act.

He couldn't go in both directions at once, and Lilli and Frank took precedence. He cared as much about Rossi as he did the girl and ignored the voice in his head that said otherwise. He'd make sure they were safe before he went out to Olaf's.

After he caught the thief, he'd turn his attention to the shooter and his connection with the stable master. And then the notes. His gut told him they weren't connected to either man.

Two hours later, he stopped beneath the tree line outside Frank Rossi's cabin. Smoke curled from the chimney into the frozen canopy overhead. The wind bit his cheeks and nose as he surveyed the quiet clearing. Nothing stirred.

Circling the area, he searched for any sign of the

stranger but found nothing. For two hours, he studied the surrounding forest before he cantered off. Satisfied the Rossi's were safe, he returned from a different direction so anyone backtracking him would be unable to find the cabin.

At dawn the following morning, he leaned forward in his saddle with his gaze on Olaf's trap line. Weary to the bone from his all-night stakeout, he rubbed his face with a handful of snow and ran his hands through his hair. One hour passed, and then two. Frowning, Max took a piece of jerky from his saddle bag and studied the situation. He could use a good, strong cup of coffee but wouldn't risk giving his presence away with a fire. The robber should be here. He tracked this thief for weeks until a pattern emerged.

Shielding his eyes against the glare of the sun on the glistening snow, he took a pair of binoculars from his saddle bag and studied the area. A blur on the far side of the trees caught his attention. A figure dressed in white appeared and leaned against a tree. Slight in build, the figure could pass for a woman. His grip tightened on the glasses in his hand.

And then another figure appeared a hundred yards to the right of the first one. Taller, thinner, and moving with caution, this figure approached the trap line. The first figure slipped behind a tree, and Max lost sight of him.

The second figure placed a gun on the ground and worked the catch on the trap.

Max tucked the binoculars back inside his bag and nudged his horse forward. He had the thief! Well, one of them. Once he had this one behind bars, he'd find the other one.

The man glanced up as Max approached and disappeared into the trees at a dead run. Nudging his horse into a gallop, he crashed through the forest in hot pursuit. The man knew the area well and used every dip and run to his advantage. Stopping beside a small clearing, Max caught a blur of black behind a clump of snow-covered bushes. Riding around to the right as if he were searching, he closed the distance between him and his quarry. The thief took the bait and charged to the left. Max caught him less than five minutes later, tackling him to the ground and pinning his arms behind his back.

Thin and wiry, the man wore moccasins with leather boot heels and beadwork.

Max grinned. "You're under arrest." Leading his prisoner with his tied hands, they walked to where the robber had left his horse. He tied the sullen man to the saddle and took the reins.

On his way back to the fort, he received a shock when he ran across Lilli and her sled not too far from Olaf's cabin. "What are you doing so far north?" He stared at her pale face as she drew her sled to a stop.

The rest of her color drained from her face. "We were robbed early this morning, and I tracked him here." Her gaze slid to the man tied to the horse behind him. "Is this the man who set the bear trap? He must be because he wears the beaded moccasins." Her face flushed, and she shifted her weight.

Anger and frustration raced through him. "No, he isn't." Max stared at her face. "But I know who did. I asked you to stay away. You shouldn't have come. Tracking thieves is a dangerous job. What if you got too close and got shot? How could I tell Frank you died?" A stone formed in his belly, and he frowned.

She bit her lip and refused to meet his gaze. "We can't afford to lose any more pelts." Glancing up at him, she shrugged. "Besides, I can do anything you can." She spat on the snow and wiped her mouth with her sleeve. "But you caught him. So there's no need for me to be anywhere but out checking lines. I'll let Papa know our troubles are over." Swearing and scratching her crotch, she turned her sled around and whistled for the dogs to go.

He remembered her persona just in time. "Bye, Willie. I'll be by later in the week. There's something I should talk over with Frank." He didn't plan to tell Lilli the shooter returned, but he figured her father had the right to know. Frank might know the connection between the shooter, Lawson, and Charlotte Adams. Unless the man spied on Lilli and not the other girl. He frowned, and his chest tightened at the thought. With this thief in custody, he would go after the shooter before he tackled the IOU mystery.

But it was not to be.

When he dismounted and tied his horse outside the guardhouse, an officer handed him a telegram from headquarters requiring him to go downriver to Fort Providence to collect a recruit. His sergeant transferred the man to help with the vast wilderness surrounding Fort Simpson. And all the recent robberies. He wanted Max to train him to survive the bush.

After turning the thief over to the fort commander, Max mentioned the shooter and asked if the commander would order his men to keep a close eye out, telling him of his suspicions. "He wore his guns low and tied to his thighs. The butts of his pistols show signs of wear."

The commander turned around. "A hired killer?

Who's he hunting?"

He frowned. "I'm not sure. He could be partners with the man I arrested today. He took a shot at Willie Rossi and set a trap on their property, but his tracks were all over. Up and down both sides of the river, by the trap lines, as well as around the cabins. Strangers make me nervous. We haven't had city folk up here before unless they planned to stay. This man walks on the balls of his feet and misses nothing. Either way, he's up to no good." He paused, wondering how much he dared tell the commander. But then, Lilli's life could be in danger, and he couldn't disobey a direct command. "I'm wondering if you'd send a patrol to the village. There's a man named Mateus there. Ask him to keep an eye on the Rossi's until I return."

"I'll speak to my men. See you in a few days." The commander lit a cigar. "I can't promise to hold your thief until you return. Once the trappers find out, he's here. They'll come for blood."

"I know. Do what you must." Max slept for two hours and packed a bag. An hour later, he boarded a canoe for Fort Providence.

Dr. Talon stopped him as they shoved off. "I have an order of carbolic acid waiting at Fort Providence. I'll need it for Frank."

"No problem." Max took his seat and studied the wilderness as the rowers assumed their positions. All the way down the river, he analyzed the last few weeks. The IOUs, Lilli, the shooter, Charlotte Adams, and Frank Rossi. He thought the shooter might be connected to the trouble coming for the Rossis, but Frank's expression remained passive. Anxious about Lilli's welfare, he prayed she'd stay out of trouble until he returned. He couldn't do anything to help her here, and after a bit, he closed his eyes. His sleepless night got the best of him about an hour downstream, and he dozed off to dream of a killer chasing Lilli through the woods. He couldn't get to her in time and started in horror as the stranger plucked a pistol and shot her between the eyes. His heart beat so hard in his chest that he expected it to break free. When he ran into the clearing outside their cabin, Frank Rossi lay dead at his feet. And then he faced the cold-blooded killer.

"Why?" The Rossis deserved better.

The killer laughed and pointed his gun at Max. "Because they're not who they say, and you've fallen in love with the girl. You swore to remain a bachelor, and this is what happens when you break your promise. You broke the rule, so you must die."

He awoke as the killer pulled the trigger. Covered in perspiration, his heart pounded in his ears as he jumped to his feet. The canoe rocked. The two oarsmen cursed, and he sat down as quick as he rose. Resting his head in his forearms, he ignored the stone in his chest. Where the hell did such a dream come from? He never planned to marry. Not after being so duped by Elsie and her innocent demeanor. Or did he? Lilli's face flushed with pleasure danced before his eyes, and he groaned. Once he arrested the shooter, he planned to get stumbling down drunk and sleep for two days. Maybe then, he would start acting like his old self again. His brother Chase would laugh his ass off if he knew a wisp of a girl got under his skin.

Chapter Twelve

Lilli raced home with her heart thumping high in her chest. She had no idea Max would be so far north at this time of the morning.

Papa wouldn't say who he robbed pelts from, so she made an educated guess by calculating the time she left him alone by the number of cabins on their side of the river. Max mentioned the cabins on both sides were robbed, too. She left four IOUs so far and had the fifth one in her pocket.

She damn near got caught three times in as many days. Did Max suspect her? Frantic for an excuse to explain her reason for being so far out of her area, she sighed with relief when she caught sight of his prisoner. The lie fell from her lips as easy as rain from the sky. Only, now he caught the real thief, Papa would have to stop his daytime activities in the other trappers' barns.

As she guided the dogs back to familiar territory, she waved at a neighbor tending his line, and the weight of the world dropped onto her shoulders. She alone would have to shoulder the responsibility of their survival. When she asked Papa if she promised to keep him in powder, if he would stop taking bundles from his friends and leaving tracks for Max to find, he agreed.

And now she had to live up to her end of the bargain.

She didn't like the idea of taking something that didn't belong to her any more than she liked Papa doing it. But in his present state of mind, the officer would catch him in a matter of days.

And he'd be hung or shot.

Without Papa's help, she couldn't produce the pelts required to keep him in opium the legal way. With her father in good health, they managed to survive, but not now. And weaning him from the terrible drug was not an option. Every time she tried, he got meaner and more violent. So *borrowing* from the doctor seemed the lesser of two evils.

Leaving IOUs in place of the medicine she *borrowed* would ease her conscience. The soldiers would take precautions against further robbery, but then, so would the trappers. And she didn't relish the idea of being caught.

Twice, she ran into Max when she went to deliver IOUs to the barns Papa robbed. Both times, he noted her appearance with a raised eyebrow.

How could she make her father's sins right when she continued to run into the over-observant officer? Sliding her feet beneath the sled, she hoped he didn't see Papa's boots on her feet. Something he said weeks ago about tracks like her father's with a longer stride gave her the idea. Wishing she hadn't stepped out of her sled did no good now. She hoped he'd search elsewhere in his investigation and frowned when he didn't.

"What are you doing here?" She didn't mean for the words to come out so harshly, and bit her lip when he slid off his horse and strolled toward her.

"Hello to you, too. I am searching for the pelt thief." He smiled down at her and stopped a foot way. But within reach.

She frowned and resisted the urge to step back.

Frustrated, she glanced up at the sky. She had very little time to get the IOU into the barn and return home before Papa woke. "Why here when you have thousands of miles of territory to search in every direction? Every time I round a corner, you're standing there." Her sharp tone made her wince.

His warm hand cupped her chin and tilted her face up to stare deep into her eyes. "I'm here because the evidence is here. I figured you liked running into me. I know I like seeing you."

Lilli closed her eyes as his breath blew across her face, and familiar heat settled in her belly. He smelled so good she wanted to cry. The heat of his body enveloped her in a cocoon of longing. "I do. I'm sorry. I didn't mean to be rude. I'm just in a hurry." She glanced up, hoping the sky would drop a plausible excuse for her being here on her head. Gazing away from his gorgeous eyes, she told her lie. "I borrowed a trap while Papa mended one of ours, and I came to return it."

"Ah, I see. I hope you're both doing okay and you haven't been cleaned out like some of the other trappers on this side of the river. I've been telling everyone to lock their barns and cabins while they're out checking lines. Leaving a dog in the barn will help deter the thief, too."

She ducked her head in case her expression gave her guilt away. 'We're doing fine. I leave Apollo or Achilles when I'm gone, and Papa has a rifle." God, she wished things were different. Without the stress of Papa and his addiction, she'd be in Max's arms this moment, kissing the hell out of him.

"Then why don't you?" He stepped closer and wrapped his arms around her.

She hadn't realized she had said the last part out loud until he enveloped her in his embrace and his mouth covered hers.

She resisted for two seconds and then gave in to the enticement of his hot kiss and mating tongue. He drank deep, and she leaned in, giving stroke for stroke. Desire settled in her belly and raced through her blood stream. She couldn't get close enough and whimpered when he shifted position. His hands roamed her body and cupped her buttocks, holding her against his arousal.

"If we were alone, I'd remove your clothes and taste all of you." He lifted a hand and rubbed the pebble of one nipple beneath the layers of binding. She gasped into his mouth, remembering the way he sucked her the night in her room.

Liquid heat settled between her legs, and she moaned with pleasure. "God, you feel good." Rubbing her hips against him sent shivers of delight through her. She rocked her pelvis against his and wondered how his hard shaft would feel inside her. She trembled against him and gripped his shoulders. She would have fallen if he hadn't thrust a muscled thigh between her legs and caught her buttocks with both hands.

Max lifted his head and held her tight against his chest. He sucked in a deep breath and leaned his head against hers. "I could lay you down in the snow and take you this moment. You're so wet for me that it drives me insane. All I can think about is the taste of your kisses, the scent of your hair, and the way your body melts into mine every time I hold you. You make noises in the back of your throat when you get excited, and it makes me wild to give you more. Making love to you will be the most satisfying thing I ever do. I can tell by the hotness of our kisses and the way you respond to my touch."

He held her until their breathing returned to normal. "I'd invite you back to my room at the fort to finish what we started, but I must speak to one of the trappers tonight. Soon, though. You and I will have things we must discuss. Without our clothes."

She froze when he mentioned the trapper and retreated to her sled. Smiling so he wouldn't suspect how her heart rose to her throat when he mentioned his investigation, she nodded. "I'm looking forward to it." Stepping onto the sled, she whistled at her dogs. "I have things I must do tonight, too. Bye." She hoped Max didn't notice her panic to get away. If he ever found out about Papa, she wouldn't know what she'd do. Max would be right to arrest him, but Papa was *her father,* and she would defend him.

"Bye." He smiled and waved as she drove away.

She didn't see him again for ten days. Mateus came by to check on Papa and mentioned Max left for Fort Providence after receiving a message from his superiors.

"The man who set the bear trap has returned." The light of the fire glinted on the older man's black peppered hair and the lines of his face. He glanced at Papa's sleeping form in the chair and shook his head. "I will stay close until the officer returns. I will let you know if danger comes."

"Thank you, Mateus." Lilli ignored the fear in her gut and spent her time sneaking into barns to hide IOUs. With Max in Fort Providence, she didn't have to worry about him catching her. With their *Dene* friend close, she could concentrate on her task without worrying about her father.

Four days later, she made an evening trip to the fort

for more carbolic acid for Papa's foot. He didn't get up much anymore and spent his time dozing in his chair or laying on his bed. When she threatened to take him to the fort, he got angry and made her give her word she wouldn't. When she suggested the doctor come to the cabin, Papa grew livid. The more people who knew their location, the more chance her uncle had of finding them.

With great reluctance, she gave Papa his dose of opium and left for Fort Simpson. With him lounging around the cabin, she didn't have to worry about him breaking his word. So far, he had kept his end of the promise.

And she kept hers.

Lilli left Zeus in the cabin with her father and took the rest of the dogs with her. Tossing a fur blanket over her bundles of pelts, she made good time and arrived early afternoon.

To find the fort in chaos.

One of the soldiers on patrol found a body five miles south of Fort Simpson. A civilian. The man had been shot between the eyes and dumped in the brush. The soldiers found no identification on the body and asked visiting trappers for information.

Lilli didn't realize she missed Max until her gaze caught on his red woolen jacket. He stood outside the fort commander's office with a shorter, dark-haired man, also dressed in a red woolen jacket.

A new officer?

Max glanced up, and their gazes caught and held. His darkened, and a small smile tugged at his mouth. Sensual blue eyes held her prisoner, and heat rushed to her cheeks. She remembered his kisses, and longing spiraled inside her. The noisy fort disappeared, and they were alone in her bed at the cabin. Desire blazed in his eyes as he kissed her deeply and carried her to the pinnacle of exquisite gratification.

Her lips parted, and her breathing increased as she stared at him.

He gave a slight shake of his head and turned to his companion.

One glance into his gorgeous blue eyes, and she forgot everything. Embarrassment glued her to her sled. She flushed again as she glanced around to see if anyone caught her indiscretion.

Max's companion turned her way, and then gave her a second look. Something flashed in his brown eyes, and Lilli's gut tightened. She didn't like this new officer she hadn't met yet, and her instinct told her to run.

Cold, soulless eyes swept over her, and a sinister smile touched his lips.

Facing the wolf frightened her less than the calculating assessment in the shorter officer's eyes.

The new man planned to kill someone, and soon. The words were branded in his expression, and a dark aura clung to him like the angel of death.

Icy fingers trailed down her spine. She should turn around and race for home as fast as her dogs could run.

But she didn't. Swallowing her fear, she guided her team to the commissary, ignoring the two men and focusing on the reason she came to the fort. Keeping her gaze averted, she climbed from her sled and untied the bundle of fur. Anxious to make her trade while all the trappers were busy with the murder victim, Lilli hurried inside.

With the lack of pelts, the fur price rose, and she pocketed an extra twenty dollars. Happy with her success, she stepped from the building into the light and put a box of supplies into her sled.

She met Max and his companion walking toward her on the boardwalk. Swallowing her discomfort, she forced a neutral expression on her face.

"Hello, Wille. I'd like you to meet Officer Finlay. He graduated a month ago and came upriver with me last week." Max turned to his companion. "This is Willie. He and his dad run a line up north."

Men shook hands, which meant she would have to touch the evil black-eyed man.

She shoved her hand out and grunted in response to Officer Finlay's greeting.

"How's your father doing?" Max meant to be kind, but the longer she stood here, the more she wanted to escape.

"Fine." She shoved her hands in her pockets to keep from rubbing the man's germs off on the side of her breeches. "He'll be looking for me, so I've got to get home."

He filled her in on the murder. "We're asking everyone to look at the victim for identification purposes. He had no papers or effects on him. Officer Finlay will show you the way." He glanced toward the fort's central building. "The commander wants to talk to me, or I'd come too. I'll see you later, Willie."

She nodded and dropped her gaze again to hide her disappointment.

"The body is this way." Officer Finlay pointed to the left, and she strolled alongside him, careful to maintain her distance.

Stepping into the fort's chapel, her gaze fell on a stiff body displayed on a wooden slab, and her heart rose to her throat.

She knew him. The man who shot at her in the woods and she warned off with an answering bullet. She glanced at his feet. He wore the same boot as her father but a smaller size. Lilli swallowed and shuffled her weight, keeping her gaze averted to hide the flash of recognition. The new officer worried her more than the dead shooter. Danger permeated the air, and she took a step to the side to put distance between them. A knot formed in her stomach as the chapel walls pressed down on her.

"Do you recognize him?" Office Finlay's gaze studied her with a strange intensity. He tensed like a predator preparing to pounce.

"No." Turning on her heel, she did her best male walk to the door. Who killed the shooter and why? Did he work with the pelt thief or on his own? And if he did, who hired him? A terrible suspicion threatened to choke her as she took hold of the latch.

"Rebecca Van Rassner." The officer's silky, soft voice sent a shiver down her spine.

"Who?" Her heart jumped to her throat, and her knees grew shaky.

This nasty man worked for her uncle. Or knew someone who did. Cold sweat broke out on her forehead.

"You know. Either you are her, or you know where she is." His tone dripped with menace.

She froze and turned to sneer at him. "Did you just ask me if I were a *girl*?" Emphasizing the word, she scowled at the man and snorted. "Most folks make fun of my thin arms, but this is the first time I've been accused of being *female*! I have a good mind to bloody your face."

He ignored her outburst. "You're about the same height and weight as Molly." Smiling into her frightened eyes, he sauntered toward her. Tilting his head to survey her from head to toe, he stopped beside her. "If I were to remove your clothing, what would I discover?"

She bloodied his nose and knocked him on his ass. "You'd find a whole lot more of this. Touch me again, and I'll kill you." No one ever accused the soldiers of being a woman, so she didn't know how a man would react. But she doubted they'd like it much. Once outside, she shut the chapel door and ran for her sled. Tucking her buffalo rug around her, she picked up her lead lines and whistled to the dogs.

Men in uniform blurred past as she sped for the fort's entrance. Her heart raced as she contemplated the situation. *Carlton Genova found them!* Did Max know Officer Finlay worked for her uncle? Frowning, she bit her lip. Max didn't know about her uncle because *she never told him.*

Setting her concern aside, she returned to her earlier worry. Did the dead man in the chapel work for her uncle, too? And if so, who murdered him? And were the two things connected? She'd pack their things and drive off in the middle of the night if Papa weren't so sick. To do so now might kill him. Lilli shivered again. Now she knew why the short man made her hackles rise. Her hands trembled, and terror broke out on her brow. Did she dare tell Papa? He would be awake soon and asking for his—

Medicine!

Lilli drew the team to a stop. God, she forgot the most important part of her errand to the fort. In her haste to get away from the evil little man, she drove off without the thing she risked her neck for. Turning the team, she whistled and followed her sled tracks back the way she came. Once inside the fort, she stopped outside the doctor's office. Checking her surroundings, she blew out her breath. Max and Officer Finlay were nowhere in sight as she committed her first serious crime.

Stepping into the doctor's office, she asked for carbolic acid and opium. She figured if she stopped buying the white powder after making major purchases of the drug the last few months, someone would get suspicious. And she didn't want to be on the suspect list for the robberies, especially with her growing feelings for Max. If he ever discovered what she did, she'd die of shame. And lose him forever.

Dr. Talon asked about Papa's health while he measured and wrapped her purchases. She lied and told him the same story she told Max. Papa stayed at the cabin to tend the line. No one knew his real condition but her.

Gathering her purchases, she packed them in her sled.

She ate dinner with Marion and made her excuse to get back to the cabin, but instead of leaving, she circled around behind the doctor's office and peeked in the window. Carrying the cloth bag she brought along for the occasion, she held her breath and took stock of her surroundings. Dark, empty, and quiet, she smiled and picked the lock.

On silent feet, she crept into the exam room and opened the correct cabinet door. She took the whole bottle of opium, and added bandages, herbs, different tinctures, and a few salves. She figured if only the opium disappeared, everyone would know who took it. Placing her IOU in plain sight, she closed the door and left the way she came.

Placing the bag under the fur in her sled, she took hold of the handle and gave a cry of surprise when Max stepped up beside her.

"Hi." His husky voice sent her pulse soaring.

He scared the hell out of her, and she took a minute to get her heart back in her chest where it belonged.

"Hi." The word came out breathlessly, and she glanced around for the other officer.

"I thought you left until I spotted your sled outside the doctor's office. I'm glad you didn't."

"We can't talk here. Is there somewhere we could go?" She didn't intend to have another encounter with Officer Finlay anytime soon.

"Sure. We could go to my rooms." His gaze narrowed on her face. "Are you in trouble?"

She ignored his questions, anxious to disappear before the other officer found them. "Do you have somewhere for my sled? I must get off the street."

"Yeah. Follow me." He led her behind the doctor's office, between the commissary and the stable. They stopped beside a barn, and he waved her inside. "This is mine. Your sled will be safe in here."

Latching the door behind them, he led her across a small open area and up the wooden stairs to his room. "In here."

He closed the door and gave her a rueful grin. "I'm sorry I haven't been out to check on Frank for a while. I've been busy since I returned from Fort Providence with Officer Finlay."

"I don't like him. He makes me uncomfortable." She shifted her feet and wrapped her arms around her waist.

Something flashed in his eyes as he turned to latch

the door. "Did he touch you?"

She shook her head. "No. He suggested I might be female, and I hit him." Max didn't know the whole story. She kept information to a minimum the one time they spoke about her past.

He stood still for several long seconds. "I'll keep him as far away from you and the cabin as I can." He glanced at Lilli. "What about the body? You recognized him as the man who shot at you?"

"Yes." She frowned. "But I don't know a name or why he fired at me. At the time, I assumed he and the thief were the same person. I haven't seen him since you mentioned he came back." She glanced down at the wooden floor. "Do you know who shot him and why?"

"Those are the answers I intend to find out. Commander Jorgensen asked me to solve the murder. I wondered if your father shot him. He's quick with a gun and got the drop on me twice. Your father's tracks were everywhere. The problem is the patrol found his body five miles south of Fort Simpson. Too far out of your range for Frank to be involved."

Swallowing against the sudden lump in her throat, Lilli shivered and glanced up at him. "I got so upset over Officer Finlay's questions that I left without Papa's medicine and had to come back. I left my sled at the doctor's while I ate with Marion." She needed an excuse for being beside the doctor's office when he found her.

"I'm glad you did." He took a step toward her and wrapped her in his arms. "If you're in danger, Lilli, I need to know."

His embrace comforted her, and she leaned in to absorb his heat. But some things were best left unsaid. The fewer people who knew her real identity, the better.

"I won't let anyone hurt you." His deep voice rumbled beneath her cheek, and she sighed with relief.

If only that were true. She felt safer tucked inside his arms than she ever had. But he didn't know who or what came for her, and she would never endanger him in her affairs. He didn't know about the stolen medicine either. Her own mother would be disappointed in her.

Mama and the long-ago day when she lost everything flashed across her mind. What if she never returned to New York or had the normal life she dreamed of? Life could be snuffed out in seconds, and dreams shattered with the report of a pistol.

The intimacy of the room and Max's proximity made her tremble with a new emotion. She had right now and no promise of tomorrow. Running her hands over his broad back, she pressed her body against his.

"When does your father expect you back?" The husky timbre of his voice made her breath catch in her throat.

In all reality, Papa would sleep for another few hours. "Not for a bit."

"Then we have an hour or so?" His grin weakened her knees and made her heart jump to her throat. "I missed you. Let me show you how much."

She could reject the suggestion in his voice and go home to her cold single bed. Or she could seize this opportunity and enjoy every second to the fullest. The uncertainty of her life and future made her choice for her. "I missed you, too." Everything but her need to be in his arms disappeared.

The night he came to her bed, she asked when he would show her more, and his answer danced in her head. *When you can scream and moan out loud. And I can pleasure you the way I'd like to."*

"What if someone knocks on the door?" Her mouth dried as she remembered the pleasure he gave her. A month of dreaming about the night in her room tightened her belly. She wanted to be with him, feel him, and touch him the way he touched her.

"They'll go back the way they came. No one will see or know." He kissed the side of her neck, and her knees turned to water.

"They'll know if I'm screaming." Her belly quivered with excitement.

He tilted her face up to his. "Then they shouldn't listen at other people's doors." His gaze darkened. "I haven't been able to get you out of my head since the night you came in my arms. I want to hold you naked and pleasure you the way I've dreamed about."

Her heart threatened to jump from her body, and heat rushed through her veins. A sudden concern made her frown. "What if Officer Finlay finds Papa while I'm here with you? I should go." Lord, she wanted to stay, but not if her father was in danger.

"He doesn't know where the cabin is. He's green as a sapling up here in the bush. Someone would have to lead him out there for him to find Frank. Your father did an excellent job if hiding the cabin. I rode the area for months and didn't find you." His blue eyes studied her expression. "Will you stay with me?" Silence hovered between them. "This isn't your father's cabin."

How could she resist such temptation? "I must be back before Papa wa— uh, is." She damn near said *wakes* and caught the word at the last second.

"I never planned to get this serious with anyone again, but I can't get you out of my head or the taste of you out of my mouth. I burn for more. But it's up to you. You can say *no* if I'm going too fast for you." He stared at her lips, and his gaze dropped to the top button on her flannel shirt visible through the opening of her jacket.

"Yes." Their gazes met and locked.

Chapter Thirteen

A slow, wicked grin crossed his face as he tugged her heavy jacket off. "I've dreamed of you and your kisses for the last four weeks. Every night, when I close my eyes, your whimpers of pleasure play in my head. I want to bury my body in your softness and drink from your soft lips until you cry my name."

Her legs buckled, and he caught her before she hit the ground. Covering her mouth with his, he devoured her lips with long, drugging kisses as he propelled her backward. She quivered when the bed pressed into her. Wrapping her arms around his neck, she held on for dear life as his tongue stroked along hers. Desire and excitement fluttered in her belly. Max smelled like the forest. His warm, musky scent enveloped her in a haze of unaccustomed anticipation. Dropping her hands to his shoulders and chest, she ran her fingers over the ridges and dips of his abdomen.

He sucked in a breath. "My turn." He undid the buttons on her shirt and drew the garment from her arms. He dropped the item to the floor and stared at her chest. Her chemise followed suit. "Now, this is cruel." Unpinning her binding, he unwrapped the strip of linen from around her chest, and her breasts sprang free.

She crossed her arms and gulped as she stared up at him. Modesty and years of being alone hadn't prepared her for this situation. Sure, he suckled her in the darkness of her room, but now that she stood here half-naked in the middle of the day, she worried about what he would think.

His gaze darkened as he moved her arms. "Let me look at you. I've imagined this moment for days." When he dropped his gaze to her heaving chest, she swallowed. "God, you're beautiful. Like a ripe peach waiting to be sampled." He dropped his head and kissed her white globes.

She trembled in his arms, willing him to suckle her like he did before, and squirmed against him. "Max." Her whisper came with a breath of longing, and he responded by closing his mouth over one hardening nipple.

She cried out and arced against him as he sucked her. Clutching his biceps, she focused on the pinpricks of pleasure his hot mouth gave her. Moisture gathered between her legs, and she whimpered. "Please…"

He did. And tugged her other hardening pebble into his mouth, giving it the same attention he gave its twin.

Boots walked along the boardwalk in front of his door and stopped.

Lilli held her breath until they thumped off and down the steps. She blew out a breath of relief and gazed up at Max with a half-smile.

She glanced at the door and back at him. "I don't want you to stop, but if someone—"

He caught her mouth in a deep, carnal kiss. "They won't. No one bothers me here unless it's urgent. But I have an idea." Walking away, he collected an extra blanket from a chest on the left side of the bed and packed it around the bottom of the door.

Lilli shivered as soon as he let her go. Without his warmth, her heated flesh cooled in the afternoon air.

Max returned to the chest for thick buffalo rugs he laid on the rug before the fire. Catching both pillows from the bed, he turned and held out his hand. "I've spent a good deal of time thinking about this moment and where I wanted our first time to be. Come to me, Lilli."

She crossed the room before her inhibitions caught up to her curiosity and cooled her anticipation. He removed his jacket and unbuttoned his shirt. Both articles flew across the room and landed with accuracy on the bed. He stood before her, naked to the waist, and she sucked in a breath as she took in the masculine perfection of his chest and arms.

Laughing, he sat on the chair and removed his boots and socks.

She gulped and sat on the floor to remove hers. Stacking them beside the chair, she gasped when he sank down beside her and gave her a sensuous smile.

"Have you envisioned our first time?" Rolling to his side, he leaned forward and flicked her erect nipple with his tongue.

She gasped and, with shaking arms, lowered her body down beside him. "No...I mean, yes...I don't—"

He chuckled. "Tell me what you want to do. Or show me." His challenge hung in the air, and she swallowed.

God, she wanted to touch him, to kiss him, to feel him around her and over her. She didn't know she spoke aloud until he rolled onto her and wrapped both arms around her.

"I am, I will, and I do." He kissed her hard, and his tongue slid into her mouth to mate with hers. His hands were everywhere, touching her, caressing her, cupping her breasts, and teasing her nipples.

Lost in a sea of sensation, she gulped when he nudged her legs open and settled between her thighs. Rocking into her, his erect shaft pressed into her belly, and she shook from head to toe in response. Her mind grappled with the picture of him sliding inside her, and she couldn't breathe.

Liquid desire dampened her pantalets, and she gave as good as she got. Stroking his chest, arms, and belly, she traced every line and ripple on his well-formed body until he caught her hand and kissed her fingers. "Take your breeches off. I want to feel you."

With trembling fingers, she complied. "If you take yours off." She managed the words despite her dry mouth.

His knowing, wicked glance never left hers as he unbuttoned his breeches and rolled off her to discard them.

He removed his small clothes with a careless flick of his hand, and his manhood stood erect and proud in the afternoon light.

Lilli gaped. She had no idea men grew so large and hard and risked a glance at his face.

He studied her through half-closed eyes, not a bit bashful about his nakedness. "I took mine off. Let's see yours."

She bent her head and struggled to free her buttons.

Max kissed her neck and down the front of her chest to her breasts while she worked them out of their buttonholes. On his side, he bent his head and licked around her nearest areola until she gasped and arched back.

"Want some help?" He took hold of her breeches and slid them from her hips. Tossing them behind him, he slid a finger under the waistband of her pantalets. "Now is your chance to tell me what you dream about, Lilli." He stripped them from her as he spoke.

"You." Lilli swallowed. "I dream about you."

He turned aside and withdrew an animal skin which he slipped over his engorged shaft. Rolling to his back, he lifted her onto him. "Show me."

She lay against him, quivering with anticipation and nervousness. His shaft frightened and excited her at the same time. Rocking her hips against him like he did hers, she gasped as his length rubbed against her femininity. She rocked again and cried out when he caught a nipple in his mouth and tugged. She couldn't breathe and shifted forward, so his arousal pressed lower on her pulsing mound. An ache grew inside her as he suckled, and she rocked. Her nervousness disappeared in a haze of delight as his hot fingers stroked over her chest and down her sides. She wanted him inside her and tipped her hips up against him until the head of his arousal slid between the lips of her mound.

Leaning back, she rocked again and shivered with eagerness. His raspy breath told her she affected him as much as he did her.

He captured her lips with a low moan and dropped his hands to her thighs. Spreading them open, he lifted her knees up to his waist. "Straddle me." His hoarse voice made her eyes fly open. Hunger glowed from his eyes as he stared at her. "God, you feel good."

She moaned in response. With every moment of their bodies, her womanhood grew more sensitive to the pleasure of his, and she sat up to rub her aching sheath the length of his thickness.

He murmured with satisfaction and rocked his pelvis

into hers. He slipped his fingers between the folds of her femininity and stroked her hard nub.

She quaked with reaction and grew hot. Liquid heat pooled between her legs as he dipped his finger into her opening. Groaning, she widened her thighs and lifted her hips. He penetrated her with his finger while she rocked against his hand. Shaking with each thrust of his finger, she could do nothing but pant against his chest. God, if his finger were this good, his arousal would shoot her to the moon. Shifting against his hand, she rode him up and down while he tugged at her nipples. If he didn't enter her soon, she'd die. Her pleasure center throbbed with need, and she lifted to stroke the length of his arousal.

He sat up and caught her by the hips. "You're so wet for me, you're making me crazy."

Her, too. Catching the head of his shaft, she guided him to her slit and rubbed him against her slickness.

He groaned and caught her hips with both hands. His slumberous blue eyes gazed into hers as he lowered her over his pulsing shaft.

She quivered and moaned with each inch of his girth and shivered with delight as she adjusted to him. He felt every bit as good as she imagined, and she cried out as he inched higher. When fully seated over his arousal, she wrapped her arms around his neck and swallowed. He stared at her as he lifted her hips and then lowered her back onto his bulging member.

Lilli couldn't breathe, much less speak, and panted against his chest.

"Do you want to ride me, or should I take over?" He kissed the side of her neck as he raised and lowered her once more.

She stared at him and held his shoulders as she

raised and lowered her body in wonder and delight. Tantalized by the pleasure each movement created inside her pulsing sheath, she increased her rhythm to both of their satisfaction.

Her heart sped up, and her breathing increased as tension built inside her quivering body. She couldn't believe he let her ride him like this and bounced up and down on him until her muscles tensed. Euphoria beckoned just beyond her reach, and she stopped to catch her breath.

His ragged breathing against her neck made her pause. "Did I do something wrong?"

"Hell, no." Flipping her over in his arms, he thrust into her hard and deep.

She screamed with rapture and lifted her hips for more.

He grunted as he wrapped her legs around his waist. "God, you feel good."

Plunging faster and deeper, he carried them both to the vortex of fulfillment. Lilli dug her hands into his shoulders as she exploded in a perfect storm of bliss.

His moan of gratification followed hers, and together, they writhed in pulsing waves of rapture.

When the last ripple dissipated, Lilli uncurled her toes and released her death grip on Max's shoulders. She never experienced so much peace and satisfaction in her life. Turning her head, she met Max's gaze.

A smile played around the corner of his mouth. "I knew our coming together would be mind blowing after the first time I kissed you. You make me crazy with lust." His grin widened. "I can't believe you hide all of this beneath a baggy shirt and breeches." He ran his hand the length of her heated flesh. "I'll have to stop by more often now I know how good we are together."

She wanted him to, too. Lilli swallowed. She didn't want this intimate moment to end, but reality returned with the darkening room. "I have to get back, or Papa will wonder what happened to me."

Disappointment flashed in his eyes. "I know." Rising to his feet, he held a hand down to help her up. "There's a basin and towel on the far wall if you want to wash up."

She took two steps before he caught her to him and kissed her hard.

"I enjoyed this afternoon more than I can say, and I wish I could offer you more than a few hours. Someday soon, I'll hold you in my arms and pleasure you all through the night. I intend to know everything there is to know about you, my Lilli. You tantalize and excite me more than any woman I've ever known. And the more I taste your kisses, the more I crave them. In the meantime, I'll keep Officer Finlay busy searching for the other thief while I investigate the murder and get us some answers. If someone is after Frank, we'll find him. I won't let anything happen to you or your father."

Thief and *murder* were the only two words she registered, and she stiffened against him. "Okay. Uh, me too." Swallowing her panic, she grinned at him. "For now, I have to go."

Washing and dressing as quickly as she could, Lilli slipped out the door with a good-by kiss and raced for home. The darkening sky told her she stayed longer than she should have.

Her mind raced with worry as she sped along the path through the brush. Making sure she doubled-back and recrossed her trail in several places to make tracking her sled difficult, she took the back road into the cabin. The one thing she didn't want to happen must come to pass before she could have the one thing she did. Max. She couldn't be with him for real until her uncle no longer hunted her. One thing she knew for certain. Officer Finlay must go. His presence filled her with terror. She could tell Max the truth, but if she did, his life would be in danger. Carlton Genova killed anyone who could identify him as a killer. At first, she didn't trust the officer enough to divulge family secrets. But now, she would never find peace if anything happened to him because of her. Her feelings for him wouldn't let her.

Glancing up, she yelled. "I *will* have the life I want no matter what you throw at me."

Snowflakes drifted down from the darkening sky.

The bleak forest road swerved and dipped before her. Crying would do no good. Papa must get well so she didn't have to *borrow* anymore, and something must be done about Officer Finlay. No way would she run away again and lose the one good thing in her life. Max. And her growing feelings for him.

Chapter Fourteen

"You've taken quite an interest in the Rossi boy." Officer Finlay made the statement the next morning while the two sat in the dining hall for breakfast.

Max shrugged. "He's young, and his father stepped on a bear trap. Running a trap line is demanding work for a man, let alone a boy."

"Or a woman." The other officer studied his face for a reaction.

Max sat his fork down and stared into the other man's face. "There's no woman up here running lines. First off, the other trappers would shoot her husband, brother, or father for allowing such a thing. And second, she couldn't do the lifting and hauling. She might keep up for a day or two, but not steady. Trap lines are a man's work." He resumed eating. "Willie tells me you asked him if he were a woman." Max shook his head. "Good thing the boy held onto his temper, or you'd be in bed recuperating from more than a broken nose."

Officer Finlay snorted. "That skinny kid?"

"That skinny kid knocked me down and damn near shot my head off when I surprised him one night. I've never seen anyone who can move as fast as Willie in a fight. Ask any of the soldiers. They give the kid a wide berth." He exaggerated, hoping to convince him to leave Lilli alone.

"All right. Do you know of any young women living

up here? There's a family I know who lost track of their daughter, and they asked me to find her." The officer took a sip of coffee and leaned back in his chair.

Max shot him a glance. "No. But then, most of the men up here keep their women clear of the fort. Too many lonely soldiers. I appreciate your concern for this family, but your job is to find the thief who's been robbing barns and leaving IOUs. If you can't keep your mind on the task I've given you, I'll send you back to Fort Providence and have you reassigned." He put the last bite of the egg in his mouth and drained his coffee cup.

Panic flared in the other man's eyes before he dropped his gaze.

Max tucked the information away. "Check with the doctor and any of the trappers trading today to see if there have been any recent robberies. Then check for cabins south of here. I'll expect a report first thing in the morning." He rose to his feet and sat his black hat on his head. Strolling from the eating area, he untied his stallion from the hitching post and mounted up with a nod at some nearby soldiers. Max left the fort and traveled south. He intended to find the area where the patrol found the body and search for answers.

A blanket of snow covered the ground, and the ice crystals at his feet glistened like diamonds in the morning light. The frosty breeze smelled of pine, nipping at his nose and cheeks. An hour and a half later, he rode into a small clearing and found blood. He knew from examining the body that he'd been shot with a rifle.

Marking out a hundred-yard perimeter from where the body fell, Max searched the ground. On the east-facing side, he discovered the butt of a cigar beneath a tree. Someone stood there for most of an hour waiting for the victim. He sniffed the wet evidence. Cuban. Cigars of this caliber were tough to find this far north. He placed the article in his saddle bag and scoured the area beneath the tree again. Nothing.

Max tied a spare neckcloth from his saddlebag around a south-facing limb above the spot where he found the cigar butt. Marking the tree so he could re-search the area once the snow melted, he made a mental note of the tree's position in relation to the clearing. Unless he found the cigar-smoking murderer by then. Nothing about the prints in the snow stood out. Male, medium height, medium weight. Any number of soldiers and trappers in the area fit the description. Wolves drawn to the scent of blood obliterated any other sign.

He climbed into his saddle and turned his stallion north. A few nights in the saloon at the fort and he'd know who the cigar smokers were. New to the area or otherwise. The commissary officer would tell him of any recent cigar shipments. He should have the murderer in custody within the next few days. Glancing up at the sun, he grinned. He could check on Frank and Lilli and be back at the fort by dinnertime. The trapper might have more information on the victim's identity. Which would help him narrow down his search. With the murder solved, he could help focus on the second thief, send the other Mountie back to Fort Providence, and focus on Lilli.

Nudging his mount, he raced through the trees with his mind on yesterday's visit. Hard-pressed to keep his mind off her sweet kisses and luscious body, he made up excuses to have a private moment alone with her. Never had a woman taken over his mind like this one did. Not even Elsie. His ears still rang with Lilli's cry of pleasure, and the taste of her in his mouth made him want more. So much more. The gratification he experienced with her far outweighed his reluctance to get involved.

Rounding the path through the trees, he came across a group of soldiers on patrol. They nodded as they passed, and Max took note of their names. The commander would give him patrol information to check against a list of smokers. And Officer Finlay could help him collect names for the list. Arriving back at the fort, he took the cigar to the commander.

"Any ideas who the murderer is?" Commander Jorgensen sniffed the evidence.

"None." He outlined his plans and left.

Officer Finlay stopped him outside. "There are no new robberies. No one here knows anything new. I think I'll ride north and talk to the trappers." His eyes grew watchful. "If you draw me a map of the cabins in the area, my investigation will go faster."

Max climbed into the saddle. "Follow the river. Did you check the ones south of here, like I asked? And I want a written report. Not a verbal one. Things have a way of being forgotten unless there's a record. See you first thing tomorrow."

He ignored the flash of anger in the other officer's eyes as he rode out of the fort. He might not have caught the intense stare when the other man asked for a map if Lilli hadn't mentioned her discomfort. He gave his word to keep her safe. Despite her insistence, he refrained from asking her father questions, but he intended to get some answers. Frank would know things she didn't. Important things that could make all the difference in keeping them both safe.

Two hours later, he entered the clearing and stopped in front of Frank's cabin. He slid to the ground and tied his horse to the hitching post. Walking around to the back of the cabin, he knocked twice and stepped inside.

Late afternoon sunshine streamed through the windows, and he waited for his eyes to adjust before taking a step. The scent of herbs, vegetables, and meat cooking made his mouth water. Frank's wet boots stood beside the door. Good. He worried the trapper might still be out working his lines. "Frank?"

Silence.

Strolling into the living area, he expected to see the other man sitting in his chair but found the room empty.

A log settled on the hearth, and he called again.

"Who's there?" The trapper's voice came from the half-open door of his room.

"Max Calhan." He strolled into the middle of the room. "I came to see how you're doing."

"I'm in here. Come on in, Marion."

Stepping through the door, he came to a stop. The other man lay on his bed with a leg propped up on pillows. Drenched in sweat, the little chamber reeked of body odor and stale air. The other man's short, labored breathing caught his attention.

"You're not Marion."

"No. Are you doing okay?" One glance told him the other man hadn't been off his bed in weeks. He frowned. Yet his boots were by the back door wet with snow and ice.

"I'm in pain, and I can't breathe like I used to. Where's my daughter?" He clutched and fidgeted with his bedclothes. His labored breathing grew louder. "She said she'd be in to give me my medicine, and she should have been back by now." He shivered and tugged the quilt higher. "Probably off whispering with Charlotte."

Max stepped closer to the bed. "Where did she go?" For Rossi to call her *daughter* concerned him as much as his disorientation.

"She said something about the dogs, but I want my medicine now! Can you get it for me?" The other man speared him with his gaze. "I'm in too much pain to wait for her. If you don't go, I will."

Max wondered if the threat worked on Lilli and noted the other man's foot resting on pillows. "Looks like your leg is getting better."

A loose strip of linen hung around his lower leg. Red, angry scars crisscrossed the area below his knee with no sign of infection or swelling.

"Look closer. The wolf damn near took my leg off. It's not better. All the infection is inside where you can't see it, and it hurts like hell. I need pain medicine. And I need it an hour ago." His voice rose several octaves, and he sat up, gasping for breath.

"I'm coming, Papa." The back door slammed, and hurried footsteps clicked against the wooden floor.

"It's about damn time." The other man growled and settled back against his pillows.

This man bore little resemblance to the trapper who cocked a pistol in his face through a crack in the door the day they met. Irritable, fidgety, sweaty, and short of breath. He must be getting too much opium.

"I'm here." Lilli swept into the room armed with white powder and whisky. She paused when her gaze met Max's. Red flooded her cheeks as she turned away and spooned a healthy dose of opium into the whisky.

Guilt, no doubt, over her lies.

Helping the invalid sit up, she handed her father the glass and stood beside him while he drank. "I'll get you some supper."

"I'm not hungry." The older man slid down in the bed and turned his back to them. "Go away. I'm tired."

Lilli stared at her father and glanced at Max. "I had no idea you were coming out to the cabin today."

He figured she didn't since she'd lied to him about her father's condition, and she wasn't happy he came by the look on her face. Max studied her. If Frank hadn't worn his boots out in the snow, she must have. If she borrowed them, why switch back to hers?

Max folded his arms, determined to get some answers.

Chapter Fifteen

Lilli's heart lodged high in her throat, and she shivered despite the heat in the room. Did he see the boots? She came in the back door and didn't see his horse out front. Shifting her weight, she contemplated excuses in case he asked. He couldn't find out about her extra activities. Not until she could make it right. Rubbing the back of her neck, she folded her arms and tilted her head toward the other room.

He followed her.

Stopping in front of the fire, she held her trembling hands to the blaze. "I'm glad you came." She hoped he didn't read guilt in her expression.

"I wanted to ask Frank a couple of questions about the men chasing him. But I didn't get the chance." He cleared his throat. "He's not any better."

The statement hung suspended in the air.

She took a deep breath and willed her heart to return to its normal rhythm. "This day has been an experience. First, I couldn't find my boots, and I had to wear Papa's, which slowed me down. Then, the dogs took a bend in the road too fast and tipped my sled. Righting everything took time I didn't have. When I got home, the fire had gone out, and I had to light it before I took care of the dogs, making Papa wait for his medicine and supper. And now he wants to sleep." Her shoulders drooped. He *had* to believe her.

"Why didn't you tell me the truth about your father? You've been out tending the line since the wolf bit him, haven't you?" His blue eyes gazed into hers with compassion.

She shrugged. "What good would it do to let everyone know the truth? Marion would worry and want him to come live with her. We can't afford to move to the fort where Papa's enemies can find him. You would feel obligated to come check on us despite all the obligations you have to the mounted police and the fort." She shook her head. "I analyzed the situation and decided to deal with things on my own. I can handle this."

"Tending the trap line and taking care of an injured old man? Most men couldn't handle the strain, let alone a woman." He shook his head. "You should have told me."

His voice softened, and Lilli resisted the urge to throw her body into his arms and weep all over his broad chest. He had the strength to shoulder the weight on hers, but she couldn't let him.

"Papa is my problem." She straightened her spine and lifted her chin. "You're not responsible for his well-being, and you can't run out here every time he needs something. Right or wrong. Like it or not, he's my responsibility."

He studied the mutiny she knew shone from her eyes and changed the subject. "Your father takes too much opium. I've seen the symptoms before. You must cut him back before his need kills him."

She wanted to cry. "I know. But every time I suggest he's taking an excessive amount or I put a smaller dose in his whisky, he knows. And gets angry." She shivered, remembering the last time.

Papa's lack of balance and disorientation saved her. He struck out when she refused to give him more and fell face first onto the tied rug in front of the fire.

He went to his room and hadn't been out of bed since.

Max listened while she explained. When she finished, he drew her into his arms and a rebellious tear ran down her face.

"You don't have to do this alone. I'm here. And I'll do whatever I can to help." Wiping the wetness from her cheek with the pad of his thumb, he tilted her face up to his.

He kissed her with tenderness, sliding his lips over hers while he held her against his heart.

Guilt, fear of discovery, and the seduction of a new lover raced through her being. God, if he ever found out the truth, she'd lose him forever. Wrapping her arms around his neck, she kissed him back with all the desperation swirling inside her. Opium, Carlton Genova, Officer Finlay, and the lot of them could go to hell. They wouldn't win. They couldn't.

He groaned and tilted her face to the side as he deepened the kiss.

She remembered the last time he held her and the way his girth filled her aching core. "Come with me. Papa will sleep for a few hours now." She took his hand in hers and turned toward her room.

He hesitated and then laced his fingers with hers. Staring down at her with a serious expression, he caressed her cheek. "I understand why you didn't tell me about Frank. But I want you to promise you'll come to me if you're in trouble. I can't help you or keep danger away unless I know where it comes from. Now I know about Frank, I can help you wean him off the drug. Give me your word, Lilli."

She longed to pour all the rest of her troubles out and let him help shoulder them, too, but she couldn't. If she did and her uncle found them, he'd kill Max without hesitation. And the concern made her chest hurt.

Allowing him to help Papa helped her. If her father could travel, they could leave before her uncle sent another assassin. But his return to health meant the end of her time with Max.

She swallowed. Gazing into his compassionate blue eyes, she nodded. "If you let me know when you plan to come, I'll make sure I'm home. I want to be with you every chance I have." She meant every word and figured they had until spring.

His gaze darkened. "Me, too. I can't get you off my mind." His hands dropped to her hips, and she gasped when his arousal pressed into her belly. "This is still your father's house."

She shivered with pleasure, and warmth spread from her groin outward." And mine."

Gripping his hand still intertwined with hers, she led him on shaking knees to her room and latched the door behind them.

Their clothes fell in a heap on the floor as their lips and bodies clung together. Her thighs trembled as she opened them wide for him, and he settled between them. They touched, licked, caressed, sucked, and stroked every inch of the other's body until they both panted with passion. He entered her in one quick thrust and caught her cry of delight with his mouth. He dipped his fingers between their bodies and pleasured her with delicate flicks against her nub while he rocked into her.

"God, you feel good. Better than I remember." She gasped as he rolled to his side and turned her in his arms. "What are you doing?"

"You'll like this." He turned her back to him and wrapped his arms around her belly. Sliding his hands down her quivering length, he dipped his fingers into her slick sheath. "Open your legs."

She did, and he guided his shaft into her from behind. She bucked forward. Her legs quivered and heat filled her aching core, surrounding him in liquid desire. Holding her hips against him, he rubbed her nub while he thrust long and deep.

Her heart accelerated, and her breath came fast between parted lips. "God." She arched against him, panting for air. "That feels so—" She couldn't speak. Her pleasure center grew more sensitive with every plunge of his hard member. Delicious friction centered around his pulsing shaft.

And she couldn't get enough. "Deeper. Harder."

He complied, and she lost all reason but what he did to her. Satisfaction came in a glittering wave of pinpoint pleasure, drowning her in euphoric delight. She gasped his name as he carried her over endless waves of exquisite gratification. Floating in a sea of ecstasy, she twisted her hand in the quilt for a lifeline.

He came a minute later and groaned into her hair as his climax claimed his soul.

Together, they lay soaked in the afterglow of their lovemaking. Sated and content, they clung together.

Lilli opened her eyes and let go of her death grip on the patchwork quilt. She stared at the opposite wall, wishing she could stay here in his arms like this forever.

But happiness and reality were two different things.

Max kissed the side of her neck and hugged her against him. "I love holding you in my arms and making love to you."

Her stomach fluttered with remembered heat. "Me, too."

Five more minutes elapsed. "I should go. I must be back at the fort before the saloon closes. As much as I enjoy holding you, I have a murderer to catch."

She stiffened. The shooter. Reality returned with a bang. "Right." She rolled away from him and rose to her feet. Shuffling through their clothes, she separated her own.

"Lilli, I wouldn't go if I didn't have to. Once I solve the murder, I'll have more time to be with you." He spoke behind her and turned her around. Sincerity shone from his incredible eyes. "I've never enjoyed being with a woman as much as you. What we do together is something I've never experienced before, and I want more. Your face fills my mind, your kisses fill my dreams, and your delightful body feeds my fantasies. But I can't have you until I fulfill my obligations. Otherwise, I'd spend every waking moment acting out those fantasies with you." Lifting her chin, he drank long and deep from her mouth.

When he lifted his lips, she sighed. "I feel the same way."

He grinned. "If I knew how good being with you would be, I wouldn't have turned you down the first night out in the barn."

She laughed. "And I wouldn't have let you."

Once they dressed, he followed her out of the room. Kissing her goodbye outside the front door, he promised to come back in a few days and strolled away into the darkness.

Lilli shut the door and leaned back. Blowing out a sigh of relief, she shook her head. If Max helped her wean Papa off the white powder, she wouldn't have to borrow anymore. For a second, the weight on her shoulders shifted, and a ray of hope entered her bosom. Returning to her room, she removed the journal she kept on who and how much she owed. Running her fingers over the tally, she cringed and could have wept with guilt. Mama would be disappointed if she could see her now. Twenty times, Papa took things from other trappers, and her heart dripped with remorse. One more for the doctor, for her sin. Five more handwritten notes were tucked inside the back cover of her journal, and she hoped she wouldn't have to use them. Placing her journal back on the shelf and the ink and parchment back inside her trunk, she missed the two little notes that fluttered to the floor and fell beneath her bed. "I plan to make it right, Mama. Please help me fix this. I know you can see the entire world from heaven. Show me what to do." Stopping on her way to the door, she whispered. "And thank you for sending Max."

Morning came too soon, and Lilli raced through her morning preparations. Anxious to be on her way, she kissed her sleeping papa goodbye and left.

A mile down the trail, Zeus growled and sniffed the ground.

Lilli stopped the sled.

Climbing out, she circled back along the path and froze. A strange horse walked along the side of the path. Someone came past her in the night and circled back several times.

Did they see Max?

Heaviness settled in her chest. The thought of him being hurt or killed hurt more than anything she experienced so far. Almost as much as losing Mama. Her eyebrows snapped together, and her heart ached.

Circling back to the clearing, Lilli made sure she brushed her tracks away like Papa taught her. No more mistakes. Not anymore.

****

Officer Finlay waited until Max disappeared into the trees before he mounted his horse. Careful to keep a safe distance between them, he followed the other officer north. He didn't give a fig about orders. He traveled to this God-forsaken territory for one reason. To find Rebecca Van Rassner.

Well, he amended, two reasons. The girl and his half a million pounds of gold. The twenty thousand pounds he earned for shooting Fingers waited for him in New York. Once he eliminated the girl, he would buy an island and retire.

He didn't believe Officer Calhan's story about Willie Rossi. Something about the boy bothered him, but he couldn't decide what. He figured if he followed the other officer long enough, he'd find the girl. Calhan knew more than he let on. He'd noted how the other officer's attention perked up when the kid rode into the fort. No man paid that kind of attention to a boy without a good reason, and he wasn't sure he bought the whole story Calhan rattled off.

Rubbing his jaw, he shook his head. For a skinny kid, Willie packed a surprising punch. If she were Rebecca, Finnegan did a hell of a job training her.

He lost sight of Officer Calhan an hour after they

left the fort and didn't pick up his trail for hours. As he circled in the general direction, Calhan appeared and rode toward the fort. Finlay waited under a large tree, sifting through his head for a reason to be here should the other man notice his presence. But he didn't, to Finlay's utter relief.

He spent a good deal of time backtracking the other officer, hoping to find a cabin or any trace of the Van Rassner's. But no luck. Around three in the morning, a wolf howled, and his mount danced with restlessness. Rather than wait around to see what happened, he turned back to the fort. A full moon filtered through the trees and lit his way back.

Calhan had no idea he could find his way through the forest and bushes. And he didn't plan to let him find out, either. Pretending to be green kept him from being a suspect if things didn't pan out the way he planned. In his line of work, a second plan came in handy. He rode through the gates of the fort as the first fingers of dawn lit up the sky. Anxious for sleep, he rode toward the mounted police's area and swore. In his hurry to follow the other officer, he forgot all about the report Calhan ordered him to present at breakfast.

He'd tack on an extra ten thousand pounds to his fee. Genova could damn well pay for the inconveniences he suffered. Beginning with Calhan. A sly smile crossed his face as he approached the stable and drew to a stop. Fingers recruited the stable master before his premature death. The man could earn his keep by preparing the report while Finlay took a quick nap. Dismounting, he strode through the stables to the back room and pounded on the door. "Get up, you lazy piece of shit. I have a job for you."

The man grumbled but knew better than to argue.

He gave his report the next morning as required and spent the next few weeks following Officer Calhan.

Then, one night, he caught a whiff of smoke and found the cabin. Calhan's horse stood outside, tied to the post, and all the candles were blown out. Walking on silent feet, he peeked in each window until he stopped dead in his tracks.

Two feet from his smiling face, Calhan held a slim woman in his arms and rocked into her naked, gleaming body. Satisfaction rippled through his like a climax. He found her. Carlton Genova would be pleased, and his stay in this frozen wasteland would soon be over.

He left as quickly as he came and hurried back to the fort.

Leaving a note for Calhan informing him he left for Fort Providence and would return in a few days, he rode out early the next morning. His boss would know the good news by breakfast tomorrow.

****

Mr. Genova folded the telegram and smiled at his old secretary. Anticipation and bloodlust shone in his gleaming black eyes.

Revenge tasted sweeter than raspberry tarts and much more satisfying. Two more traitors to go before his dreams became reality, and he couldn't wait.

Glancing up at the gilded ceiling in his office, he held his crystal-cut glass high and made a toast.

"Here's to you, *Dad*. I hope you're watching from hell as I rid the world of your stench. You believed you left my *sisters*—" He sneered as he said the words, "protected and safe. But you didn't count on my cunning. Only Eloise and Molly's daughter, Rebecca, are left." He laughed out loud. "And I just found Rebecca."

Closing his eyes, Carlton envisioned the old man shaking a furious fist in his face, and he reveled in the gratification the image gave him. If he focused, he could still hear the plea for mercy from the last family member he caught, and his breath quickened. He revisited Louise's terror often before he drifted off to sleep.

His secretary paled and shuffled backward as if what he read on the boss' smiling face terrified him.

"Inform Mr. Finlay he is to keep the girl under observation, but he is not to touch her until I arrive. I will handle Miss Van Rassner and her father. Pack my things and get me on the next train north. My fortune awaits." He snapped his fingers to emphasize his impatience, and the old man stumbled in his haste to reach the door.

Carlton smiled and downed the rest of his whisky in two swallows.

Once he killed Molly's daughter, the other sister would be no trouble. He ordered her death two days ago and expected good news any minute. Rising to his feet, he strolled through the vast home that once belonged to his father, humming a popular tune. In a few weeks, he would be master of his heart's desire. Murder, revenge, and gold, glorious gold.

Chapter Sixteen

Over the next few weeks, Max came every three or four days, depending on when he could leave the fort undetected. Officer Finlay didn't have any new leads on the second thief for lack of activity. The robbing stopped as suddenly as it began, and Max wondered why. Even the handwritten IOUs offered no new clues. The ink and paper were standard, and no one recognized the handwriting.

Max sighed and sipped his beer. He studied the saloon and wished he were in Lilli's bed. The Cuban cigar proved to be more popular than he anticipated. Twelve soldiers smoked the exact ones due to an unexpected shipment around Christmas. Patrol logs yielded no results, either. None of the soldiers smoking cigars were on any patrol before the murder. Nothing changed in the last month but his feelings for Lilli.

Every time he took her in his arms, the experience rocked him to the soles of his standard-issue boots. She occupied his mind and his dreams every hour of the day. And he couldn't wait until the next time he visited her cabin.

They came together in a blaze of passion and melted in the flames of desire. They became one in the dark and gloried in the perfection of their joining until he couldn't think of anything but her and how she made him feel.

The problem was Frank. Though they worked hard

to get his addiction under control, the older man figured out how to get more. He worried about her father as he swirled his whisky in his glass. One breakthrough would be nice about now. The more he wanted to be with Lilli, the more the solution eluded him. Commander Jorgensen grew impatient for an answer, and he did as well.

But Max couldn't shake the feeling he missed something. He interviewed everyone he could think of and found no new clues about the murderer's identity. And all the while, Lilli and Frank could be in trouble. The stone in his chest hardened whenever he pictured her in danger, and he couldn't shake the feeling of impending evil.

The last time he visited Lilli, he bent to pick up his boot and discovered two IOUs under her bed. White-hot anger pumped through him. Lilli and her father had a hard enough time making ends meet. He held the notes up. "Why didn't you tell me the bastard got to your fur too?"

Every ounce of color drained from her face. "I, uh. It's my problem. You have enough to worry about." She bent to retrieve her breeches, and he got distracted by the enticing view of her behind for a few seconds.

He didn't agree with her assessment. "I'll find him, and when I do, he'll pay for hurting you and every other trapper in my division." Tucking the notes in his pocket, he shook his head. "I want your word you'll leave this thief to me. Don't go hunting him like you did the last one. It's too dangerous."

She turned to study his face. "Okay."

He let the matter drop and took his leave.

January disappeared, and in the first two weeks of February, the sun came out, melting the snow. Hoping no new storms dropped more on the crime scene, Max planned to leave early and go over the area where patrol found the victim one more time. Perhaps a new clue lay beneath the blanket of white, and with the snow melting, he had high hopes. Wishing something would happen in either case, he rose to his feet and sauntered to the door. For years afterward, he would remember his wish and the evening that followed, which brought the beginning of the end.

Twice over the past three months, he caught Officer Finlay on his back trail. When he questioned the other man, he produced a plausible excuse, but Max got the feeling he lied for whatever reason. Taking extra precautions, he made sure he covered his tracks whenever he visited the Rossi's.

He met Finlay on his way out of the dining area following breakfast. The other man hadn't been to bed yet. "You find anything new?" He faced Finlay and took in his rumpled uniform, drooping eyes, and uncombed hair. The scent of alcohol hung like a gray cloud around the man.

"No. More of the same. A couple cabins were robbed upriver. Same method. Same note." He held out two familiar IOUs, and his gaze sharpened as if waiting for a reaction.

Max took the IOUs and glanced at them. One piece of paper had a familiar coffee stain. He met the other man's gaze. "Did you take these out of my room?" He had a desk in the fort's main building, but his private rooms were off-limits.

Finlay shifted feet. "No." He refused to meet Max's eyes and ran his hand through his hair. He looked ready to drop.

"Then where did you get them?" All the IOUs were on the table in Max's room. Eighteen in total. If he discovered the other man poked around in his private rooms, he'd flatten his face and send him back to headquarters in disgrace.

"They were left at the cabins like all the other ones." Finlay's eyes darted to either side as if searching for an escape route.

"And yet, from the sight and smell of you, I'd guess you spent your night in the saloon." He narrowed his gaze. "How did you make it out to the cabins and back so fast? And why aren't you out investigating?" He could see why. The other man drooped with fatigue.

He had no use for the other officer. Out here, a man had to trust his partner to protect his back. And Robert Finlay had no one's interest at heart but his own. He proved the point with his frequent trips to Fort Providence.

The other officer shrugged. "I sent a patrol out. I think the thief must be disguised as one of them, or we would have found him by now."

Max glared. "You sent soldiers to do your job? When did these alleged new robberies occur? I don't see anyone in pursuit, and no alarm has been sounded." He studied the man's face. "If you didn't go out to the cabins, how did you get the notes or know about the new robberies?"

Officer Finlay shrugged. "One of the soldiers."

Lazy officers were a liability. As were liars. He wouldn't know the truth until he counted the notes in his room. Anger pumped through him. "Finding this thief is the reason you were assigned to me and the Northwest Territory. Your position with the Northwest Territory

Mounted Police is probationary. I cannot recommend a man who disappears without warning and wanders off to the bar when he has a job to do. Nor will I recommend a man who doesn't follow orders and passes his responsibility onto others."

The air thickened as the shorter man faced him.

"Follow your assignment, or you're finished." He hoped Finlay planned to take a swing so he could flatten the lazy ass.

"Yes, your grace." The other man gave a mock bow and walked away.

"Officer Finlay, there's a man with Commander Jorgensen asking for you." A private fell into step beside the other officer, and they turned toward the commander's office.

Max shook his head as they walked away.

Honest to God, he'd like to punch Finlay in the mouth. He had the distinct feeling the other officer came north for a different reason. One with no connection to him or the mounted police. The missing girl and her family? If so, who were they, and what were they to him? Max frowned. Finlay always rode north despite being ordered to check cabins to the south. Unless he left for Fort Providence. He should ask more questions about the other man's fascination with cabins to the north.

He turned as a horse whinnied nearby, and a sudden notion struck him. The other officer did make a good point. Mr. Lawson ran the stable and disappeared often over the last few months. He hadn't questioned him yet about his involvement with the murder victim. Suspicion grew. If the thief were a soldier or someone living in the fort, he'd been looking in the wrong direction.

As he saddled his horse, he considered the gleam in

the other man's eyes and wondered what Finlay knew and wasn't telling him. On impulse, he strolled back to his room to count the notes on the table. Sixteen. Tossing the two Finlay handed him onto the table equaled eighteen. They were all accounted for.

Setting them beside his half-written report, he remembered the two notes he discovered beneath Lilli's bed and placed them on the desk, as well. Max grimaced and glanced around his room, checking for any other inconsistency. Everything was in order, but knowing the bastard had been in here made him mad as hell.

He wanted the other man gone. Sitting down, he added a few comments about Officer Finlay to his report, penned his opinion of thieves, and signed his name.

A soldier knocked on the door, informing him Commander Jorgensen wished to speak to him. With a sigh, he rose to his feet. The crime scene would have to wait another hour or two. So much for getting an early start.

The commander offered Max a seat while they discussed the robberies and the murder. One officer smoked the same brand of Cuban cigars and had been on leave the day the patrol found the victim. Commander Jorgensen wanted Max to be present when he questioned him.

They asked about the man's choice of cigars.

"Officer Finlay gave it to me. He said once I smoke a Cuban, all other cigars will taste like nothing but weeds. And he's right." The soldier glanced up. "I didn't want to try it, but all the other men did. The majority wins every time."

Max's gut tightened. "How many soldiers did Officer Finlay give cigars to?" His mind raced with the knowledge and Lilli's dislike of the man. His recruit had a tough time following orders and disappeared on a regular basis. Suspicion danced in his mind.

"My whole company and some of the others. None of us have seen those kinds of smokes before." Clutching his cap in his hands, the young soldier shuffled his feet. "Am I in trouble?"

"No. Not from me." Max rose to his feet. He planned to find Finlay and get some answers. Everything slipped into place in his mind's eye, but he required proof before he made an arrest.

"You're dismissed, soldier." The commander waved the soldier out the door and turned to Max. "There's something else. You wanted to be informed of any new arrivals. A city man arrived earlier this morning with several of his men. I offered them space in the guest quarters, and my men informed me they plan to visit a family he knows in the area. Officer Finlay volunteered to show them around. They left my office a few minutes before you arrived."

Max nodded." Thank you." Saluting, he left the room. He had no idea who these visitors were or why they came. His mind raced with possibility as he considered all the odd times he found Officer Finlay skulking around and the lame excuses he made. Were these men connected to the missing girl or her family? He wanted answers, and he wanted them now. Growling with frustration, he went in search of Officer Finlay.

And found no sign of him anywhere.

After an hour, he gave up. Glancing up, he checked the sun's position. Noon and he hadn't even made it out to the murder site yet.

An hour later, Max climbed from his saddle and

searched for the tree he marked. Studying the hundred-yard radius, he mapped out search squares in his mind. He found nothing until something shiny flashed in the sun. Bending down, he retrieved the copper casing from a lever-action rifle. The standard issue weapon for the Northwest Territory Mounted Police. His gut tightened with both satisfaction and trepidation for being right. Officer Finlay had a lot of explaining to do.

Going over the timeline in his mind, he ticked off the events as they happened to make sure he didn't miss anything.

The murder took place the day following Officer Finlay's arrival at the fort. As he worked through the scenarios until his meeting with the commander earlier in the day, he stopped on Jorgensen's comments about the newcomers. No doubt he went with them. His horse hadn't been in the stalls when Max checked. And he wanted to know why.

****

At two in the afternoon, Lilli held her breath and waited for Officer Finlay to leave the commissary. She didn't like the man and avoided him whenever possible. She sighed with relief when the cocky officer walked away toward the bar, allowing her to carry in her bundles of fur to trade. With the trap robber gone, their fur numbers climbed back, and Mateus took over Papa's part of the process. But not enough to keep her from committing one final sin.

Finlay would report their location to Carlton Genova. She would need money to move them out of her uncle's reach and keep them alive until she came up with another plan.

Half an hour later, she emerged, tucking gold coins

into her pocket. Preferring to do her borrowing after the sun sank, she came early to keep her name off the suspect list. If everyone knew when she visited the fort, when she traded her fur, when she bought medicine, and when she visited Marion, they wouldn't suspect her of robbing the doctor.

She bought enough opium for one week and tucked the packet in her saddle bag. As she tugged the strap tight, Doctor Talan stepped out onto the boardwalk and locked his door.

"Are you leaving?" She gave the older man a wide smile as she climbed into her saddle.

"Yes. There's been an accident. I'll return in a few hours if you need anything else." He hurried off in the direction of the commander's office.

Lilli tucked the information away and clucked to her mare. Riding for Marion's, she decided to visit Charlotte until close to dusk before she borrowed from the doctor one last time. They changed the lock and added more patrols, but she had to do it. She had no choice.

When Charlotte answered the door, she gave Lilli an intense stare and motioned for her to follow. In her room, she told her Officer Finlay cornered her the previous week and asked about Rebecca Van Rassner and her father.

"I told him I knew of no such persons, and he gave me this." She rolled her sleeves up to reveal a burn on her upper arm.

Lilli cried out. "I'll kill him!"

Charlotte shook her head. "I didn't tell, and if you attack him, he'll know I lied."

She could have wept over her friend's bravery. "Did you tell your mother?"

"No." The girl took her hands in hers. "Listen to me. I told you so you know to stay clear of him. I've seen him following Officer Calhan, and I've been scared he'll find your cabin." She paled. "I think he works for your uncle."

Lilli thought so, too. In the same instant, she knew who killed the man the patrol found south of the fort. But how could she tell Max unless she revealed her secrets? He would never look at her the same again.

A lump formed in her throat. The extra tracks she found across the path and near her window belonged to him. "I do, too." She told Charlotte about the tracks. As she whispered the words, her gut tightened.

Her uncle could be on his way to the Northwest Territory even now.

A new worry struck her. "Are you all right, Charlotte? Did he do...anything else?" She had to ask and swallowed hard as she waited for the answer. If he laid one finger on her friend, she'd cut his manhood off with her knife.

"No. But he frightens me." She frowned and squeezed Lilli's hands. "If your uncle knows you're here, does that mean you're leaving?"

Heartache shot through her with the force of lightning. "Yes. Unless I find him before he finds me. If I don't, he'll kill Papa and me." Swallowing the pain, she smiled at her friend. "And anyone who helped us. Including you and your mother. But I won't let it come to that. I'll take care of all of this. Don't worry, and I'm sorry about your arm. You're the dearest friend anyone could ask for. And so brave. I don't know how to thank you for all you've done for me."

Charlotte's eyes filled with tears. "Be careful. I can't

bear to think of anything happening to you."

"It won't." Charlotte's news accelerated her plans. She must get what she came for and get back to Papa. Giving her friend a quick hug, she left through the back door and hurried to the doctor's office. Once she had Papa's opium, she would find Max and tell him what Finlay did to Charlotte. He would keep the other officer busy while she dealt with her uncle.

Chapter Seventeen

With her mind racing over possible scenarios, Lilli picked the door, took what she came for, and closed the door behind her.

A soldier yelled, "Hey you! What are you doing by the doctor's back door? What do you have in that bag?"

Glancing up, she swallowed and ducked around the corner. She'd been so occupied she strolled out in plain sight!

If they caught her, Max would find out her terrible secret, and the notion scared her more than facing her uncle. She envisioned him giving her the same narrow gaze he gave the first thief and shivered. She couldn't bear the prospect and would rather die by her uncle's hand than face Max's disillusionment. Frowning over her thoughts, she probed the wound and discovered the cause.

She loved him!

Somehow, during Papa's sickness and her frayed existence, she'd fallen head over heels for the kind, handsome officer with the gorgeous blue eyes.

Shock rippled through her as she hugged the side of the commissary. Images of the many nights he held her, the tenderness of his touch, and the way he made her feel special raced through her mind. How could she not love him when he held her so tight, listened to her rambling, helped her with Papa, and made love to her so thoroughly she became part of him? For the first time since her mother's death, she was whole, loved, and complete.

God, what a mess.

Peeking around the corner to gauge her chance for escape, she bit back an exclamation of despair. Soldiers swarmed the area, and Max's room stood a hundred feet to her left.

She had to let him know about Finlay so he could protect Charlotte in her absence. For her friend had one thing correct—if Carlton Genova knew their location, they must leave. And quickly.

One good thing about this whole situation, no one would search for the thief in Max's room, giving her time to gather her wits. Charlotte told her Max left the fort a couple hours ago, traveling south. He must be going out to recheck the murder site now the snow melted. He mentioned his desire to do so a few nights ago when he held her in his arms.

With him gone, she'd have time to leave him a note about Charlotte and Officer Finlay. Making sure no one witnessed her movements, she worked her way along the side of the building.

Keeping to the shadows, Lilli ran up the two steps to the door and stepped inside. The room smelled like Max, and she groaned as memories of being in his arms assaulted her. God, what she'd give to be there right this minute. But she never would again if he discovered her secret.

She leaned against the door and listened to the noise outside. After a few minutes, she glanced around the room and took note of a stack of papers. The top paper gave a detailed report of the robberies, listing times and places. Her name leaped from the page as the thief, and the report bore Finlay's scrawling signature. He didn't know about Papa and blamed her for all of it. Lilli closed her eyes as the room shrank and darkness enveloped her. The end of her existence loomed over her head.

Her gaze dropped to Max's report and focused on the last paragraph.

I will have the guilty party in custody before the end of the day. A hanging will take place within the week. Thievery will not be tolerated, no matter who the propagator is. No person has the right to relieve another of their property and shall find swift judgment. Officer Finlay was in charge of the investigation while I focused on the murder. More will follow on this subject. I know who the thief is. Once this matter is put to rest and the guilty party is buried, I anticipate a leave of absence.

She couldn't swallow. Nor could she breathe. Her eyes dropped to several IOUs on the table beside the damning report, and her entire world crashed down on her.

Max already knew!

Officer Finlay's voice broke through her thoughts. "The thief went that way! I saw a figure beside the commissary a few minutes ago."

She blinked back her emotions as shock rippled through her. The room swayed around her, and she gripped the table to stay upright.

Lilli plucked Finlay's damning report from the table and flung it into the fire. She experienced a small flicker of satisfaction as the flames licked the paper to ashes. Then she threw all her IOUs in too. The less evidence of her guilt, the better.

Disaster threatened her from every direction, and despite her promise to Charlotte, she couldn't stay.

Somehow, she must get to Papa without being discovered and get them all to safety. Then, she'd think about Max and what life without him would mean. Being with him meant the hangman's noose, and a more horrifying thought never existed. Glancing up, she prayed her mother would intervene and closed her eyes for the briefest moment.

Quickly, she wrote her note about Charlotte and left, keeping to the shadows. One soldier almost caught her, but she ducked behind a barrel until the activity died down.

"Close the gates! Don't let the thief leave!" one man yelled, and feet ran toward the front gate.

Rounding the corner of the commissary, she caught sight of Officer Finlay hurrying toward the stables and stepped back into the shadows. Gripping the bag of borrowed medicine from the doctor, she waited until the man left. Her mare stood inside the stables a hundred feet away. Her heart beat loudly in her head, and her knees wobbled as she forced her breathing to slow. She could do this one more time. When the silence stretched for several minutes, Lilli sucked in a breath of courage before leaving her hiding place.

Slipping between the commissary and the stable, she hurried inside to her mare. Tucking her ill-gotten gains into her side to avoid detection, she walked through the open door and into the stable master. Surprised, she side-stepped with her head down and mumbled an apology, which turned to a cry when he caught her by the arm. Tossing her bag of stolen medicine into the stall behind her, she glanced up and stiffened.

An evil grin crossed his face. "I caught ye now, and I'll get the reward Genova offers for ye."

Her brain added up his comments, and the sum made her frown. Two words stood out—

Genova and *reward.* Doubling up her fist, she drew back to strike, and everything turned black. She fell to the ground in a heap.

****

Dim light from a flickering candle on a rough wooden wall met her gaze. The musty scent of stale air and the pungent odor of unwashed flesh made her wince. Her wrists were tied behind her, and she lay on a hard wooden bench.

Turning her head toward the low murmur of male voices, she froze.

The stablemaster spoke with Officer Finlay in the corner, and her heart sank.

"Welcome to my cabin, Miss Van Rassner." Mr. Lawson's lips curled in a sneer when he said her name, and she sucked in a breath.

"I don't know what you're talking about." She sat up and lifted her chin with pride at the way she kept her voice steady.

Officer Finlay chuckled. "We know who you are. Denying it will do you no good. Lawson wouldn't believe me when I told him about you and Calhan doing the blanket hornpipe in your cabin at night while your father sleeps in the other room."

"You have me mistaken with someone else." She used her deepest voice and added a healthy dose of disgust. Her heart threatened to choke her. Finlay followed Max as she suspected. Shrugging, she glanced away as if uninterested in the conversation. She allowed her gaze to wander around and discovered she sat in a small one-room cabin heaped with dirty dishes, dried food, and filthy men's clothing. A lone unmade bed stood against one wall, and a tiny two-person table sagged under the weight of dirty dishes in the center of the rough wooden floor. She fidgeted with her jacket, sliding it up so she could reach under the slit in the back to her knife hidden in a special pocket.

Then Officer Finlay blocked her view. "Is that so?"

Before she could guess what he planned, he yanked on the neck of her shirt and sent buttons flying in every direction.

"Get your hands off me, you filthy twat!" She roared with anger, wishing her hands were free so she could knock the ass on his.

He gave an evil chuckle and slid the blade of a knife under the edge of her chemise. "Ever see a kid wear one of these?" With a twist of his wrist, he slit through her delicate new chemise and binding. Her breasts tumbled out, to the delight of both men. "You were saying?"

Lilli swore and bucked against her bindings. "If my hands were free, I'd teach you what happens when you touch someone without their permission." Images of Charlotte's burn raced across her mind, and her earlier rage returned with a vengeance.

The officer sneered. "Your little charade is over. Did I mention your uncle arrived at the fort this morning, and I drew him a map to your cabin?" Delight spread over his leering face.

Horror raced down her spine. Now she understood the gnawing feeling she had in her gut when she woke this morning.

Carlton Genova was here!

She couldn't get enough air, and her heart beat so hard and fast she feared it would burst through her ribs.

"Stay calm, Lilli. Keep a clear head. That's the only way to outthink the bastard." Papa's training echoed in her ears.

Dropping her chin, she took a deep, shaky breath. She *could* do this. Shaking her head to clear her mind of the grisly reenactment of her mother's murder, she shrugged as if uninterested in the conversation.

"Mr. Genova ordered me to entertain you while he took care of your father. He's doing clean up at the cabin, and you're going to wait here until he gets back." He traced a line down her cheek with the tip of his right pointer finger." I hope you said everything you should to your papa because you won't get another chance. Not in this life." He chuckled. "Get comfortable. Your uncle has a surprise for you." His gaze dropped to her naked chest. "I might, too."

She bet he did. But she had one for them as well. Refusing to dwell on his comments about her father or surrender to her fear, she swallowed and lifted her chin. Papa had a few tricks in his bag, and wouldn't be an easy kill. "Go ahead. If you want to die."

"I keep imagining Calhan's face when I tell him I took you hard before your uncle killed you." Finlay dropped his finger to her neck and down to circle around one nipple.

Lilli sucked in a breath to calm her raging fury. "You don't frighten me." She lifted her chin in challenge as she twisted her wrists together. She lengthened her fingers to the handle of the blade. "Papa is smarter and stronger than you think. Carlton Genova doesn't stand a chance. As for me? Touch me again and see what happens."

Officer Finlay laughed in her face. "Is this the same

man who hasn't been off his bed in months? The one who requires all the opium you steal from the doctor? Your uncle has three seasoned killers with him. Who do you think won?"

Her heart lodged in her throat, and fear beaded on her forehead. *He knew about Papa's sickness!*

She tugged on the handle of her knife and lifted it free.

Finlay leered at her. "I've been following you for weeks now. I know about Officer Calhan's trips to your bed. You must be something under the covers for him to hurry out to you like he does. But don't worry. He won't miss you once he reads my report."

He didn't know Max had already read his report.

Her heart thumped so loud she worried he'd hear it. She couldn't allow emotion to surface, or she'd drown in the depths of her sorrow and misery. Lilli put a neutral expression on her face as she turned the knife in her hand. She tried not to think of Max and what he must think of her, or of Papa and what he might be going through at this exact moment. Finlay must be silenced. Without Papa or Max, she had no one and didn't plan to give either of the men facing her a reaction.

"As for touching you…" His hand dropped to the tie on the front of his breeches. "You hold her for me, Lawson, and I'll hold her for you."

The blade sliced through the tight twine-like paper and fell to the floor. Anger and fear raced through her, pumping her full of adrenaline. She shot to her feet, surprising the gloating officer. He staggered as she planted a foot in his stomach and kicked.

Recovering his balance, he roared and launched toward her, striking her face.

He missed when she stepped back.

She thrust upward with the knife, plunging the blade between his ribs.

Surprise, admiration, and then fear flashed in his eyes as he fell to the floor.

Lilli glanced around as Mr. Lawson rushed toward her. She threw a chair at his head and dove for the door.

He caught her before she made it two feet and swung her around to face him.

She grabbed the handle of a frying pan from the nearby table and hit him over the head. The big man dropped like a sack of grain, hitting the corner of the table as he fell. Blood pooled beneath his head. Shooting a glance at Finlay to make sure he couldn't chase her, she ran out of the cabin and threw up all over the ground. The sight of blood still made her sick. Even evil blood.

Finlay groaned behind her and then grew still.

Lilli raced to the hitching post, untied the nearest horse, and swung into the saddle. Kicking the horse with both heels, she raced away as if all the wolves in the forest were on her heels.

Half an hour later, she stopped and glanced down at her ruined shirt. The cold made her shiver. Or was it shock?

Trembling with reaction, she took stock of her situation. Buttoning the heavy jacket, she thanked God they didn't remove the item, or they would have found her knife. And taken it. She vomited again when she considered what would have happened if they had.

Would they hang her for killing a Northwest Territory Mounted Police Officer? She had no one to verify her story of self-defense. With her thievery the subject of everyone's attention, she might not get the sympathy she deserved for killing Finlay.

Lilli bit her lip as her mount side-stepped.

The officer seemed certain her uncle killed Papa. No doubt he came to do so, but did he succeed?

She glanced north toward danger and then south at freedom.

Several hours passed since her uncle rode to the cabin. She had no hope of getting there before him. Her father had planned for this moment for years and would have an escape plan in place. At least, the old papa would. The sick one, she didn't know about.

An image of her father as she left him this morning flashed through her mind. Groggy, glassy-eyed, and disoriented, he lay on his bed and stared at the opposite wall. He ignored her questions and admonitions to be careful and grunted when she kissed him goodbye. Pale, thin, and unmoving, nothing about him resembled the man who fathered her.

Indecision tightened her chest. Which way?

She glanced up at the starry sky. "Mama, show me what to do."

Chapter Eighteen

Lilli closed her eyes and fought for control while she raced toward the fort. After all this time, her uncle found them. In Papa's weakened condition he didn't have a snowball's chance in July of fighting off her uncle's men.

After the incident in Winnipeg, Papa made her promise to run away as fast as she could if her uncle found and cornered them.

"I'll keep them busy. Your job is to get away as far and as fast as you can." His deep voice brooked no argument.

"But they'll kill you." She could barely get the words past the lump in her throat.

"Then I die knowing I saved you. If you come, they win. Make my sacrifice count." He wore as serious of an expression as she'd ever seen.

Lilli argued with him for two hours and ended up giving her word. She didn't like it now any more than she did then and swallowed. Grief constricted her throat, and she blinked back her tears. Under normal circumstances, she'd run to Max for comfort and advice. But now she couldn't even do that. Were she to meet him face to face, she'd see disappointment and judgment in his eyes right before he arrested her. Nausea rose in her throat. She knew his views on stealing and shuddered.

She also stabbed a Northwest Territory Mounted

Police officer and didn't know if her blow had been fatal. If he died, she'd be tried for murder. An act she knew wouldn't be overlooked and one more reason to put some distance between her and Max.

If Finlay lived, he'd tell Max about her. Then, he'd know where to come to arrest her, and she would have no more places to hide. Every direction she looked, she lost.

And Papa. How she would miss him and the time they spent together. Wiping tears from her eyes, she approached the fort with trepidation. Carlton Genova made sure he killed every person connected to his victims. She had no idea how many men came with him and what their orders were. She had to warn Marion of the danger.

Feeling more alone than she ever had, she slipped to the ground outside the walls and let Lawson's horse loose. The less evidence tying her to Lawson, Finlay, and the incident in the cabin, the better. She had enough guilt on her shoulders.

The gates were closing, and the last bit of traffic for the night waited in line. Lilli slipped into the back of a waiting wagon and drew a rug over her body. The soldiers questioned the owners about their business at the fort and warned them about a thief believed to be within the walls.

The man with the wagon had trading to do the next morning, and they allowed him entrance. She breathed a sigh of relief as the wagon rolled forward. When they stopped, Lilli slipped out of the wagon bed and made her way to Marion's, keeping to the shadows.

In the background, one of the soldiers yelled they found a riderless horse dripping with lather, and the gate burst into new activity.

Charlotte answered at the first knock and stared at Lilli. "What happened? You look awful."

"I am awful. My uncle's men are here. Finlay gave them directions to our cabin earlier today. He said Papa's dead. They'll come for me as soon as they discover I'm not there. I must leave as quick as I can." She slid the latch closed and followed Charlotte to the kitchen, where Marion prepared dinner. "But first, I must speak with your mother."

The kind woman wiped her hands and gave Lilli a warm hug. "Tell me what's happened."

And she did. From start to finish, she confessed Papa's true condition, his thievery, and her lies to cover what they did.

"Once I get my inheritance, I plan to pay back every person. I won't sleep at night until I do. I know what I did is wrong, and I will make all of it right. But first, I must escape before my uncle's men find me." Her voice died away, and after several long moments of silence, Lilli risked a glance at Marion's face. "There's something else. Carlton Genova kills every person connected to his victims. The whole fort knows Papa and I stay here. And Finlay already approached Charlotte. You're not safe. Neither one of you. Not even here, surrounded by soldiers." She dug in her pocket and withdrew the coins she collected earlier with her fur. "Take this and go first thing in the morning. My uncle's men will chase me first before they circle around to find you, so you have time. But you must promise to leave before evening. Your lives depend on it."

"I see." Pale as frost, Marion clutched trembling hands in her lap. Tears slipped down her cheeks, and her knuckles grew white. Turning her head to stare into the fire, she wiped her tears away with the back of her hand.

"The old Papa would have given the killers a good fight, but the one addicted to opium couldn't even stand up to a stiff breeze. He made me promise to escape if this ever happened. But now I'm worried about you. If…" She swallowed hard, not wanting to say the words but knowing she must, and started again, "Will you give this to one of the soldiers to see Papa is buried in a proper manner?" Taking her last two coins out, she placed them on the table beside her.

The older woman's chin came up." Of course." She hesitated. "He told me if anything happened to him, I should give you the letters." Pale as the moonlight shining down on the fort, she rose to her feet.

"I thought Papa had them." Someone sent her father information, but she didn't know who.

"No. I do. He didn't want anyone to find them if they found him. They would lead to you and whoever is helping him." Marion turned away and left the room. Several minutes passed before she returned with a packet of letters tied with a string. "They come once a month from Frank's associate in New York. They may contain useful information to help you escape." A small smile turned her mouth up. "And how to get home."

Lilli took the bundle with shaking hands. Reaction to the events of the day caught up to her like a runaway locomotive. "Thank you, Marion, for everything. For being so kind to Papa. And to me." She swallowed hard. "One other thing, if Officer Calhan asks, you know nothing." Forcing the words past the knot in her throat, she rose to her feet. "Promise me you'll leave first thing. I couldn't bear to be the cause of your deaths, too." The weight on her shoulders increased, and she buckled under the strain. Giving Marion and Charlotte a quick hug, she turned to the door. "I must leave before I am discovered."

The older woman frowned. "How? The gates are closed for the night, and the soldiers are busy searching for the thief." She rose to her feet and glanced out her little window. Her chin trembled. "We will hide you until morning, and then we will all go on the first boat to Fort Providence." Although her voice remained firm, her movements were short and jerky. She bit her lip and cleared her throat. "Your uncle won't have time to find you. Or us."

A man's boots came down the wooden walk and stopped outside the door.

Marion's face drained of color, and Lilli held her breath.

Charlotte put a hand to her throat and sucked in a breath. All three women stared at the closed door and waited.

He knocked with a short rap and then tried the latch.

Three pairs of eyes stared at the closed door.

The man knocked again.

Wiping terror from her forehead with the back of her hand, Lilli scanned the other two women's faces. "Go hide. Don't come out no matter what you hear. I'll talk to whoever this is. And don't hide under the bed. Any villain with intelligence would search under there the very first thing."

The man on the other side of the door shook the latch again. After a moment or two, the boots walked away, and the three women gave a sigh of relief.

It was short-lived.

Two minutes later, another knock sounded on the door. "Willie."

Lilli tip-toed to the door. "Who is there?" Fear broke out on her forehead and dripped down her cheek.

"Mateus." The deep voice penetrated the silence of the room.

Lilli blew out a breath of relief, and after Marion nodded permission, she unlatched the door. "Come in."

The older man stepped into the room and glanced around at the three women. His black peppered hair gleamed in the firelight as he tilted his head and whispered to Lilli. "All dead." His eyes glowed with compassion. Twisting his hat around in his hand, he nodded at Marion and Charlotte.

"There may be more." She couldn't breathe. Nodding her head in his direction, she swallowed hard. "I must leave the fort."

"I will take you downriver tonight. Come." He held a leathered hand out to her. "With me, you are safe."

Turning to gaze at her last two friends, she smiled. "I'll be in touch."

****

When Max arrived back at the fort, the gates were closing for the night. Soldiers patrolled the area in greater numbers than usual. Every wagon in and out got searched because of a robbery earlier. One of the soldiers motioned for him to come over to the area beside the stable. "We tracked the thief this far. We don't know where he went from here." The man walked around searching for more clues.

"Have you considered Mr. Lawson might be the thief? Your tracking led you here. I'm willing to bet you will find the stolen goods hidden in the stable somewhere." Max nodded.

The man had to be involved, and this proved him right. He glanced at the soldier. "Get some of the others to help you, and let me know what you find." He paused. "Any sign of Officer Finlay?" The sooner the cocky junior officer left his command, the better. The other man disappeared. Again.

"No, sir." The soldier motioned toward the stable. "His horse is gone."

The man glanced his way. "The Rossi kid's horse is in there. Do you think he's involved?"

"No. The kid is too busy taking care of his dad and their traplines to get into too much mischief." He gazed at Lilli's mare and frowned. Why would she be here this late? *Unless she came to see him.* "When you find Officer Finlay, let me know." He didn't doubt the soldiers would have Mr. Lawson in custody before the night ended.

"Yes, sir."

Suddenly, in a good mood at the prospect of seeing Lilli, he saluted the soldier and strolled toward his rooms. He couldn't wait to take her clothes off and climb into bed.

With the proof he had in his pocket, he could arrest Officer Finlay for murder. With both investigations over, he could put in his paperwork for a release. He considered staying with the police for the rest of his life until he met a skinny kid named Willie. With his mind on courting Lilli, he strolled into his room a few minutes later and stopped.

Someone had been in here.

His gaze swept the room and dropped to his desk. His report and the IOUs were gone! Perplexed, he walked to the fire and noted the corner of a burned sheet of paper peeking from beneath the grate. Whoever came burned his report and the thief's IOUs. Scowling, he scoured the room for any other missing items and growled with frustration. The curved knife his father gave him no longer hung on his mantel. No sooner did he catch one thief than another appeared. Unless Officer Finlay had something to do with this. Drawing the latch, he sat on the bed and stared at the room.

And where was Lilli?

Damn, he thought his woman would be here waiting for him. Unless whoever took his blade frightened her away. But why would her horse be here? And who would sneak into his rooms and take his blade?

A memory chased across his mind. He had the blade out one day when Frank and his friend Mateus came to the fort. The native man commented on the blade and asked to examine the weapon. With reverent hands, he stroked the curved blade like a lover before returning it to Max. Did the older man take it?

Max frowned. Who would burn his report and why? Strolling back over to his table, he picked up a small note tucked inside his book. Lilli's fragrance clung to the paper, and his gut tightened. He scanned the note and scowled. Officer Finlay burned Charlotte trying to get information about Lilli. Rage raced through his veins as he left his room and hurried over to Marion's. One more reason to get the man the hell out of the Northwest Territory.

He tried the latch and discovered the door locked. Used to walking inside unannounced, he frowned. When did Marion start locking her door? He tapped again and waited. No sound came from within, and Max scowled again. The other officer better not be inside threatening them. He rattled the latch and knocked again. After another minute of silence, he strolled away. If Lilli were inside the cabin with Marion Adams, she would have answered the door. Where could they all be?

Once he arrested Officer Finlay and made his report, he would ask Lillian Rossi to marry him. Something he swore he'd never do again. Not after Elsie.

But Lilli was different. Poles apart from Elsie. No two women could be more opposite than those two. Light versus dark, weak versus strong, docile versus headstrong, compliant versus stubborn.

Max shook his head. Lilli was loyal, honest, and kind. She'd give her last piece of bread to save a life. Yes, she lied. And in that respect, the two women were alike. But Lilli had good reason. He didn't know if *he* possessed the strength and fortitude to deal with Frank Rossi and his addiction.

And she did it on her own.

Who cared that she made questionable choices? Anyone would under the same circumstances.

He knew she loved him by the way she leaned against him when they walked, the breathless way she said his name when he held her, and the way she smiled at him when they lay together in the dark. Her touch soothed and excited him, and her kisses made him crazy for more. He dreamed about her luscious body and the noises she made when he loved her. He couldn't get her off his mind, and the sooner she admitted her feelings for him, the better.

He never believed he'd find a woman he couldn't live without until he met her. And he didn't plan to let her get away. Frank Rossi might take some convincing, but he'd win in the end. They belonged together. Nothing could be simpler.

Whatever trouble came for the Rossi's, he'd handle, and they'd make a life together wherever Lilli wanted. Satisfied with his vision of the future, he scoured the fort for any sign of Officer Finlay or Lilli.

When he passed the front gate, he paused. Soldiers had one of Lawson's horses by the reins. The animal frothed at the mouth, and his sides were lathered with sweat. His hanging head and labored breathing told Max he'd been running hard.

"Where's the rider?" He stopped in his tracks. His mind raced with possibilities.

"We don't know. One of the men found him outside the gates a few minutes ago. We sent a patrol out to see what they could find."

Lilli, Marion, Charlotte, Lawson, and Finlay—all missing. Running to the stable he saddled his horse and raced for Lawson's cabin. The stable master would know Finlay's whereabouts. If either bastard touched any of the women, he'd kill them both.

At the cabin, he kicked the door in. He found the stable master dead from a blow on the head. One broken chair and rope on the floor had his undivided attention. One victim, not three. This accounted for one woman but where were the other two? His rage rose to new heights when he found the buttons of Lilli's shirt scattered around the broken chair.

What the hell happened here?

His gaze fell on her knife lying on the filthy floor beside a strip of her chemise and her binding. Her clothes were lying in a puddle of blood, and his heart stopped. He would recognize the articles anywhere. Fury raced through him as he bent to retrieve the blade.

He couldn't breathe.

The whole scene played out in Max's mind. Lilli's mare was in a stable back at the fort. Lawson had abducted her, and she escaped, making him pay with his life. So where did she go? And where were Marion and Charlotte? Rising, he stepped outside to investigate the perimeter. He found where Lilli threw up a moment later. Relief swept through him like a tidal wave. No blood accompanied the vomit. She wasn't the one injured.

He knew Lilli had a delicate nature when it came to blood, and there was no doubt in his mind this was where she lost her supper after killing Lawson. Horse tracks raced away to the north and the south at a dead run. The rider going north left a trail of blood and rode Finlay's horse. The rider going south didn't.

The other officer could be anywhere. Wounded, the man wouldn't get far. He'd catch up to him as soon as he made sure Lilli was okay. The other officer had a lot to answer for.

Lilli would go to the fort to find him after the scene at Lawson's. Somewhere, he missed her in the dark.

A full moon lit the countryside, and he thanked the universe for giving him light. Tracking Lawson's horse from the cabin back to the fort, he lost the trail a couple of times and then found it again.

He arrived outside the gates of Fort Simpson at three in the morning. He checked his room, and she hadn't been there. His gut tightened. She had to be at Marion's. He strolled to her cabin and knocked on the door. He wouldn't rest until Lilli was safe and unharmed.

Marion answered his first knock and peeked out, clutching her dressing gown to her chest. "We're both fine, but Lilli's gone. Her uncle is here. The one who wants to kill her." Her chin rose in defense."She had to go away."

Max's heart jumped to his throat. "The men who came to the fort yesterday are Lilli's *relatives*? She told me someone wanted to kill her father. She didn't say they were family." He frowned. "But you're telling me *she's* the one they're after? *She's* the one they want to kill?" Now he knew why Finlay volunteered to show the newcomers around, why he rode north after the situation at the cabin, how he got his wound and his reasons for being in the Northern Territory. Lilli was the girl he came to find.

Marion nodded. "I'm worried." Her chin dropped. "Lilli said Officer Finlay told her they killed Frank. The poor dear broke my heart. You could see her grief nearly killed her. I couldn't sleep a wink." When she glanced back at him, her face lost all color. "I'm wondering if you would go out to the cabin and check on him? But please be careful. Officer Finlay works for her uncle. He asked Charlotte about Lilli and hurt her to make her talk. I think he's been following you."

He swallowed hard. "He has been. I've caught him a couple of times." He glanced at the sky. The sun wouldn't be out for a couple of hours, and he had a lot of ground to cover. "I know what Finlay did, and I'll make sure he never touches her again." God, he wanted to shoot the smug little man right between the eyes. An idea occurred to him. "When did you have this talk with Lilli?"

"Around supper time last night." Marion gripped his arm. "Please help her." Her big brown eyes filled with tears. "Her uncle shot her mother, and he can't kill her, too." In short, terse sentences, she gave a brief description of the tragedy.

Max took a deep breath. "I found blood at Lawson's cabin. Is she hurt?"

"No." She explained about the cabin.

Relief sifted to the bottom of his standard-issue boots. "Where did she go?"

Marion shook her head. "I don't know. She wouldn't say."

In his gut he knew she spoke the truth, and his chest tightened so hard he couldn't breathe.

"She won't come back unless her uncle's gone. Will you arrest him so he can't find Lilli and kill her?" Marion's plea struck him like an ax.

Max nodded. "Yes. And then I'll find her and bring her back. I swear it." He'd do more than arrest the bastard. So much made sense about Frank Rossi and his insistence they keep their identity a secret. "You and Charlotte stay out of sight until I get back. There's no way to tell what these men will do."

"Lilli said the same thing. We are going to Fort Providence on the first boat. She made us promise." Marion clasped his hand. "Thank you. But please don't die. Lilli would never forgive me."

He closed the doors and climbed into the saddle as anger throbbed through his body. Whoever the hell this Genova man was, he just bought a whole heap of trouble.

Chapter Nineteen

Max reined to a stop beside a giant oak and swallowed the ache in his throat. He couldn't believe what he saw. He stared at the bloody scene surrounding the cabin across the clearing. Silent and foreboding in the morning sun, the hum of flies and the scent of death made his eyes water.

A body lay beside the window in an unnatural position. Max frowned. Dear God, what happened here? Drawing his weapon, he raced across the clearing and paused when he caught sight of Officer Finlay. The man lay on the path between the house and the barn with his throat ripped out. His eyes stared up at the sky, and his face wore an expression of terror.

Rossi's dogs didn't do this. Large paw prints six inches across circled the body and disappeared into the forest. Wolf.

Why weren't the dogs going crazy? Striding into the barn, he stilled. All ten dogs were dead, still corralled in their stalls.

Max leaned against the barn to get control of his emotions. The silence made his heart beat louder in his chest. These men were ruthless and as cold-blooded as lizards. They killed everything and everyone.

Returning to Finlay, Max sank to his haunches and studied the body. The man had two stab wounds. Both were in the chest, but one had been made with a curved blade. A blade like his. The other was made by Lilli.

The larger wound looked nastier. Slid between his ribs like a professional fighter, the killer must have struck his heart.

He followed the trail of blood through the trees with his gaze. The other officer must have come upon the cabin unaware the wolf followed the trail of blood left by Lilli's knife. The wolf's tracks walked on top of Finlay's.

Max's gaze narrowed. Someone surprised the other officer by bursting out the back door and stabbing him with the curved blade. Too weak to fight, Finlay turned and fell to his knees before the waiting wolf pounced. The animal tore his throat out before he could draw his weapon and fire.

Max frowned to the depths of his soul. He wanted to arrest the bastard and make him pay for what he did to Lilli and Charlotte. But as deaths go, having his throat torn out by a wolf would have to suffice. Lifting his revolver, he tapped on the cabin door with the barrel.

No sound came from within.

Cracking the door, he peeked inside. Nothing moved as he stepped through the door. His heart thumped in his chest at what he might see once he searched the cabin, and he swallowed hard. Keeping his back to the wall, he stepped around two more bodies, both stabbed with a curved blade, before entering the living area.

Frank Rossi lay dead in his chair. An elegant man dressed in a gray woolen suit lay in a heap on the floor beside the chair. They both had guns resting at their sides.

Cold sweat broke out on Max's forehead. Gripping his revolver with trepidation, he opened Lilli's door with his foot. Closing his eyes for a second to gather strength, he ignored the stone in his gut and walked inside.

He didn't believe she'd run from a fight and worried she would come to this one. He thanked the universe she hadn't.

Her clothes were missing from the hooks on the wall. Frowning, he stared at her room. When did she have time to pack? Unless someone did it for her. He found Mateus' tracks all over the area outside.

Strolling over to her chest, he lifted the lid and froze.

There, inside a small basket, sat a sheaf of familiar parchment and a bottle of ink. A half-written IOU had been stuffed beside the feather quill. All this time, he suspected Lawson, never her.

Max sat back on his heels in disbelief as memories flitted through his mind. He remembered Lilli showing up when he arrested the first thief and the surprise on her face when she caught sight of him. The day he discovered her father's wet boots beside the door when Frank hadn't been out of bed for weeks came to mind and her excuse. The two IOUs he found under her bed popped up next. He remembered her pale face and trembling hands when she faced him.

Why didn't he see the obvious? He ran a hand over his face as he realized how close he had come to catching her on several occasions. And her book. She wrote in the thing every night before blowing out her candle. He glanced at the shelf beside her bed. The empty shelf. She must have taken the diary with her wherever she went.

Swallowing hard, he dropped his head. Why hadn't she trusted him enough to confide in him? The insult struck deep. He would have produced a solution. He let out a deep sigh and set the parchment back inside the trunk.

He'd find her. One way or another.

Wandering back into the living area, he placed a blanket over Frank Rossi's body and closed the door on his way out. A detail of soldiers would bury the bodies, and he'd make sure Frank had a decent burial. He spent some time studying the tracks around the house and yard until he figured he knew what happened. The strangers rode up to the cabin and took up defensive positions. They breached the cabin and waited.

Max sucked in a deep breath. They waited for Lilli.

Thank God she didn't come.

After several minutes, he resumed his inspection of the area.

Finlay rode in, followed by the wolf. An unknown assailant, possibly Mateus, killed the two outside guards and one inside the cabin with Max's curved blade. The man in the woolen suit and Frank shot each other. Which left Officer Finlay standing outside the back door. And he knew what happened to him.

The unknown assailant had small feet for a man and walked on the balls of his feet. He used the blade with precision and accuracy, impressing the hell out of Max. And whoever the assailant was, he still had possession of the blade.

Mounting his horse, Max rode back to the fort. Perplexed about Lilli's whereabouts. Where would she go? Finlay told her they killed her papa so she wouldn't come back here. Not with her uncle in the area. Did she know he died?

Her mare stayed at the fort all night and all day. Wherever she went, she didn't take her horse and left the fort sometime before the gates closed the previous evening, according to Marion.

He figured the deaths at the cabin occurred sometime after dark. How else would a wolf sneak up on someone without them knowing?

The mystery of who stole his curved blade and killed her uncle's men remained unsolved.

Max discovered the silver-haired man in the woolen suit was Carlton Genova. A cutthroat businessman who had a reputation for violence. His superiors considered the man's death a mark of excellence for the entire mounted police force and offered him a medal. Which Max declined. He wanted answers, not decorations. He understood the reason Lilli robbed the doctor. Medicine for her father's leg and his addiction to the drugs had to be expensive. She couldn't provide the number of furs required to keep them both alive and pay for medical bills.

Max sighed. He could even understand her reluctance to talk about her past. Being present at her mother's murder had to be the worst nightmare anyone could imagine.

And she lived through it. His superiors updated him on Genova's reputation, and he had witnessed the gore at Frank's cabin. Her father did the only thing he could to keep her safe. Take her as far north as he could and keep her in disguise. And somehow, her bastard uncle found her anyway.

He would have taken precautions if he'd known the truth, and the fact she didn't trust him enough to tell him hurt worse than he imagined.

Everywhere he turned, he met her smiling face and beautiful eyes. He missed her laugh, her husky voice, and her sense of humor. But most of all, he missed holding her in his arms.

Marion and Charlotte didn't have the answers he required. They knew little more than Marion told him before he rode out to the cabin. And when she offered coins for Frank's funeral, he shook his head.

"I'll see to it. Save the money for Lilli. She'll need it."

Frank Rossi had the best burial the Northwest Territory and money could provide. Beside his plot, they buried the dogs he loved so much and burned the cabin to the ground with Carlton Genova and his men inside. The man didn't deserve to have his memory preserved.

Perturbed over the identity of the stolen blade-wielding killer, Max went over every detail in his head.

He knew Lilli had come to his room and left a note about Charlotte. But she didn't take the knife because she didn't go out to Frank's cabin. She didn't have time to.

He suspected Mateus of stealing his curved blade or Finlay. For he had proof the other Mountie had been in his room, and he found Mateus' tracks outside the cabin. But Finlay didn't possess the skill to wield the blade with any degree of success and sported a wound made by said knife.

When he searched out Mateus, he couldn't find him, but the soldiers reported opening the gate for him around nine in the evening. As far as Max could tell, Mateus arrived at the cabin after the killing, although he couldn't find the man to ask him.

Max had no suspects and no Lilli.

He knew why she didn't come to him when she discovered her uncle had arrived at the fort. She read his report and believed he planned to arrest her. Her remedy was to disappear without a trace. Frank Rossi did the same every time Genova found them and taught Lilli everything he knew.

If Max had the chance to talk to her one more time, he'd explain he could never do such a thing. Together, they would have figured it out. If she'd only given him the chance. Which she didn't.

Max ignored the stone in his gut and punched another hole in his belt.

He had no appetite and couldn't sleep even though he drooped with fatigue. The days melted into one another in an endless array of tasteless, colorless, joyless hours of never-ending nothingness.

His superiors issued an order for Willie's arrest for robbing the doctor. And with a heavy heart, Max hung it up at the fort. Every day, he walked by the board and wanted to rip the offending notice off. He loved her and would give his life to keep her from harm. If she'd have him.

And then, as if by magic, velvet bags with money and handwritten apologies appeared in people's barns and houses, paying back the notes Lilli left, all with the initials RVR. He knew Frank robbed the pelts. She robbed the doctor and took responsibility for the lot.

Marion and Charlotte claimed to be in the dark as much as anyone on where the money came from. And Max reported each incident to his superiors with a smile of satisfaction. If he could find her, he'd let her know her uncle died, and she didn't have to run anymore.

For six months, he patrolled the Northwest Territory searching for Lilli and found nothing. No sign could be found of Mateus either. Both individuals disappeared like a mist in the forest. Max never found out who took his blade or where it went despite the hours he spent going over every detail. Whoever killed Genova's men had it still. When he found the blade, he'd find the killer.

For a while, he toyed with the idea Lilli might be the one, but the time limit didn't fit. In between her time at the fort when she robbed the doctor, got abducted by Lawson and Finlay, and then returned to the fort, she didn't have the time to gallop out to the cabin, murder her uncle's men, and then return. Too many witnesses placed her too far away from her cabin to be the murderer. Besides, she didn't have the stomach for it. He would have found vomit everywhere.

And so, the mystery prevailed. His superiors wanted to give the killer a commendation as soon as he discovered the identity. But after six months of searching, he gave up.

When fall rolled around again, he turned in his resignation and paid for a trip to Quebec. From there, he traveled to New York City to spend some time with Connor.

His heart ached with the loss of Lilli, and he concluded some time with his family would help with the pain. And he wasn't disappointed.

Connor had his hands full with his competitor's daughter and her crusade to ruin his shipping business. Max spoke French from his time with the trappers and joined several conversations as an interpreter.

The girl had his brother firmly by the heart, and Max smiled over the fanciful notion. He recognized the expression on Connor's face because his own reflected the same emotion every morning when he gazed into the mirror.

Two weeks after he arrived in New York, his older brother invited him to a party for some heiress.

"No thanks." He would prefer to stay at the house

and enjoy the quiet evening alone.

"Come one. Going out will do you good. You mope around like an old man. If anything, you're grumpier than I am. Maybe some girl will catch your eye, you'll fall in love, and spend the rest of your life following her around with a silly expression like our two younger brothers." Connor smiled and waved at his collection of wool suits. "Take your pick. I know you didn't pack evening wear, and my wardrobe is at your disposal."

He couldn't say no. Connor shot down every excuse until he stood outside a two-story stone house in a wealthy neighborhood dressed in Connor's best navy blue suit and leather shoes. Eyeing the expensive lighting, red carpet, and servants waiting by the front door, he turned to his brother. "Who is this person?"

His brother shrugged. "Rebecca Van Rassner. She came into old money recently after being away for a few years. I agreed to come because having good connections in my business is important. Besides, you need to get out and get over whoever she is."

Max had nothing to say.

They strolled up the stairs and into the elaborate entry hall. Gilded plaster adorned the walls, and thick Persian rugs covered the floor. Liveried servants ushered them down a long, tiled corridor to a massive ballroom flooded with New York's elite. Golden chandeliers hung from a cream and gold ceiling. Gilt-edged mirrors and portraits hung on the silk-covered walls while the gleaming wooden floor reflected the light up above.

Women clothed in every color of silk strolled the room laughing and sipping champagne from glass flutes. Accompanying them were dapper gentlemen in woolen and silk suits with embroidered vests. White shirts with winged collars and darker-colored bowties completed their attire. An orchestra played soft music in the corner, and laughter filled the room. The scent of freshly cut blooms, heavy toilet water, and cigars wafted past.

Déjà vu settled over him, and he resisted the urge to turn around and walk away. If Connor didn't insist they come, he would have stayed behind.

Connor handed Max a glass of champagne from a passing servant. "Let me introduce you to our hostess. I see her over there." He wove his way through the crowd, and Max followed. He didn't like being this close to so many people. Especially wealthy people.

Some inner voice warned him a minute before it happened. Intuition tightened his gut as the people in front of him stepped aside.

And then he saw her.

His heart jumped to his throat and threatened to choke him. Tremors shook his hands and knees. He couldn't believe the vision before his eyes and blinked back his surprise. He chased all over the Northwest Territory searching for her, and she'd been here the whole time.

Her tinkling laugh settled over him like angel dust, making his mouth dry. His gaze swept over the back of her, hungry for more. God, he missed her. His body stiffened in response, and he focused on the back of her head as he followed Connor. He knew the shape of her shoulders, the dip of her waist, and the curve of her hips.

They stopped a foot behind her, and Max couldn't breathe. He caught one whiff of her delicate perfume and froze as memories of her in his arms washed over him. He knew how predators reacted when delicious morsels emerged from the grass upwind. And he had his in his sights.

She stopped talking and straightened. An expectant silence filled the space between them as she turned in slow motion and met his gaze.

"Miss Van Rassner, this is my brother, Max." Connor stopped beside him to make an introduction.

Max's eyes wandered over her beautiful, flushed face and dropped to her soft pink lips. Resisting the urge to take her in his arms, he allowed his gaze to roam her body. God, she personified temptation, smelled like an aphrodisiac, and lured him like a siren to her side. Her beauty increased beyond his ability to withstand, and he came close to dropping to his knees. "Hello."

The crowd disappeared, and they stood alone, staring into each other's eyes.

God, the difference between this vision of feminine splendor and the waif he first met astounded him. Draped in pink silk, her gown clung to her curves like a lover's caress. Her ebony hair, coiffed in the latest fashion, rose high on her head and glinted in the overhead light. Her pink cheeks and delicate complexion gleamed with health. Elegant, dainty, and dripping with jewels, her entire being screamed wealth and privilege. In his mind's eye, he compared her to the baggy breeches-wearing, foul-mouthed youth who scratched his crotch and choked on whisky. And Max couldn't contain his grin.

Her face turned red and then paled. "Hello."

Connor nudged him as he stared from one to the other. "You didn't say you were already acquainted."

Max studied her face. "I'm not sure we are now." He ran his gaze over her luscious figure one more time and noted the blush on her cheeks. "I met her first as Willie, second as Lilli, and now as Rebecca. I would need to know how many more names she answers to before I can determine whether we know each other or not." She astounded him with her diversity, and he had to force his mouth closed so he didn't gape in amazement.

"Just Rebecca." A tinge of pink danced across her cheeks, and her gaze dropped.

Her breathless answer encouraged him, and his grin widened. She wasn't as immune as her lifted chin suggested. He spent months wondering how she would react when they met again given the circumstances.

Max extended his hand. "I am pleased to meet you again, Miss Rebecca Van Rassner." As he said her name, his mind clicked. *RVR. I'll be damned. She sent the money and paid them all back on her own.* He figured Marion knew more than she let on. She must have delivered the mysterious velvet bags to each person on Lilli's list.

He took her cold, trembling fingers in his and raised them to his lips. With slow, deliberate action, he kissed each finger while he stared into her eyes.

A flash of desire raced across her face, and she withdrew her hand from his. Taking a hasty step back, she bumped into the table behind her. "Thank you for coming to my party. If you'll excuse me, I have an important matter to address."

****

Rebecca stared at the refreshment table as her best friend Emily babbled about the different types of wine she enjoyed. Cake, pastries, and fruit punch blurred before her eyes. Staring at the sea of faces around her, she wished she were back in the Northwest Territory in her cabin. She missed the solitude of the forest, the smell

230

of pine trees, and the hot, sweaty nights she spent in Max's arms. Would he ever forgive her for what she did?

A hanging will take place within the week. Thievery will not be tolerated, no matter who the propagator is. No person has the right to relieve another of their property and shall find swift judgment.... Once this matter is put to rest and the guilty party is buried....

Buried. She swallowed and glanced around at New York's elite gossiping in small groups. They didn't know what she did, either.

Not that it mattered. She didn't know ninety-five percent of the people swarming her home. Mr. Astor, Emily's dad, sent the invitations and decided who to invite or not. She'd been away too long to know.

He stopped beside the two girls. "Is everything all right, Rebecca? You look pale." His black peppered hair glinted in the light of the golden chandeliers, and his blue eyes smiled into hers. Dressed in gray wool, he oozed wealth and confidence.

"I am fine." She gave him a wide smile and placed a piece of cake on a small, gilded plate. "I'm just not used to so many people in one place." She had her old life back. And she had the money that came with it. But she lost the man. And none of the eager young men of her acquaintance measured up to Max.

Mr. Astor nodded. "Let me know if you need anything. I'll tell the waiters to inform the guests the party ends at eight. Unless you grow weary beforehand. In which case, I'll make the announcement and ask everyone to leave."

Lilli shook her head. "Eight sounds good."

She studied him as he strolled away to find the head waiter and give his instructions. Mr. Astor met her at the train depot when she arrived and gave her a place to stay until they could meet with her family lawyers. He escorted her to the meeting and stood by while she claimed her mother's wealth.

He had been the trusted source Papa mentioned so long ago, and his last letter to her father confirmed her suspicions. Mr. Astor kept her father informed of Carlton Genova and the situation in New York. The letters Marion handed her on her way out of the fort warned her father of her uncle's plans to visit the Northwest Territory and listed every detail of his dealings with her mother's family.

Only Carlton Genova arrived before the letter and killed her father. Weary and heartbroken, Lilli couldn't remember the boat ride downriver or much of the train ride to Quebec. She'd been too upset about Papa's death, leaving Max, and what her fate would be if he caught her. Somehow, Mateus got her to Fort Providence and onto a train bound for Quebec.

Mr. Astor telegraphed her with news of her uncle's death a week later and wired her money to make the trip home. She didn't know what she would have done without his kindness, support, and help.

She sent the Astors a telegram from the train station in Quebec with her expected time of arrival in New York, and they both met her at the depot.

A sigh escaped the depths of Lilli's being.

Once she settled into her old home, she sent money to Marion and Charlotte. Every individual in her diary received a velvet bag of coins for repayment and a note of apology. She made sure every person she borrowed from received more than the cost of what she took. With every coin she tied into a velvet bag with a note of apology, the weight on her shoulders diminished. Marion's last letter assured her the last bag had been delivered, and the trappers no longer wanted to hunt her down. The wanted poster at the fort with her picture disappeared, and she was free, at least of the robbery charges. She never learned anything about Officer Finlay's death other than the soldiers buried him at the fort.

She jerked back to the present when a tall man with blond hair and broad shoulders strolled past. Her heart collided with her ribs, and the room swung around her head. But the man wasn't Max. Although her heart called to him and her gaze kept watch for his broad shoulders, she doubted she would ever see him again. For she had no plans to go north again. Ever.

Emily made some joke about the whipped cream on her cake, giving her a white mustache, and Lilli laughed.

And then she felt him.

Every muscle in her body tensed, and the hair stood up on the back of her neck. The air around her crackled with awareness, and she couldn't breathe. Gripping her plate until her knuckles turned white, she set it down on the table and took a deep breath.

Turning, she met the object of her dreams and desires, looking more handsome than any man had a legal right to. Her knees clacked together, and her body shook. God, she missed him. Her heart jumped into her throat and threatened to choke her.

She swallowed and allowed her gaze to sweep over his gorgeous body before she tangled with his blue eyes. Desire and knowing burned in his blue depths. Plucking a glass from a passing waiter, she downed the champagne in one long swallow. She had to get the hell out of there before her emotions fell all over the floor in front of him. His heart-breaking smile made her heart do double time, and her belly flutter with awareness. She knew how a body starved of food would eye a first meal and licked her dry lips.

Did he come to arrest her? Anxiety broke out on her forehead as she risked another glance at his face. But his eyelids dropped over his eyes, hiding his expression. He didn't look like a man seeking justice.

Then he took her hand in his and kissed her fingers.

She couldn't stop her eyes from drifting closed as his hot lips moved over her trembling hand. She wanted to lead him upstairs to her soft feather bed and strip the clothes from his gorgeous body. He would be all warm and bronze, glistening in the light of the fire as he took her in his arms and rose over her…

She jerked her hand away,

"I, uh, think we need more champagne. I'll find some." Turning, she hooked the edge of the tablecloth on her heel and tripped. She gripped the edge of the table for support as his hand closed around her elbow.

"I'll help." His deep voice shivered down her spine, turning her insides to jelly.

His touch burned through her thin silk sleeve, and she took a hasty step to the side.

Lilli believed she'd have better control than this should they ever meet again. In her dreams, she did and had plenty to say to him in a level, no-nonsense tone of voice. But now the moment arrived. Her traitorous body wanted to run into his arms and beg him to never let go. Grabbing another glass from a passing waiter, she downed the new contents in one swallow.

Max's eyebrow rose, and she flushed.

"You can't come with me. I, uh, must go alone. It's a single job. Meant for one person." She didn't mean to sound rude or talk so fast and flinched when Connor Calhan chuckled.

"I think you skipped telling me the most important part of last winter." His grin widened as he gazed from one to the other.

This conversation required a lot more alcohol. Setting the glass on the table, she signaled for another drink.

Her dearest childhood friend and keeper of all her secrets stood beside her, grinning like a clown. "Why can't he help? He's better looking than I anticipated." She nudged Lilli in the ribs and whispered in a not-so-quiet voice to Max. "Are you Becca's Northwest Territory Mounted Police Officer?" She inspected him from head to toe and took a step forward.

"I am." A slow grin lifted the corners of his gorgeous mouth. He shot her a sideways glance. "*Becca? Is this another one of your names?*"

Heat rushed to her face, and she lifted her chin. "Yes. I forgot that one. Only Emily calls me Becca." She frowned. "And my mother."

Her best friend stepped between them. "Hello, I'm Emily Astor." Extending her hand, she shook Max's and whispered to Lilli. "Let him help. I'll bet a few of his kisses will lure you from your melancholy. They would me. I can see why none of the men in New York receive a second glance from you. Not after knowing *him*."

"None of them?" He stepped around Emily and offered an arm. "Let me…help."

Visions of his hard mouth descending to hers made her pluck her third glass of champagne from a passing waiter and down the contents like she did the other two.

The world whirled around her head. A groan escaped to her consternation, his satisfaction, and his brother's interest.

"Our two younger brothers will be overjoyed when they read my telegram tomorrow morning. I can hear their *I told you so's* from here." Connor Calhan's lips twitched as he clapped Max on the shoulder. "I'll leave you to it. I see my competitor over there, and I have an issue to discuss with him." He smiled at Lilli. "I'm looking forward to getting to know you and hearing the story of how you two met. Until we meet again, Miss Van Rassner." He kissed her fingers, and Max's eye twitched. "Uh, huh. Just what I thought." With a chuckle, he strolled away.

Emily stared from one to the other. "I think I should go, too."

"No." Lilli caught her arm. "Please stay."

"Are you afraid to be alone with me because of what *I'll* do or what *you'll* do?" Max's deep voice made her go weak in the knees, and his suggestive tone did crazy things to her insides.

"Both." Swallowing to ease the sudden dryness of her throat, she held onto Emily with a death grip.

"As fascinating as this is. I plan to mingle. I think you should go take your officer out to the gardens and show him around. You owe him that much." A smiling Emily unclasped her hand.

"Traitor." Lilli couldn't resist the comment as her sworn-to-protect-her-heart-at-all-costs best friend disappeared into the crowd, leaving her alone with the enemy.

Chapter Twenty

"I spent the last six months scouring the Northwest Territory for you, and all the while you were here." He tucked her arm in his. "I missed you."

The champagne made her legs wobble. Or was it him? She risked a glance at his face. "Why after…what I did. I read your report the day—that day." Speaking about Papa still hurt, and she skipped any reference to him. She hated small talk, and coming back to New York reminded her how much. Squaring her shoulders, she tackled the most important subject head-on. "I know you know about Papa's activities and my robbing the doctor. I know what you think of me, and I know you want justice, but I won't go back." She met his gaze without flinching, and her chin held high. Her heart beat in her throat as she stared at the man she loved. "I have a life here, and I plan to stay in New York. I'll pay whatever fines you want to charge. But you're wrong, you know. I did have a valid reason to take the things I did. I had no choice."

"I know." He tucked her arm back through his and continued their walk along the garden path. "If you confided in me, I would have helped you." His deep voice sent shivers down her spine.

She stopped and turned to face him. "Would you? I know what you think of thieves. And I am one." She closed her eyes as her memories of the time, the area, and the situation swallowed her whole.

"Yes." His quiet answer made a knot in her stomach. "But I know why."

He led her to a curved metal bench beside the path and sat down beside her. "I had no idea things were as bad for you as they were until the doctor showed me your IOUs. Why didn't you say something all those nights we were together? I have money. I would have been more than happy to help." He laced his fingers with hers, and she sucked in a breath at the way they were so intimately entwined. His gentle voice washed over her like a warm bath on a winter night.

"I didn't think you'd understand. And I don't like to ask for help. The less you knew, the better." Her chin dropped. The nightmare of Papa's illness and the uncertainty of what to do raced through her mind. "Uncle Carlton would have killed you, too." Her heart rate accelerated, and her breathing grew shallow as the old terror re-played vivid scenes best left forgotten.

He glanced at her and frowned. "I learned the truth about your uncle from my superiors when I reported the incident at your father's cabin. Imagine how I felt when I discovered how much you kept from me." Leaning back, he shook his head. "If I knew, I could have kept you safe. Your uncle never would have found you. He never would have made it out to the cabin or your father."

She shook her head before he got done talking. "You don't understand how my uncle does things. He has people working for him everywhere. Like your officer friend. Either way, he would have gotten to me. To us. He found us two times before we moved to the Northwest Territory. Papa's quick thinking kept us from being murdered both times. Carlton Genova planned to kill me and everyone connected to me. I couldn't put your life at risk for mine." He had to see the truth of what she said.

"Why not? I would, I will, and I do." He gazed deep into her eyes and stroked a finger down the side of her cheek, making her suck in a deep breath.

He'd die for her. She drowned in the sincerity of his gaze. God, he smelled good, and the heat of his body drew her like a fire on a cold northern night. "I'm not going back." He said all the right things, and she squeezed her eyes shut, hoping to hang on to her resolve. She had so much liability and horror hanging over her head for such a long time that she had a tough time adjusting to a life without fear.

"You don't have to go back unless you want to. All the charges against Willie have been dropped." He squeezed her fingers and smiled. The intimate connection made her tremble with awareness.

They shouldn't sit so close together and tempt the chains around her heart. For once, she gave in to the fire of desire raging through her bloodstream. She wouldn't stop.

"Are you saying I'm free?" She tasted the words, and they were delicious. Her heart thudded against her ribs when he leaned closer.

"Willie is." His hot gaze devoured her.

"There's nothing more you want me for?" She had to hear him say the words again.

"I wouldn't say that. I want you for plenty of reasons. One or two come to mind that I want to discuss with you in detail." His gaze darkened as he stared at her lips, and she resisted the urge to lick them.

"What sort of things?" After the past year, she required reassurance.

"Well, for starters, the way your kisses affect my ability to function. When I get a daily dose, my heart rhythm is steady and strong, my mind is as sharp as a throwing knife, and my body burns with energy. I've had the displeasure of finding when you're not around, I can't think, I can't sleep, and I can't breathe. I can't even eat. Nothing satisfies me, and every day is a dull repeat of the day before. My entire world is dingy and black. I can't do without you in my life and in my bed."

She swallowed the lump in her throat. "Same." Her heart hit her chest in a rapid staccato as she waited for him to continue. One by one, the chains dropped, and she shivered with hope.

"This isn't the most romantic place or the best time, but I can't risk losing you again." Dropping to one knee on the cobblestone path in her family garden, Max retrieved a diamond ring from his jacket pocket and held it toward her. "Will you, Willie Rebecca Lillian Becca, and whatever other names you go by, Rossi Van Rassner, make me the happiest man on the planet by agreeing to be my wife. I can't live without you. I didn't know how lonely and sad life could be until I lost you. I spent countless hours going over every track, every piece of evidence, every moment of the day you left, hoping for a clue on how to find you. But I found nothing. You disappeared like a fantasy lover in the night, and my heart hasn't been the same since. I don't care what you did, who you did it to, or why. I don't care where you came from or where you've been. I only care about this moment and the future. A future with you." He gave her a lop-sided smile. "My little brother told me I'd find you.

That you'd fulfill me in ways I never dreamed of, and I laughed. But he was right."

Her empty hand shook so badly she tucked it under her skirt so he wouldn't notice. Good thing her skirt covered her clacking knees, and the neckline on her gown covered her pounding heart. She licked her dry lips. "You carry a ring in your jacket pocket? Did you know I would be here? Or do you keep it on you for emergencies?"

He shook his head. "I ordered the ring the last time I traveled to Fort Providence. I've carried the thing in my pocket ever since and planned to ask you to marry me as soon as I caught the thief. I had it with me the day you snuck into my room and left the note about Charlotte. I'm surprised you didn't see the little box beside my report and guess."

She had too much on her mind at the time to pay much attention to anything but getting away. The sincerity shining from his incredible blue eyes told her he spoke the truth, and she swallowed. "You planned to ask me to marry you even though you knew what I did? That I stole medicine from the doctor?"

He gave her a tender smile. "Yeah. I did. I figured we make a hell of a team together. But then the whole thing went to hell." He squeezed her fingers again. "I love you, Willie Rebecca Lillian Becca Rossi Van Rassner, with all my heart." He paused and leaned forward to kiss her fingers one at a time. "I'm hoping for an answer soon. I don't know if I can take too much more uncertainty."

The touch of his lips sent tingles through her entire body. She choked on the love welling in her heart. Nothing mattered but this moment and this man. "Yes, I will marry you. I love you too, Max Calhan."

He slipped the band of gold onto her third finger and rose to his feet, drawing her up with him. He grinned. "*My* full name is Maxwell Victor Calhan, but you can call me anything you like as long as *husband* is one of them."

Chapter Twenty-One

They were married a month later, on the first of October, in New York.

Max's family in Chicago came by train a week before to help with the arrangements. His brother Reese clapped him on the back and grinned. "Welcome to the married side of the family."

Reese's wife, Shanna, a slim blonde with blue eyes and the mother of his twin girls, Mary and Maggie, gave him a hug and welcomed Lilli into the family with a wide smile. Her butler, Giles, came with the family to help with the arrangements. And they all stepped aside to allow the man to work his magic. Reese and Shanna claimed the man had connections with the supernatural because of his ability to whip up miracles, but the thin man would deny it and say, "It's what butlers do. They observe and adjust to fit the circumstances. I observe and take the necessary steps. Quite simply, I am the best there is." And they all agreed.

His youngest brother, Chase, arrived from Texas a few hours later accompanied by his beautiful brown-haired wife Rose, and their one-year-old son, Samuel Tucker Calhan, who they named after Chase's dead partner. The boy had brown hair, blue eyes, chubby cheeks, and a wide grin.

Chase grinned and rocked back on his heels. "Now, tell me again what you said when you caught Rose's bouquet at my wedding?"

All the brothers stood six feet and had blond hair and blue eyes, but Chase. His were amber with gold flecks.

"Not a damn thing. As I recall, I spent the evening sipping whisky with Connor." Max returned Chase's hug and caught Lilli's slow smile from across the room, where she spoke with Maggie, his mother, and Madelaine, his older sister.

He couldn't wait for the wedding night, and neither could she.

"Liar." Chase gave him a good-natured slap on the back. "I want to meet the amazing woman who convinced you to marry despite your reluctance to join our happy ranks." He smirked. "She scooted Elsie out of the way and got under your skin, didn't she?"

Max nodded." Oh yes. In more ways than I believed possible."

As Lilli made her way over to his side, he grinned. "Chase, meet the love of my life, Willie Rebecca Lillian Becca Rossi Van Rassner, soon-to-be Calhan." He kissed her hard and drew her into his side. "I liked her best in her oiled breeches and flannel shirt. She answered to Willie then and swore like a soldier."

His darling flushed as bright a shade of red as her silk gown and shook her head at him. "They don't want to hear that story."

"Oh, yes, we do." Maggie, the Calhan's mother, a lithe figure in her early fifties with graying blonde hair, and Madelaine, their only sister, joined the group as they took their seats in the elaborate drawing room of Lilli's newly inherited house. Madelaine was five feet four and slim with curly dark hair, vivid blue eyes, and a widow. She had a fifteen-year-old son, Jeremy, who towered over her with laughing blue eyes and dark hair.

White and gold satin settees faced each other in front of a massive white and gold marble fireplace. Golden chandeliers hung from the gilded ceiling, and two large windows faced the rose gardens at the front of the mansion.

When the pair finished their story, Reese frowned. "Did you ever find out who stole your knife?"

Max shook his head. "I have gone over the situation many times and concluded Mateus, Lilli, and Frank's friend, took my knife and killed the men Carlton Genova brought with him. I found his tracks all over the area later, and he's the only one not accounted for. He hasn't been around since the day Lilli's father died. I haven't found the blade either. Whoever has the blade did the killing, and I think Mateus is the one."

Silence filled the room.

"Well." Maggie rose to her feet. "I am so happy you found Lilli, and thank goodness her uncle didn't succeed in his awful plan. Think what we would have missed out on."

With a smile in Lilli's direction, she left to go unpack.

****

Lilli's heart beat high in her throat the whole time they told their story. She waited for judgment or criticism for her wrongs, but none came. Every member of Max's family hugged her and made her welcome, and she couldn't believe her good fortune.

Over the next week, she listened to the other women tell their stories and discovered they had much in common. Her love for Max grew moment by moment, and she thanked the stars and Mama for sending him to

Papa's cabin that day.

The week flew past as they prepared for the glorious day when she became Max's wife. And then she stood in the church facing Max in her white satin gown and slippers. She held a bouquet of red roses and wore a heavy lace veil that once belonged to her mother.

In the months since she left the Northwest Territory, her hair grew past her shoulders and could be twisted up in an elegant knot. She wore diamonds in her hair and ears to match the diamond on her finger.

Max's eyes gleamed with love and desire as he spoke his vows in a deep voice and slipped the matching band onto her left hand.

She said her vows to him, loving every minute of this magical day, and then they were married.

He swept her into his arms and gave her a thorough kiss to the amusement of his family and the shocked silence of her last remaining aunt.

"Congratulations, my dear. Your mother would be happy you found such a strapping man to care for you." Aunt Eloise kissed her on the cheek and made her excuses to be on her way.

Her best friend Emily congratulated her next and, in an undertone, asked if Max had any more brothers.

Lilli chuckled as she returned the hug. "Just Connor, and from what I hear, there's a certain French captain's daughter giving him problems down at the docks."

"And wherever else she puts her nose. The girl has no sense of propriety or inclination to follow the rules." Connor shook Max's hand and hugged Lilli. "Believe me, there's nothing going on between us. The girl is nothing but trouble."

Max and Chase exchanged glances.

"If you say so, big brother." Chase hugged them both and turned to Shanna. "Where's Giles? I want to know when he starts planning Connor's wedding. I want to place a bet with anyone who wants in."

Everyone laughed but Connor. "If he does, he'll be wrong. I don't plan to marry, and if I did, it wouldn't be to Gabrielle Blanchart. The woman is a pain in my ass."

Lilli glanced up at Max. "Why would Giles know before Connor?"

"He follows his gut and hasn't been wrong so far." Max slipped an arm around her waist and whispered in her ear. "He ordered a cradle for us yesterday."

She froze and glanced up to meet the burning desire in his eyes. "Are you serious?"

"Yes. I'm thinking we should leave soon so we don't disappoint him. Want to go practice making babies?" His breath blew across her cheeks as he drew back to smile into her eyes. The love and passion burning there took her breath away.

"I do." Months of abstinence had her trembling like a blade of grass in the wind. "But we have a wedding dinner to attend first."

And with a groan of frustration, he agreed.

Soft notes of an orchestra met them when they returned from the chapel following the ceremony. Tantalizing whiffs of roast duck, roast pig, and roast beef floated on the air, combined with the mouth-watering aroma of fresh baked rolls and sweets. Footmen in black uniforms ushered the guests through the halls of the Genova Mansion to the ballroom, where Giles had long white linen-covered tables set up for the wedding dinner. Red roses twisted together with white calla lilies ran the length of every table, and ornate centerpieces featuring the flowers overflowed golden vases in the center of each table. Gold dinnerware, utensils, and gold-rimmed glasses sat in perfect formation before each guest, along with heavy black linen napkins.

Lilli sighed with delight. This moment she dreamed of every night in the Northern Territory, and she sucked it all in with every fiber of her being. Delight and golden happiness raced through her body, and her heart told her everything would be all right. Somewhere close by, Mama could see her and approved. She knew about Max and what a wonderful man he was. Papa could see her, too. And his smile wrapped around her heart, erasing all the aches and suffering she endured.

God, this felt good. And so did Max, sitting beside her. All her dreams came true, and in a short while, they would go to the master bedroom and make love as husband and wife. After an eternity of longing, loss, and heartache, the golden life she longed for surrounded her. And soon her husband would, too.

She considered all the ways she wanted to love him and took a sip of wine to wet her suddenly dry mouth.

Max glanced at her and choked. "I think we've stayed long enough. Let's go."

Their exit didn't go unnoticed, and they waved to their joking guests as they retreated down the corridor to the stairs and up to the master bedroom.

Lilli had the room redone in red and mauve, adding cherry furniture and thick Persian rugs following her return to her childhood home. Now, the room vibrated with romantic elegance, which enhanced the anticipation of the moment.

One of the servants turned down the oil lamps on either side of the down-filled bed, and the fire in the marble hearth flickered, filling the room with warmth and intimacy.

Max swung her into his arms as they crossed the corridor into their new life together.

As the gilded door swung shut behind them, he turned the latch and devoured her with his eyes.

Lilli sucked in a breath. She longed for this moment for months and believed she would never again lay in the circle of his embrace.

He lowered her to her feet and tilted her chin up to stare into her eyes. "Mrs. Calhan." Tugging on the laces at the back of her gown, he kissed her bare shoulder, sending shivers of desire through her. "I love the sound of your new name and plan to use it often." Her ties came loose, and he stripped her bodice to her hips. Running his hands down the length of her bare arms, he held her against his heart. "I think you have too many clothes on."

She agreed, and soon they stood in the middle of the floor with their clothes in a heap around them.

He stared at her naked body in the gleam of the fire and stroked her breasts, waist, and hips with the tips of his fingers. "God, you're beautiful. I used to dream of seeing you like this when we were together in your room. I envisioned how you'd look standing proud and bare to my view."

She returned his interest with a heated inspection of her own.

His chest and arms rippled in the light of the fire, and his manhood jutted out in magnificent form from his slim hips. Muscle bunched and bulged with each movement, and his skin glowed with golden, supple silkiness. Her gaze dropped to his loins, and heat filled her belly.

Her mouth dried as she measured him with her eyes. She lifted her gaze to the lust burning in his. "I want you." She remembered how his girth filled her and carried her to the pinnacle of exquisite pleasure until she cried out with rapture.

Seven months was a long time to go without your lover. Especially one as exciting as Max Calhan.

She traced the ridges on his abdomen and chest. "You're perfect. I remembered how you looked without your shirt, but now I find I'm mistaken. You're so much more than I remembered." He tantalized her in the soft light, and she leaned forward to taste him. Salty, smooth, and aroused, she ran her fingers up the bulge on his arms while she kissed and licked her way across his chest.

"I've dreamed of you every night since you disappeared and searched everywhere for you. You have no idea how much I longed to take you in my arms again." He kissed her neck and ears as he caressed her breasts. His voice broke off in a moan as she licked around one of his nipples.

"Me either. Emily is tired of hearing me talk about you. I did so every waking moment for the last six months. I couldn't get you off my mind. Even when you wanted to arrest me, I would have gone to bed with you one last time. I don't believe I'll ever get enough of you."

"I know I won't. I never stopped caring about you or wanting you in my bed. Even after I discovered what you did. My one regret is that you didn't allow me to share your burden. Because I would have, and I do. Whatever happens, we face together from here on out the good times, the tough times, in sickness and in health, dressed or undressed." His voice rasped with pleasure at her touch. Giving her a wicked grin, he bent forward and licked the hardening pebble of her rosy nipples and tugged one into his mouth.

Her knees buckled when he drew on her, and he caught her to him. His manhood prodded her soft belly as he held her by the hips, and heat moistened the juncture between her legs. Raising on tiptoes, she wrapped her arms around his neck and rubbed against him.

He took her mouth in a deep, satisfying kiss as he angled her backward to the waiting feather bed. Clutching her buttocks, he wrapped her legs around his waist and placed her in the middle of the bed.

She clung to his broad shoulders and kissed him back with all her pent-up longing, regret, and passion.

He followed her down, settling into the cradle of her pelvis. Lathering her breasts with his tongue and lips while he rocked against her, mimicking the mating act. She moaned and opened her legs wider, anxious to feel all of him inside her.

She stroked his back, arms, and hips with her fingers, marveling at his strength. And then gasped when he moved his mouth across her ribs and down to her belly. He sucked and kissed his way down her body while she arched and moaned against him. Her breath came fast between her parted lips, and her blood sang with desire.

His erection pressed into her and then probed lower when he did. An answering pool of heat filled her aching sheath. Lilli moaned. "It's been so long. I want you inside me, Max."

He grinned and kissed his way to her hips and lower until his mouth hovered above her mound. She knew what he planned to do and lifted her hips to meet him halfway. His tongue stroked her sensitive nub before his lips closed over her and suckled in gentle nips.

She cried out, gripping his head to her as he led her along the fiery rim of pleasure and satisfaction. She burned for him in ways she didn't know were possible and cried out when he flicked her with his tongue. Glorious gratification shimmered just out of reach as he thrust his tongue into her in a steady rhythm.

"I want…" She gasped when he replaced his tongue with two fingers and returned to her nub. His hands, lips, and tongue took her over the edge a second later, and she screamed as her release rocked her to the core of her being.

He rose above her with a grin on his face as she uncurled her hands and toes. "Turn over for me.

She did, and he took her from behind in one long surge. Her sensitive body contracted and clung to his girth like a second skin.

Max moaned and rocked into her, gritting his teeth at the pleasure her body gave him.

She responded with a moan of her own and lifted her hips for deeper penetration. They surged and withdrew in an ever-increasing rhythm, reveling in the delight their friction created.

She fell over the edge into the most brilliant gratification a few minutes later, and he pumped hard and fast as he followed her into pure bliss.

They clung together, gasping for breath and riding the waves of satisfaction until the last ripple disappeared and left them weak, hot, and completely sated.

"God, I missed you." Max rolled to his side and tugged her into his arms.

She smiled, too spent to move more than a few

inches. "Not as much as I missed you. Without you and without Papa, I was more alone than I ever have been. It's been a dreary world for me until the night of my party when you walked in and breathed life into me again."

He smiled into her hair. "You are the one who gives me life. I had to punch two new holes in my belt because I couldn't eat or sleep. Even the commander commented on my haggard appearance." He yawned and lifted the satin comforter over their gleaming, naked bodies. "Tonight, with you back in my arms, I will get the first real sleep I've had since you left me."

She didn't like his comment. "I didn't leave *you*. I left the situation. There is a difference."

He didn't think of the way she phrased her answer until much later.

Chapter Twenty-Two

They spent a month touring Europe and making love every chance they got.

Lilli liked to try new things, and before they returned, they had made love in the back of a wagon, in the bottom of a boat, behind a waterfall, in a castle, in a cottage, in a lake after dark, and along the seashore.

She didn't like the sand and spread a blanket to keep the grains from going places they shouldn't.

Max laughed but didn't argue. He loved every second of their time together and her willingness to try new things. He preferred letting her ride him because all his favorite parts were right within easy reach of his lips. He would hold her hips and guide her when she got too close to finding her pleasure and couldn't move. Then he'd turn her over and plunder her from behind or roll on top of her and wrap her legs around his waist.

Tired, happy, and so in love, he thought of nothing but Lilli and how to make her smile. They returned to New York and their new life together.

The darkness, terror, and trauma of the past disappeared, and his love's smile grew wider as they discovered she carried his child.

Max accepted Connor's offer of employment and joined his older brother in the office.

Things went smoothly until one day when Max received a letter from his superiors asking him to come back to the Northwest Territory to give testimony of the events leading up to Frank Rossi's death.

Commander Jorgensen found Mateus, and they held him in a cell for questioning. The Northwest Territory Mounted Police wanted definitive answers on who killed whom, and Max wanted his blade back. His father gave him the knife before he left for battle the last time and lost his life in an ambush.

Max wanted answers as well. Only the killer who wielded his blade knew who killed who and what happened at the cabin. Everyone had their theories, but he wanted the truth.

And he figured Mateus could give it to him.

Searching in the wardrobe for a valise, he found an old, worn one in the back corner and decided to take it instead of one of the more expensive ones.

Lifting the bag to the floor, he wondered why it weighed so much.

He opened the catch and discovered a cloth-wrapped bundle in the bottom. Lifting the object out, he unwrapped the length of cotton cloth and received the shock of his life. He stared in astonishment.

His stolen curved blade lay in his hands.

"How in the hell…?" Turning the blade over in his hands, he ran his fingers over the intricate carving on the handle and traced his father's initials, JMC. Jonathon Matthew Calhan.

"Darling. Where are you?" Lilli walked into the room and froze. Her eyes darted from the blade to his face. Her throat worked as she met the question in his gaze. Every ounce of color drained from her face, and for a minute, he thought she might faint.

He stared from her to the blade while his mind raced

with possibilities. "*You* killed your uncle's men?"

She sucked in a breath and nodded. "Yes." A long, silent minute passed. "Will your superiors arrest me?"

He had her in his arms a second later, holding her tight against his chest. "No. They want to know the truth, and they plan to *commend* the man who killed Genova's evil crew, not prosecute him. Er, her, you." He stroked her back as he shook his head in disbelief. "Why didn't you tell me? How did you do it? You have such a violent reaction to blood; I have a hard time believing you're the killer. I've gone over that day and the following night so many times in my head. I know it all by heart." He stared into her eyes. "How?" He asked again. "You wielded the knife with such precision. I can't comprehend how the killer could be you."

Lilli blew out a breath of relief and gave him a small smile. Everything would be okay. "Papa taught me. I found there's a difference between shedding blood and defending family. My rage over Mama's murder burned the whole time I fought with the men responsible."

"But you didn't have enough time to ride out to the cabin…." He ran a hand through his hair. "Why didn't you say anything about what happened?"

"I didn't tell you because I believed I would be charged with murder, and I never wanted to go back. I can't. There's too much emotion with Papa…and…everything."

Max kissed the top of her head. "No one will touch you. I won't allow it. But I do want to hear this story. I'm certain my brothers do, too. But first, me." He squeezed her to him and kissed her hair.

"Okay. What do you want to know?" She lifted her face to gaze into his eyes. and he sucked in a breath at the love and trust shining in her blue depths.

"Everything. But first, let's get you comfortable." He took her arm and led her to the overstuffed satin settee in front of the fireplace.

Although barely three months into her pregnancy, Max treated her like a glass doll and wouldn't let anyone get close to her but him.

Tucking a coverlet over her knees, Max ordered tea and took a seat beside her.

"Start from the beginning, when you rode to the fort to borrow from the doctor one last time." Pouring her a cup of fragrant tea, he tucked her into his side and urged her to tell her story.

****

Lilli sipped her tea and glanced at Max. She wanted to tell him for such a long time but didn't know how to begin. He believed Mateus took the knife and she hadn't told him the truth because she didn't know how he would react. And losing him would never be an option.

Encouraged by his loving touch and concern, she took a deep breath and closed her eyes. "After my talk with Charlotte and my visit to the doctor's office, I went to your room to hide from the soldiers searching for the thief. And to leave you a note about Charlotte.

"I spotted Finlay's report informing you of my identity and naming me as thief. I couldn't face losing you or your affection, so I burned the evidence. Men came down the boardwalk outside your door, and I discovered I left my knife in my saddle bags. I worried I would be caught and searched for a weapon. I took your knife from the mantle and tucked it in my belt for safekeeping. The footsteps walked away, and I left your room. I didn't know my uncle found me until Finlay and

Lawson held me captive."

Lilli took a sip of her tea and sucked in a deep calming breath. "When I returned to my mare, I collected the stolen medicine and retrieved my blade from my saddlebags. I tucked the blade into my belt as Lawson approached me. I tossed the bag with the medicine into the stall behind me right before Finlay hit me on the head, and they took me prisoner." She related their talk and the threats the two men made. "I used my blade on Finlay when he rushed at me. I believed I killed him and worried I'd be hung for murder.

"The blood did get to me, and I threw up outside the door. I didn't know my blow killed Lawson, either, until later. When I escaped, I took the first horse I could find and galloped south toward the fort. I kept thinking about Papa. My uncle would be waiting for me if I rode out to the cabin. Papa might already be dead, and I'd be next. Uncertain of what to do, I stopped and asked Mama for help. A falling star fell to the north giving me the sign I waited for. I turned around and rode hard toward the cabin without giving the matter another thought."

Max shook his head. "How? I made the calculations, and you didn't have enough time."

Lilli shrugged. "I rode the trail between the cabin and the fort for four years and could ride the distance blindfolded. I don't think anybody else could have done the same thing except Papa. The old Papa. A full moon lit the trail, and I raced full speed through the forest.

"When I came to the edge of the clearing, I stopped and analyzed the scene. Five horses stood outside, tied to the hitching post. I checked to make sure my blades were where they should be and checked my gun. I crept toward the silent cabin with my eyes and ears open.

Everything seemed so peaceful. Moonlight bathed the roof of the cabin in silver, and smoke curled from the chimney as it did every night. An owl hooted above my head, and a gentle breeze nipped at my nose and cheeks. Calm settled over me, and nothing mattered but saving Papa.

"I made my way to the cabin and peeked in the window. The fire flickered in the hearth, and Papa sat in his favorite chair. He hadn't come out of his room in weeks, and his appearance in the living area made me nervous. I leaned forward, hoping to catch a glimpse of the enemy. And then the barrel of a gun pressed into my temple.

'Hand me your gun. Do it real slow, or I'll blow your head off,'" she imitated a deep male voice and swallowed.

"He whispered in my ear." Her hand shook as she lifted her tea to her lips. Setting her cup down, she gave Max a smile. "Don't frown. There's nothing you can do now but listen."

He nodded. A muscle ticked along the edge of his jaw, and she put a hand on his. "I'm fine."

"I know. Go on with your story." He pretended to sip his tea in a relaxed manner. His facade would have worked if the handle of his cup hadn't snapped in half.

Lilli caught the cup before it spilled and set it on the table. "I can stop if you'd like."

"No. Keep talking. I must know what happened." He smiled at her, and she relaxed. "I'll keep my rage in check. Tell me the rest."

"He told me to hand him my gun butt first and nudged my head with his weapon. The metallic click of the hammer being pulled back terrified me, so I handed him my gun." She risked a glance at Max.

He sat silently, opening and closing his fists with his head down. "Go on."

"I dropped my hand to the handle of the knife tucked inside my pocket and waited for the right opportunity. My terror left me the second I gripped the handle, and Papa's training took over.

"'I don't know why you're scared of her. She's nothing but a skinny female.' The man beside me called to a shadow on my right as he dropped the hammer of his gun and tucked it into his belt. Then he relieved me of mine.

"'Now hold still.' The man took a piece of twine from his pocket.

"I never pay attention to orders and slid the curved blade between his ribs. He dropped to my feet with a cry of surprise. I turned as another man strolled into view and glanced down at the body by my feet.

"'Stupid fool.' He turned and aimed a gun at my chest. 'Unlike him, I know about your surprise attacks." Chuckling, he pointed toward the back door. 'You uncle would like a word with you.'

"I knew I would be dead if I didn't produce a plan quick and whistled for Zeus. He couldn't come because I hadn't taken them from the stable all day, but I wanted to stall for time. The man struck me, and I stumbled.

"'Now, none of that. Haskin and Burney are taking care of your dogs. I hope you aren't too attached.' His voice sounded anything but remorseful as I regained my balance following his blow.

"'My dogs don't like strangers. They'll kill the men inside the barn.' I smiled when shouting and growls filled the night silence. Whistling again, I called. 'Kill,

Zeus.'

"And received another blow. Staggering, I swept my leg wide, hoping to trip my escort, and landed on the ground with a thump. I shook my head to clear my senses. The man picked me up and tossed me over his broad shoulder as if I were a doll. He carried me into the cabin and dropped me on my feet in the middle of the living area.

" 'Marvin, make sure Calhan didn't follow her.'

"I remembered my uncle's voice from the day he murdered Mama, and a cold sweat broke out on my forehead. I searched the room, taking in the tall, thin man with the silver hair and unsmiling face dressed in a gray woolen suit standing beside Papa's chair. Now, I had a face to put with the loathsome voice. A burly man approached from the window and stood behind me, blocking my escape. I glanced at Papa.

"'Stiff and silent, he gave me a slight shake of his head. His glazed eyes and pale face told me his whisky glass contained opium. I wanted to weep with frustration. If Papa were in his right mind, Carlton Genova would be dead.

"'You have me. Leave the boy alone.' Papa glared at my uncle. They had already had a conversation because blood poured down my father's face from a wound on his head.

"A thin smile spread across my uncle's face. 'Drop the pretense, Finnegan. I know this is my niece. Officer Finlay has been extremely helpful in acquiring your location. But now I have her, I have no further use for you.' Then, he lifted his arm and shot Papa before I had a chance to react." Lilli clenched her trembling hands in her lap and dropped her gaze to blink away her tears.

After all this time and everything that happened, Papa's death still made her queasy inside.

Max lifted her onto his lap and tucked her head beneath his chin. "God, I'm sorry. We can talk about this another time. I don't like to see you so upset."

The strength of his arms around her and the heat of his body warmed her chilled heart. "I'm okay. I wanted to tell you, and I should have ages ago. I'm sorry I didn't. At the time, I thought you planned to arrest me and see I paid for my crimes like Elsie should have."

"Nothing about your situation resembles hers in the slightest. You killed to defend your father. She killed for greed."

Telling him the truth soothed the last of her troubles away, and she relaxed as the tension drained from her heart and body. Drawing courage from Max's embrace, she continued.

"'No!' I shouted when he shot Papa. I couldn't believe the nightmare started all over again! In my mind, Mama's murder played out. As I rushed forward, the burly man behind me twisted my arm behind my back. Twirling, I used my momentum against him and knocked him to the floor. Then I ran across the room and threw my body across Papa's. Gulping down my terror, I searched along the side of his body for the pistol he always kept with him. My hand curled around the butt as Carlton Genova's chuckle filled the room. I'll never forget what he said or the way he gloated.

"'Success is such a sweet reward. I admit, your father gave me many sleepless nights, but, as you can see, he is no match for me.' He caught me by my shoulder. 'I don't have the time to savor this moment as I'd like to or as I planned. Your mounted police officer has the habit of showing up at the wrong time, and I must be off. There's another sister to kill and money to collect. You understand.' He tugged me around to face him as he spoke.

"I cocked the gun as I swung around and shot him between his eyes, freezing his shocked expression for all time. 'I do understand.' I couldn't resist saying the words, although I could hardly get them past the lump in my throat.

"Reaction made my hands shake, and I remember choking on a sob as I wondered how I would survive without Papa. But my surprises were not over yet. The man I knocked down rose to his feet.

"'Get the girl!' Officer Finlay's voice boomed from the back of the house, and when I turned, another man rushed inside.

"One knocked my gun out of my hand. He tossed it, and it landed beside Papa's chair. We struggled for a minute before I had the chance to slide your blade between his ribs. I spun on my heel and killed the other one an instant later. Like Papa taught me. As I stared down at their bodies beside my feet, I wondered how many more men my uncle had with him. No more noise came from outside, so I crept forward and waited. And I had no idea where Finlay went.

"My heart beat so loud in my head I couldn't hear a thing until a lone wolf howled nearby. I shivered. It seemed to me predators roamed everywhere that night. Inching toward the door, I stepped outside and froze.

"Officer Finlay stood in front of me with his gun aimed at my chest. He took a step toward me, and I knocked his gun away as I slid your blade into his heart.

"Officer Finlay stumbled and mumbled some threat

about cutting me to pieces before he fell to the ground.

"I stepped back to the cabin and latched the door. Sinking to the ground, I wrapped my arms around my knees and gave way to my terror and grief. Papa was dead, and I had no one. Tears rolled down my cheeks as I relived the terror of the night Mama died. My years alone with Papa as he moved from place to place to protect me filled my thoughts.

"And then Mateus appeared from the direction of the barn with the news all the dogs were dead. He shook his head. "You must go. All of this is bad medicine. I will check for more bad men, but you must leave tonight. Go. I will find you at the fort."

"A million thoughts raced through my mind. At the very least, I could be charged with four counts of murder. Mateus was right. I had to leave, and quickly."

Max interrupted her. "I thought Mateus came by once a week."

She shot him a glance. "When he discovered how sick Papa got, he came every day and took over…the process."

He nodded. "Go on."

"I reentered the cabin, packed my valise with the few clothes I possessed, and paused beside my shelf. I withdrew the book containing the amounts and people Papa and I borrowed from. Tucking the book on top, I snapped the valise closed.

"All the way back to the fort, I gave way to my emotions. Papa taught me how to fight, how to survive, and how to live. I could never thank him enough for all he did to keep me safe. But after all his efforts, Carlton Genova got him in the end. Bitterness filled my heart, and I cried harder. Would things have turned out differently if I kept Papa away from the opium? All the sins I committed to help him and the risks I took filled my mind, and I groaned with remorse. In my mind, I would make it all up to them once I went home. And then it hit me. Uncle Carlton no longer threatened me. I could go home!"

Max squeezed her. "You didn't kill Finlay. The wolf did." And he told her what he found in the cabin. His kisses on her hair calmed her soul and made telling her story easier than she anticipated.

"I tasted the idea of life without fear and stirred it around in my mind, savoring the sweetness of freedom. But freedom meant leaving you and all you meant to me." A tear betrayed her and rolled down her cheek. "I agonized over what happened, what could never happen, and what I must now do.

"You knew the truth about me and planned to arrest me on sight. I couldn't stay, not after what you wrote to your superiors about me and what I did. Or at least I believed I did after reading your report. I had no idea you were convinced Mr. Lawson was your second thief. Seeing hatred, disappointment, and judgment in your eyes would kill me, so I left.

"Back in New York, I could access my mother's money, pay back all my IOUs, and make a different life. But I knew in my heart I would never recover from you. There would never be anyone like you again."

She told him about her return to the fort and how she turned Lawson's horse loose to avoid being tied to the whole affair.

"That must have been one hell of a ride. No wonder we found the animal lathered and nervous right before we closed the gates for the night. So much makes sense."

Max's footsteps were the first ones outside Marion's door before Mateus appeared to take her to Fort Providence.

"So Marion and Charlotte knew the whole time?" Max shook his head.

Lilli kissed his cheek. "No. I didn't tell them where I planned to go until later. I worried more of Uncle Carlton's men would come and made Marion swear to get her and Charlotte out of the fort. When I did wire Marion with my location, I made her promise not to tell. I worried you would come after me and arrest me for Finlay's, Uncle Carlton's, and his men's death." She sucked in another breath. "Did Marion and Charlotte leave like they promised? If my uncle or his men discovered they were connected to me in any way, he'd kill them, and I worried for weeks about their safety. And yours."

"They went to Fort Providence." He shook his head. "And once we confirmed all Genova's men were dead and no longer a threat, they came back." He frowned. "You knew your uncle was dead. Why didn't you go back to New York?"

She gave him a smile. "Word of his death had to reach New York and the rest of his men in order for me to be safe. I had no way to know how many more were searching for me with orders to kill."

"You're a smart lady." His face darkened. "You have no idea what I went through afterward. For months no one told me a God damned thing, and now it all makes sense." He paused. "It also explains why Mateus disappeared without a trace. But why come back now?

She shrugged. "I sent word of our marriage to Marion. She must have told him, and he decided such a union meant he could return to his old life with no fear of being held for questioning."

Max chuckled. "I believed he had the knife and killed the men at your father's cabin."

"No. He sent me away while he checked for survivors. Afterward, Mateus came to Marion's to assure me Carlton Genova's men were all dead. He knew a way out of the fort and took me downriver. I remember staring up at the sunrise and thinking the quiet morning promised a beautiful day that would be enjoyable if my life weren't so messed up.

"I prayed for Papa, the dogs, Mama, and the life I left behind. Once I commended their souls to heaven, I prayed for you and what we would never have together. Or so I supposed at the time." Her voice drifted off on a sigh.

He made a low noise in his throat, and she hastened to add. "If I knew then what I know now, I would have raced toward you instead of away from you. I made a list of desirable attributes in a mate, and you are everything I dreamed of finding. And more. Except fighting. I believe I could whip your ass if I weren't with child. But don't worry. I will give you instructions once our baby is born, and we'll have you in top form in a few months."

Max chuckled. "We will have to wait until then to put your boast to the test. I bet you a romantic week in Paris. I can hold my own without your instructions." He nuzzled the side of her neck as he talked, and she went hot all over.

"I'll take your bet and raise you a weekend in bed. I know a move or two I haven't used on you yet." She shivered with anticipation as his lips kissed the length of her collarbone.

"Is that a fact? How about showing me these moves now? I don't know if I can bear the suspense of waiting until our babe appears to find out what other talents you have." He rose with her in his arms and strolled toward the bed.

She laughed, and they spent a most satisfying afternoon loving each other until they fell apart, panting for breath. No longer carrying the weight of the world, she rejoiced in her newfound freedom.

"I believe you owe me a week in Paris." Lilli turned to her side and ran a finger over his damp chest.

"How do you figure?" He tucked her into his side and caressed her growing belly.

She gave him a wide grin. "You bet me you could hold your own without instructions, and I'd say you accomplished that quite well." She flushed as she remembered how well.

"I'm happy to accommodate you, my dear." He yawned and tucked the coverlet around them both. Gazing into her eyes, he held her as though she were the most precious thing in his life. "You're beautiful, my Lilli, and it doesn't matter what name you go by. You're the most desirable woman in the world to me."

She fell asleep with a smile on her lips. She had her home, her life, and most of all, she had her family right here beside her.

Did life get any better?

Epilogue

Jonathon William Calhan arrived on July fifteenth to the delight of the entire Calhan family. Healthy, chubby, and good-natured, everyone wanted to hold and cuddle him.

Max and Lilli argued for weeks over his name. Lilli wanted the babe to have one name to avoid confusion, and Max insisted upon two.

"Jonathon is perfect. We can call him Jonathon, Johnny, or John. William also gives him options. Or he can be William, Willie, Will, Liam, or Bill." Max sent Lilli a wicked smile.

Lilli gave him a quizzical look. "Think of the poor girl he falls in love with and what she'll have to go through. I think a straightforward name such as Hank or Tom would be better. No one can shorten it or get it confused." She kissed the top of the baby's black hair. "I feel sorry for your future wife already."

"If Johnathon had been a girl, I would have named her Elizabeth. She could go by Eliza, Lizzy, Beth, Betty, Bess, Betsy, Ellie, and a few more I wrote down."

"Are you serious?" She glanced at him and laughed. "You're incorrigible."

Max chuckled. "Since we had a son, I settled for Jonathan. Think of all the fun he and his future wife will have getting the name straight. I did. And I wouldn't change a thing for all the single one-syllable names in the world. To me, you'll always be Willie Rebecca Lillian Becca Rossi Van Rassner Calhan. The love of my life and the keeper of my soul. With you, I have everything. After all, what's in a label? A Lilli by any other name will forever be mine despite the moniker."

Max smiled at the woman he loved, astounded at the changes in his life. He thought of his past relationship, his determination to never marry, and his views on the law.

Riding north was the best decision he ever made. For he found a Lilli growing amid the thorns. A flower of immeasurable wealth that seeped beneath his defenses and destroyed the wall around his heart. He discovered morals, honesty, and integrity weren't divided by class. But by individuals. Each person made their own destiny, and he had his. No longer did any of the past matter. For he held the future here in his arms. And eternity stretched before him, filled with family, joy, and love forever.

For the first time in his entire life, complete satisfaction filled his soul. He held the entire world when he held her.

A word about the author...

I enjoy reading, knitting, crocheting, quilting, and faux painting. I love sitting on the beach and watching the waves rush toward my bare feet. I could do it all day long and not tire of the soothing melody of the water.

Roses, calla lilies, plumerias, and gardenias are my favorite flowers of all time. At one time I had a hundred rose bushes in my yard, and I miss them every day. And the smell of them in the air.

My dog Mozart sits beside my desk and keeps me company while I write.

I occasionally bake when the mood strikes me. Which isn't very often in all honesty because I consider cooking and baking necessary evils. Not necessities. LOL

I have been married to my best friend for forty-one years and he is my greatest fan/critic. I don't know what I would do without him. My family is my greatest support and I love every minute I spend with them. Life is a journey and I can't wait to see where it leads me next!

Thank you for purchasing
this publication of The Wild Rose Press, Inc.

For questions or more information
contact us at
info@thewildrosepress.com.

The Wild Rose Press, Inc.
www.thewildrosepress.com

www.ingramcontent.com/pod-product-compliance
Lightning Source LLC
Chambersburg PA
CBHW052021020726
47501CB00004B/1176